Weapon of Tyrants

The Last War: Book Four

Sylvie Grayson

For information write to
Great Western Publishing at
sylviegraysonauthor@gmail.com
http://www.sylviegrayson.com

ISBN: 978-0-9947345-7-0

First Great Western Publishing paperback printing
March 2017
10 9 8 7 6 5 4 3 2 1
Great Western Publishing is a registered trademark of Sylvie Grayson.
Cover art by Steven Novak   novakillustration@gmail.com
Printed in the USA

DEDICATION

This book is dedicated to Anna Markland, bestselling author of Medieval romances including *Hearts & Crowns, Conquering Passion*, and *Dark Irish Knight*. Anna, you have been so generous with your knowledge about writing and the publishing industry, your constant care and encouragement. I would never have gotten to Book Four of The Last War without your inspiration and steady support. Thank you so much.

- Sylvie Grayson

-

Rain Man, Lies He Told, Book Two

Don't Move, Lies He Told, Book Three

Game Plan, Lies He Told: Book Four

My Best Mistake

Moon Shine

Find Sylvie Grayson at her website - www.sylviegrayson.com And on facebook at - facebook.com/sylvie.grayson.
Find her books at Amazon - amazon.com/author/sylviegrayson

Praise for Sylvie Grayson's books

I've been reading Sylvie Grayson - can't seem to put them down. How do you come up with these exciting mysteries? Very fun reading!!

Suspended Animation

Wow! This book is amazing, its very well written and the characters are very well developed. This is my first book by Sylvie Grayson and it won't be my last. I was hooked from the first page and this book was very hard to put down.

Interesting characters, family conflicts and divided loyalties make this a book that kept me up half the night

Legal Obstruction

I loved this book! I've found my new favorite author.
Emily is a fiercely professional woman who is on her own and determined to protect her little family. Joe is a solitary guy who often doesn't deal with problems until they are front and center. But boy does Emily wake him up. Add in a wildcard assistant and a few unsavory characters and I was up all night finishing the book to find out what happens.

The Lies He Told Me

If you are a fan of the heartwarming craftiness and domesticity of a Debbie McComber romance, and the intense intrigues of Danielle Steele, you'll enjoy the writing style of Sylvie Grayson; where the bad guys are not heartless, and the good guys are virtually flawless.

Just a quick note to let you know how much I enjoyed your book. You drew on your vast experience as a result of being a female, a wife, lover, mother, business woman, lawyer, friend, gardener, homeowner, compassionate and caring individual. It was an intriguing read which kept me guessing and very interested. Well done, Sylvie.

The Last War: Book One, Khandarken Rising
The General of Khandarken sends his son, Dante, to investigate the situation. When Dante meets the lovely Beth she eyes him with suspicion. But he won't stop until he solves the tangle of motives, fueled by greed, which threaten Beth and her family. I enjoyed this book very much. The well-developed characters and sensuous love scenes make this a page turner. I look forward to reading Book Two and Book Three

… this story is one of a kind and couldn't be truly compared to anything but itself. It has so many unique characteristics. The personal relationships are intriguing and different from many other fictional relationships. The names are cool, the plot gets thicker with each page, and I loved the author's style. It became evident that I was addicted to reading the book once I was sad to be finished. I'm going to give this a strong recommendation. It's my kind of book.

The Last War: Book Two, Son of the Emperor
I am a big fan of The Last War series. I loved Book One, the story of Major Dante Regiment and

Beth Farmer. The dystopian world Grayson has created, where women are scarce and Clones are used to replace them, where the Emperor has finally been defeated but his son takes up the fight, just gets better in this second book.

...Thrills abound on the race to freedom and home. I can't wait for Book Three. Grayson has great imagination, the fantasy series is awesome.

.

ACKNOWLEDGMENTS

To Steven Novak, novakillustration@gmail.com for his great book covers.

To my critique group for their hard work and willing contribution.

To my family for their constant support.

. .

Weapon of Tyrants

The Last War:
Book Four

Sylvie Grayson

.

CHARACTERS

Adjudicator, Julianne, wife to Abe Farmer, daughter of Little Harry Adjudicator, teacher of origami

Adjudicator, Little Harry, deceased, Julianne's father

Advisor, Frank, lawyer in the City

Anatoliy, nickname Toll, assistant to Chief Constable Cownden Lanser

Aqatain, Emperor, deceased

Balcomb, Ms, Governor Maude's secretary

Barrington, General, also referred to as Barrington the Benevolent, rule of Legitamia

Carlton, Emperor, son of Aqatain, succeeded his father

Clone, an artificial woman to provide sex for men who cannot find mates, since women have become so rare in the former Empire

Duncan, former Assistant Chief Constable of Khandarken, deceased

DuSatoy, strongman of the north of Khandarken, Sable Maude's business partner, running for election as Leader

Elkon, General of Emperor Carlton's troops in Legitamia

Elliott, former head of the Constabulary Board and supporter of Cownden Lanser

Farmer, Bethlehem, sister of Abe Farmer, wife to Major Dante Regiment

Farmer. Abe, brother to Bethlehem Farmer, husband to Julianne Adjudicator, owner with sister of Farmer Holdings

FitzGibbon, Deputy Leader of Khandarken and Acting

i

Leader after Harold Master's assassination

Hannan, cook at Farmer Holdings at the manorhouse

Hart, Mildred, widow, mother of Puntledge Hart, companion to General Paulo Regiment

Hart, Puntledge, Chief Adjudicator and Chief Judge of Appeal Court, son of Mildred Hart

Hawker, Jade, father of Loyal Hawker, father of Selanna Nettles, uncle of Abe and Beth Farmer

Hawker, Loyal, son of Jade Hawker, works undercover for Governor Frank Maude and Cownden Lanser

Holmes, Brentwood, friend and colleague of Saxby Wordsmith, his shop, 'Holmes Books and Documents' is in Old Towne

Lanser, Cownden, son of Jessalyn Lanser and Emperor Aqatain, Chief Constable of Khandarken

Lanser, Jessalyn, member of the former nobility of the empire, lives in Adar Silva, mistress to Aqatain, mother of Cownden, sister to Judson

Learmonth, Jack, head of wealthy distillery family, owner of Learmonth Hotels, running for election as Leader

Makulski, runs an illegal gambling operation in the Western Territory

Malahide, Dante Regiment's administration officer

Master, Fanny, daughter of Ms Master and Leader Harold Master of Khandarken who was assassinated in an aircart bom returning from Gilsigg, Legitamia

Maude, Frank, Governor of Southern Territory of Khandarken, was in military for Emperor Aqatain but changed sides to join the rebellion partway through The Last War

Maude, Sable, son of Governor Frank Maude of the Southern Territory, runs a brothel business from his establishment north of Khandarken inside the Legitamia border

Men's Club, an exclusive club in Old Towne of the City where the senior men meet

Moiselle tribe, of the Jiran nation

Ms Hawker, mother of Loyal Hawker, wife of Jade Hawker who is deceased

Ms Maya, housekeeper for the Master family

Nettles, Selanna, a sookie, wife of Cownden Lanser, step daughter of Dr Harris Stuke

Nikesh, long-time buddy of Damian Stuke, both on the Helmcken Trail and in the Western Territory

Norcross, Governor of the Collaros Territory

Ooievaar, Dante Regiment's right hand man in military

Penrhy tribe, of the Jiran nation

Penrhy, Shandro, Prince of the Penrhy tribe of the Jiran nation

Phelong, Governor of Foothills Territory, town of Buckley

Radha, Chief Investigator of the Khandarken Constables

Ransom, men's tailor in Deep Creek, informant for Dante and military, worked under Paulo during the War

Regiment, General Paulo, head of Khandarken military, fought in the Last War for Aqatain, but changed sides to join the rebellion partway through.

Regiment, Major Dante, second son of Paulo, serious military man, second in command under his father

Regiment, Virgil, General Paulo Regiment's oldest son, deceased

Rutman, longtime Constable, now Lead Constable in the Southern Territory

Saffi, Assistant Chief Constable after Duncan's death

Shafoneur tribe, of the Jiran nation

Stonsifer, Dr, works at hospital in the City

Stuke, Harris, Dr, medic in The Last War along the Helmcken Trail, father of Damian Stuke, step-father of Selanna Nettles, nickname Da for his children

Tasha, friend of Fanny Master

Thames, worker on Farmer Holdings, head of a team of dispossessed who live in Farmerville

True-May, Collier, elected Leader of Adar Silva

Waite, ex-military, now works as enabler for Sable Maude while also working undercover as an informant for Dante Regiment

Weisner, Mr, tutor for Abe and Beth Farmer on Holdings as they were growing up, tutor for Boulter

Wordsmith, Saxby, bookbinder who lives in Old Towne, friend of the Farmers and Brentwood Holmes

Zhang, Chief of Police of Legitamia

. .

Hawker

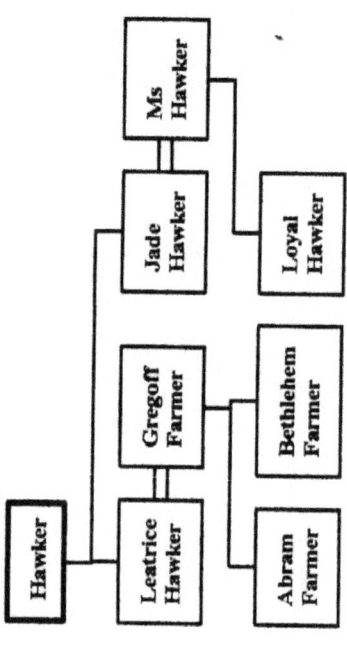

General Paulo Regiment

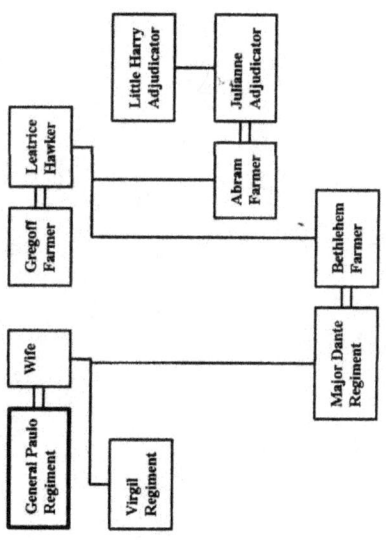

Aqatain

CHAPTER ONE

Fanny Master reached for her mother's hand as their official transport approached the crossing of the Violetta River. Their driver slowed for the turn and then speeded up for the slight rise onto the bridge, following the vehicle ahead where their guards rode.

This was their first outing since Father's death, and it had been very hard to maintain a cheerful face while they toured the Children's Corral on the south side of the river. The Corral was a charity her mother helped found years ago to care for orphans in Khandarken, many of whom had lost their parents during the Last War and the bitter aftermath.

But Mother had had no interest in anything since Father perished. He had died from a lethal aircart bom just inside the Legitamia border right after the international meetings held in Gilsigg. As Leader of Khandarken, Harold Master had been sorely missed and the event had thrown the newly-formed country into something of a crisis.

The family had been in crisis as well. General Paulo Regiment, head of the Khandarken army, knew the rest of the Master family was targeted for death, just as their father had been. Because of that, they had guards riding ahead of their transport as they traversed the City, and a Constable driving their vehicle. But no one knew who had placed the order to have them killed, or why.

Today Fanny had set out to pry Mother loose from the house and back to some kind of involvement in the outside world. Maybe this was a good start, because Ms Master had finally begun to show some interest in how the children at the Corral fared.

There was a loud screech from the giant wheels as their transport suddenly swerved sharply on the planks of the bridge. Fanny turned in surprise to look through the plexi window. A large black armoured hydro-truck appeared as if out of nowhere, ploughing sideways across the track toward them. She stared straight into the eyes of the driver's menacing gray gaze as he aimed straight for the side of their transport.

The Constable driver yanked the wheel in the direction of the bridge railing, and gunned the engine to try to speed past the oncoming menace. Fanny was struck dumb with panic. But their driver's actions were too little, too late. The hydro-truck slammed into the side of the transport, sending it skidding and spinning into the bridge support.

Fanny opened her mouth, but words never had a chance to leave her lips as the crash of armour against armour rang in a never-ending bell of attack. As their advance guard drove on, seemingly oblivious to the collision, the railing beside them gave way like weak plexi under the force of the impact. The transport shot through the gap, silently sailing far out over the dirty waters of the Violetta River like an aircart taking wing. Was this the end, then? Had their enemy found them and delivered the death knell, as feared?

Fanny cringed at her mother's fierce grasp on her arm, and dimly heard the bellow of rage from their Constable driver who was fighting to get out of his harness. They seemed to travel endlessly over the dull brown water churning below. Her mother's fingers simply slipped from her arm as they reached the surface of the river.

The impact was stunning. The transport stopped as if hit by a battering ram and they were thrown forward and then back against the rear seats like rag dolls. The side door popped open as they sank like a stone.

Water rushed under Fanny's pale blue dress and over her head. She floated beneath the surface for what seemed a long time. She was alone, having washed out of the transport through the open door. Watching the heavy vehicle slowly disappear into the watery depths below, Fanny was confident Mother had also escaped. Weeds swept past her, tangled in clumps under the water. Bits of debris sailed above her head, momentarily blocking the light. One shoe was gone. Her arms hovered at her sides as her skirt drifted about her legs as in a dream. Even then she wasn't alarmed. She floated, forgetting to use her limbs.

When her head finally bobbed to the surface, she greedily sucked in a huge gulp of air and water, and promptly spewed it back up. Arms and legs thrashed as she struggled to grab another breath. Suddenly she was fighting for her very life. Battling the pull of the river, she fought to reach the shore.

What seemed like hours later, Fanny lay on the muddy bank between rotting wharves that clung to weak pilings. She'd barely managed to pull herself half out of the water, the weight of her dress like an anchor holding her back. Panting, she laid her head among sparse blades of grass and wondered where Mother was.

When she came to again, it was close to dusk, the sun showing as a red orb in the west. Shivering, she staggered to her knees, her skirt dragging at the edge of the river. With fading energy, she pulled herself the rest of the way onto the bank and lay gasping for oxygen, resting against the broken carcass of a fish boat with the topside stripped bare.

Water wept from her clothes and she shook in an early evening breeze. Her hair had pulled free of its confinement and hung in wet ropes around her shoulders. Her brain seemed to freeze over, and she slept where she lay in the mud of the bank.

CHAPTER TWO

When Fanny woke again it was dark. A halo of light showed off to the side and proved to be a warehouse where, judging by the sounds coming from within, work was still being conducted. She dragged herself to her feet, leaning on the hull of the boat to steady herself, then crept forward. Through the doorway, two men could be seen applying a coat of colour to the hull of a fish boat that was supported on stilts above their heads.

"That's it, then," one man said. "We can polish her tomorrow when she's good and dry." They began to pack up their buckets and brooms. Fanny shuffled into the dark corner behind a stack of barrels and wondered if they would notice her. But the men grabbed jackets and slid the wide door closed, locking it as they departed.

Panic grabbed her throat and squeezed it closed. Now she was locked in. What if she needed to get out? How would she escape? Sliding to the floor she leaned her back against the wall. Mother would be worried. She had to get word to her somehow.

In the night, she became aware of a low meow and the nudge of a furry beast against her hand. A cat had crept into the warehouse. It curled on her legs, purred for a while, and as Fanny petted its warm coat, it snoozed in her lap.

~ * * * ~

"What do you mean, you didn't notice?" Cownden Lanser slashed the air with his hand in a fierce rage. "Tell me again what happened. And you'd better not leave anything out." Disbelief fought with anger in his gut. How could something like this escape his control in his own country?

It was bad enough that he'd been flying home from the meetings in Gilsigg, Legitamia, in one of the Khandarken aircarts when Leader Harold Master died. No, Cownden wasn't responsible for their security in a foreign land. Nor did he have access to examine their aircarts during the visit there. But he was the Chief Constable! It was unthinkable that that explosion had happened on his watch.

Yet what he was hearing now brought new anger up his throat. He motioned impatiently at the young Constable standing before him and pointed at his assistant, Anatoliy, to take notes.

The Constable straightened his spine. "We had been to the Children's Corral this morning, Sir. Ms Master has not been well and it was the first outing in weeks." His face was pale and sweat dripped down his temples as he took a shallow breath.

"We were coming back from the south side of the City, I was driving the guard transport and had Fellows with me. Wil was the driver of the Master vehicle. We turned onto the bridge and I gunned the engine to make the climb. I can only think the sound of the engine drowned out what was happening behind, Sir."

The young man stopped and stared desperately into Cownden's eyes. Cownden gave a demanding nod for him to continue.

"We heard a bang, Fellows said *what was that*. I looked in my reflectors but couldn't see the transport because an old black hydro-truck had pulled in behind me. So when we got to the other side of the bridge, I pulled off to wait for Wil. Meanwhile Fellows was using his beltlink to find out where the hell... Sorry, Sir. He was trying to locate Wil, but there was no reply to his message."

Cownden swore under his breath. "And the hydro-truck?"

"What about it, Sir?"

"Who was in the truck?!"

Cownden's bellow nearly blew the Constable out of his boots. He swayed and one hand fluttered to his forehead to wipe at the moisture gathered there. "I don't know, Sir," he muttered. "I climbed out to look back for Wil and the truck carried on. When it passed, that's when I was able to see behind. The bridge railing was gone, smashed and hanging out over the water."

Cownden motioned tiredly to Anatoliy, who escorted the Constable out. It was already dark. He had no hope of any of his crew finding something until daylight, but they had to get moving if they were to set up the rescue operation for the break of dawn. It seemed unlikely anyone had survived. How would the women manage to extricate themselves from the transport once it hit the water? And even if they did, how would they get to safety? Perhaps the driver had escaped and could tell them what had happened. This was a nightmare.

He glanced longingly at his voicelink. It would be another night away from his new bride. Selanna would be sleeping now, he'd best not wake her.

CHAPTER THREE

Early morning came and with it a dim light from the upper windows of the warehouse. Fanny shivered and unsteadily managed to get to her feet. The cat was gone. The men would be back soon and she had to vacate the premises before they found her. She didn't know who was friend or who was enemy, and she couldn't take the chance to find out. Her life, and her mother's life, depended on making the right decisions. Searching, she found a half-eaten pané sandwich and quickly devoured it. A single door on the side opened into an overgrown alley. And on a hook beside the door hung a worn jacket. Slipping it over her shoulders, she was soon lost in the back lanes of Old Towne.

Her family had already been under attack. Her father's murder was a devastating event that they hadn't recovered from. But this new assault was even more astounding. *Who was after them, and why?* It had become very personal. She would have to find Mother and go into hiding until this was over.

Would she be safe in the collapsing streets of this ancient part of the City? Her bare feet were tender on the old cobblestones. But her dress had dried. Her hair must be a mess, the pins long gone. Running her hands through the snarls, she smoothed it the best she could.

Sitting on the low wall in the central park square of Old Towne, she listened to the fountain gurgle behind her and warmed herself in the sun. Soon she would have to pull herself together and find her mother. Soon they would have to make a decision about where to go and what to do until these attacks were over. That was when she learned her fate.

This was the best part of the old quarters on the 'wrong' side of the Violetta River. The cobblestone lanes led off from the fountain in all directions like the spokes of a wheel from the hub. An old fellow in a dated pinstriped suit paused near the fountain to feed the pigeons. The birds leaped and dove around him as he scattered seeds on the pavement.

Before long she spied a second man emerging from one of the lanes. He approached, a large leather-bound book under his arm. "Holmes," he said with upper crust diction, "thought I'd find you here. Just laid my hand on a decent copy of that book you were looking for."

The pinstriped suit shifted on the fountain wall, his shoulders hunched. The man's face grew long. "Won't need it now, Wordsmith. Things have changed. It's a disaster, really."

Wordsmith stopped in his tracks, his eyes keen. "What? What has happened?" Cautiously he glanced around, but must not have noticed Fanny where she sat still as a mouse while the shade of the lotus tree stole over her.

She should get going, but it was pleasant here, and there was nowhere to go. She was still trying to come up with a plan. *Was it safe to go back home and see if Mother was there? Would they have taken her to the hospital? Should she call General Paulo Regiment?* He was the one who had guaranteed their safety after Father died, and look where that had gotten them.

Fanny turned her head to watch as the man continued. "It has been devastating news."

Wordsmith examined his friend for a minute, then dropped the book on the wall and sat beside him. "Tell me."

"My client is dead. The one who wanted that book. She's dead. She and her daughter both died in the Violetta River yesterday. They pulled the transport from the water this morning and their Constable driver was still behind the frontboard. They're arranging a dive now to recover the bodies."

Fanny's breath caught in her throat and it wouldn't go in or out. She tried to cough, but nothing happened. It was as if she really were drowning. Jerking upright, she finally pulled in some air and bent over in despair, waiting for the dizziness to pass. Mother had died in the river. She was dead.

Fanny should have known. It wasn't likely that they both managed to swim to shore and pull themselves out of the muddy waters. Her heart

11

cramped in her chest and she massaged the spot to try to ease the pressure. *Mother was dead.* Now she had no family at all.

~ * * * ~

Only sheer determination kept Fanny moving in the days that followed, picking up a pair of rubber plastic boots sitting untended at some back door to replace her lost shoes, finding a sack with an apple core and half-eaten leg of fried olinguito in it for her next meal. Her thoughts jumbled, she just kept moving. If she was moving, they couldn't find her, could they? The threat was still out there, waiting for her to slip up.

On unsteady legs, she worked her way out of the City and away from the Catastrophic Ocean. As she travelled further into the Southern Territory, she became weak as a kitten, her only goal to find a safe place to hole up until she could figure out what to do next. But when she saw the sorry sight, something in her heart wouldn't let her walk by.

The child was sitting in a dry ditch at the edge of the dirt road amongst clumps of dead grass, humming to himself, with his filthy head pressed against a crumpled grey blanket. Fanny glanced around but no one else was in sight. He paid her no heed as he explored a thread in the blanket with his thumb nail.

"Hello, there," she called softly.

He looked up and grinned, little teeth white against grubby cheeks, then immediately grabbed the blanket and tugged on it. "Wake up," he whined. When he looked back at her, his face was haggard. "She won't wake up any more."

Fanny looked more closely. There was a still body at the bottom of the incline, partially hidden by the deep grass, legs sticking out from beneath the blanket. Fanny's gaze flipped back to the little boy as she slid and stumbled down the side of the ditch. Kneeling, she placed a hand on the motionless foot and shook it.

There was no doubt the owner was dead, the woman's body stiff as a board. There were no obvious signs of trauma to the woman's head or face, but Fanny was no doctor. She didn't know what to look for.

The boy was thin and listless as he watched her for a moment and then seemed to lose interest. He resumed his humming, picking at the stitches in his dirty ill-fitting shirt. Fanny stared at him in indecision. She was so weak she wondered if she could pull herself out of the ditch, let alone take on the added care of a child.

He gazed up at her with strange yellow -brown eyes, then just grabbed her hand and held it. As she knelt in the brittle weeds, frozen with indecision, she heard a low rumble nearby, like the sound of a tryke engine on idle. Cautiously she raised her head and looked around.

Through the tall grass and low shrubs, she spotted the huge mottled hide of a mountain cat. The large head slowly swung in her direction, and one round ear twitched as if to flick away an insect. The golden eyes with a slit in the iris, eyes just like the small boy's, seemed to gaze directly at her for a long moment as her breath caught in her throat. Her heart thumped heavily in her chest. Had she survived the Violetta River only to die in the jaws of a lion?

Then the strange yellow eye slowly closed and the big head swung away. When she blinked and looked again, the cat was gone. It was a moment before her heart slowed and her breathing returned to normal.

She'd had no choice but to take the boy with her. Rummaging through the woman's things, she found a piece of ident. The name—F Winthrop.

Fanny couldn't believe her good fortune. She had her own ident still, it hadn't washed away in the river, but she was mortally afraid to use it in case the Master name was flagged. But now she had Boulter with her, who was too young to have his own ident, but was listed on his mother's document And she had a new name. It would take a lot to recognize her now, wouldn't it?

CHAPTER FOUR

*T*he grinding noise came from the far wall. Alarmed, Damian struggled to rise from the bed but found his hands were already tied behind his back. He must be strapped securely to the pallet because he couldn't move. The grinding grew louder as if it was approaching where he lay, then the clicking started off to the left. He twisted his head wildly, trying to dislodge the blindfold fastened over his eyes. It was no use. He was bound so tightly his hands were numb.

When the whirring commenced, he could almost feel the machine drawing closer and hovering over his face even though he couldn't see a thing. It was right above him now, inches from his head. If only he could get one hand free he might be able to shove it away. As he tugged against the tight bonds, he felt the skin break under the rough rope and blood ran down his wrist to pool in his palm.

He wanted to howl, to bellow in fright and rage. But he couldn't get his lips apart. There was a bundle of cloth stuffed *in his mouth and his jaw was tied tightly shut. Ominously, the clicking stopped and that's when the grunting began, slowly growing in volume till it filled the room with noise. This was the sound he feared the most, the sound that gave him nightmares. He waited for the first harsh blow to connect with his skull.*

Damian Stuke came suddenly awake. He was drenched with sweat and a thin blanket was tangled tightly around his body as if he were a mummy in a coffin. His lungs heaved for air and his heart pounded heavily in his chest. The light was just starting to show at a window to his left. *Where was he?*

Then he recognized the place, the small house he rented in Bereford, near the Jirani border of the Western Territory of Khandarken. Turning his head, he saw Nikesh snoring faintly on a pallet against the far wall. This is where he lived, this was where he worked for Makulski, the gamer.

Sighing, he rolled over and heaved the blanket off his sweaty chest. Nikesh stirred and opened his eyes.

"Damian. Are we on duty?"

"Pretty soon," he muttered. "I'll be first in the garderobe." He staggered down the hall on unsteady legs and stepped into the grungy facility, pulling the door closed behind him. He leaned on the shelf under the water basin, staring into the plexi mirror propped against the wall.

A tall lean man stared back at him. His light brown hair needed a barber, but his sideburns were neatly clipped along his jaw. The muscles stood out on his heavy shoulders as he tightened his grip on the counter. His brown eyes were most noticeable due to the deep marks gouged beneath them.

Da was a doctor and worked with many of the dispossessed in Bereford. He had his own way of helping his patients deal with mental stress and night dreams. But Damian hadn't been taking his medication. He didn't like the way it made him feel. And the treatments that his sister Selanna gave him worked miracles but she'd recently married Cownden Lanser and wasn't available to attend to his sorry hide right now.

He splashed his face with cold water and used a towel to wipe the sweat off his chest. He could handle this. It wasn't anything new, just a left over from the Last War. Many men had the same problem.

More pressing was the fact that Selanna had married the Chief Constable of Khandarken and Damian worked for the biggest crook in the Western Territory.

CHAPTER FIVE

Many weeks later in Deep Creek...

Fanny stopped at the edge of the open field of yellow parched grass and turned to the little boy at her side. "You have to promise to stay here, Boulter. There's no choice. Promise you won't leave and that you'll be here when I come back for you."

Boulter glared up at her with a ferocious frown between his small brows. "I said I would, didn't I? I don't know why you don't believe me."

She knelt and straightened the collar of his outgrown yellow shirt, tucking the tails into khaki pants that were clearly too big for him. "I do believe you, sweetheart. I really do." She leaned forward and kissed his thin cheek. "I just worry. That's what mother's do."

The frown faded and a little smile appeared on his pursed mouth. He liked it when she talked about being his mother. It seemed to soothe something in his heart. She patted the dog, a long-legged dark brown Penrhy hound that sat on its haunches beside Boulter. "Stay with him, Mickens. Don't let him out of your sight. Keep him safe."

Shouldering her bag, she stood and pointed down the field. "There's a playground for the school children at the other end. See it there? You could play on the swings and slides while the other kids are in class so they don't bother you. And your lunch is in the sack. Don't share it with Mickens. He can find his own. He catches mice and rabbits for his lunch."

That sack held all the food she'd managed to scrounge for the day. But she knew her words fell on deaf ears. Boulter always shared even the meagre meal she packed for him. He didn't like to think of his dog going hungry. But she had her hands full just feeding the two of them, let alone that rangy hound that had inextricably attached itself to them some weeks ago. It was a strange beast, never growled or barked, but she'd heard it make a clicking noise in its throat sometimes and she'd learned to listen for that sound. It was usually a warning of some kind.

"All right, Boulter. Give me a kiss. I'll be back as soon as I can, but it might be late. Ms Hawker is very fussy and she doesn't let me leave until everything is done just so." She leaned down to receive a wet smack on her cheek. Tears threatened and she threw her arms around his narrow shoulders in a fierce hug.

That kiss was so sweet and trusting. She prayed she could live up to what he needed in the way of care.

Hurrying across the jumble of transit tracks, she walked quickly up the road to the cross street. At the corner, she turned to look over her shoulder in time to see Boulter and Mickens disappear behind the back wall of a huge building that bordered the expanse of brown grass. Its clerestory windows glinted high in the walls. She didn't know what the structure was used for, but had noticed there were always a lot of men hanging around the entrance. It could be a hall for the dispossessed. The men were not in uniform of any kind that she recognized, no sellers outfits, no military dress, nothing formal at all. And many of them walked with a limp or had other obvious injuries. Hopefully he'd be able to stay out of their way. Such men weren't the best kind of company for a small boy.

She walked faster. If she was late for work, there would be no end of trouble. Ms Hawker was a strange woman, but had proved to be a useful way station in the downhill slide that had become Fanny's life in the last months. She had found work with Hawker, not full-time but enough to keep body and soul together. For now, that would have to do. She wouldn't be here forever. At least, that was her plan.

Her employer was a knitter and weaver, and Fanny had been trained not only in weaving techniques but also in fabric design. Although she tried not to show it, Ms Hawker had been impressed with her knowledge. It had added greatly to the persuasive powers during her negotiations for a wage. Ms

Hawker had given in surprisingly early in the discussion, obviously anxious to hire her as an assistant.

Fanny climbed the two steps to the door of a small, deceptively tidy-looking home on a side street of Deep Creek and tugged the bell-pull attached to the post near the entry. Slow footsteps approached from within, followed by a scuffling noise, and the door finally opened. Ms Hawker stood there, a knitting needle stuck through her streaked gray hair which was scraped back helter-skelter into an untidy knot on the back of her head. Her robe was creased as if she'd slept in it, and she wore loose slippers on her feet.

"You're late." Her wide mouth turned down in a frown of annoyance.

Fanny moved inside, forcing the woman to take a step backward into the pile of bags blocking the hallway behind her. "I am not late. I'm right on time." She slid her thin shawl from her shoulders and hung it on the overloaded coat rack by the entrance, glancing up to catch a reluctant smile on her employer's face which was quickly erased.

"Well, you're almost late." Ms Hawker turned and stamped her way through the crowded space past stacks of boxes, piles of bags and old books to the large open room at the back of the house.

Fanny followed, setting her tote on the floor inside the doorway. "No," she replied. "A person is either late or they're not. I'm not late." Her tone was very firm. She'd discovered early on that she could never let Ms Hawker get away with a thing. It was a constant struggle, but she refused to be badgered for something that wasn't true and for which her employer would try to penalize her.

Ms Hawker glared and pointed to a chair. "Sit there. Here is what I hope to get done today. The rug you have on the loom is for Julianne Adjudicator, Mr Abe Farmer's wife. It's almost finished, I need it completed this morning. She's anxious to have it delivered today. Then I have an order for three bed throws, all in llama hair, for that shop downtown. Better get busy."

Fanny sat and made herself comfortable but didn't begin work. The mention of Julianne Adjudicator always gave her cramps in her belly as alarm sizzled down her nerves. If she ever happened to run into Ms Adjudicator face-to-face, she was positive Julianne would recognize her on the spot. Although now she went by the name of Fanny Wingham, that likely wouldn't protect her. She'd known Julianne most of her life, both at school and later in the social circles of the City.

If she were recognized, she'd have to run again, as fast as possible. Maybe she wouldn't even have a chance to take Boulter with her. The very idea was enough to give her nightmares. She took a deep breath to calm herself.

Glancing around the room, she noted nothing had changed since the last time she was here. Piles of raw wool and flax lay on the floor in an uneven jumble. There was a full set of shelves against the back wall but they were almost hidden from view by the bales of spun yarn and bolts of fabric that filled it. The floor was littered with scraps of coloured strands and swirls of thread discarded from the busy and productive needles. At the end of the day, she'd gather it up and spin it into yarn she could use to make Boulter a sweater. Fanny waited, her hands in her lap until Ms Hawker turned back to her, outraged brows raised at the lack of activity.

"What are you waiting for? We've got a full day ahead of us."

Fanny firmed her lips. "Ms Hawker, this rug is not almost finished. It is at most half done. You know that. It won't be finished today. You know that as well. It's a four-day job, and we are two days into it." She waited, knowing how annoyed this would make her employer, but also aware that if she didn't get the truth on the table, she'd be yelled at or penalized for not getting the work done that she supposedly should have completed.

Ms Hawker stared in astonishment, then looked back at the loom. "Oh, by all the angels, you are such an obstinate girl." She huffed for a minute, then nodded and plopped herself into the other chair by the window. "Well, get busy then. Obviously you're slower than I thought. We won't get it done tomorrow if you don't begin today, which means you'll have to stay late to complete it."

Fanny smiled to herself and picked up the first shuttle wound with a rough dull green wool. If she had to stay late, Boulter would have a long day on his own, but she'd have enough money for groceries. And the chances of running into Julianne Adjudicator were very slim. She lived with her husband on the

Farmer Holdings land far to the east of Deep Creek, close to the Catastrophic Ocean.

She began to weave, every few minutes referring for design detail to the painting on the easel beside her. There was silence in the room save for the sound of the shuttle sliding and clattering against the weaving frame, and the click of needles as Ms Hawker knit and rocked in her chair. The motion and low sounds were soothing and Fanny began to relax. Tension slowly eased from her neck and shoulders as she moved into the rhythm of the rug.

"This colour green is especially kind to the eye," she commented presently. "It's a little less vibrant than in the picture and therefore the colours of the dresses and robes will stand out that much more pleasingly."

Ms Hawker smiled. "Yes, it was a good choice." She rocked and knit. "You're a clever girl, Fanny. It was your idea to use that colour."

Fanny laughed low. It was always thus. They would begin the day with a confrontation over some issue and she would have to make her employer back down or she'd get bowled over. Yet when the dust settled, Ms Hawker was really a very nice woman, just unable to deal with anything when she got her ire up. "Did you get up on the wrong side of your bed this morning, Ms?" Fanny teased.

Ms Hawker frowned. "Don't go there." But then she relented and gave a small smile. "I might have. I had a nightmare last night, and when I woke I couldn't get back to sleep. I wasn't sure I'd even be able to have you here today. I thought I'd be too tired."

"Ahh. I'm sorry, Ms." Fanny glanced up to catch a fleeting look of pain on her employer's face. "I shouldn't assume I'm the only one with nightmares." She bit her lip, hoping she hadn't opened a door that should be kept locked shut. Her past was as secret as anyone's. Most people in Khandarken had stories they preferred not to tell.

"Yes. I guess a lot of people have them. The war went on so long, no one escaped damage, did they?" Ms Hawker sent her a piercing glance.

Fanny shook her head in agreement and sympathy. But her own betrayal had come much later, after Khandarken became its own country with an elected Leader who was her father and the promise of law and order amongst the people. That promise had turned out to be a lie.

"You don't have to worry, Ms Hawker. If you're tired and want to rest, you know I'll keep working until the day is done. You trust me, don't you? Otherwise you wouldn't have me come so often and do this weaving for you. Your reputation rests on my handiwork."

Her employer nodded. "True. If I need to later, I'll lay down for a while."

Fanny dropped the shuttle and bent to pick it up off the floor. Maybe she should seize the opening her employer had just handed her. "I just wish you'd let me bring my son with me. Boulter is a good boy and no trouble at all. As it is, I have to leave him in the field near the transit station while I'm here. It would be so much better and safer if he could come with me."

Ms Hawker's face went hard. In the light from the window, it looked like it was made of stone, save for the sudden heat high in her plump cheeks. "No." Just the one word. She rocked harder. "No children."

Folding the needles together, she slapped them down on the table with a muffled thump as the half-finished garment tangled in the sharp tips. "I'll see to our mid-day dinner." She left the room in a slow shuffle, her slippers slapping against the wood floor.

CHAPTER SIX

*T*he grinding noise began again and Damian writhed in the tight bonds that secured his wrists and ankles. They hadn't blindfolded him this time. That only made it worse in some ways. He could see the machine approaching along a rail above his body, rather than just trying to imagine where it might be hovering.

He didn't know when it would strike, it's chrome arms folded back at an awkward angle. Someone stood behind the sheet of darkened plexi, manipulating the machines and regulating the speed of attack. As he watched, one arm slowly unfolded and a pincer-like probe emerged, pointing at his chest. He opened his mouth to scream...

Opening his eyes, Damian glanced desperately around the sparse unfamiliar room. He suddenly recognized the space. This was the barracks at the back of the fighting arts training studio, situated near the transit yard. He'd arrived here in Deep Creek, Southern Territory of Khandarken, a few days ago and was scheduled to begin training once he finished the registration procedures.

He gasped a few deep breaths and sank weakly back against the pallet. What had he been thinking, to leave Bereford and his group of long-time cronies to start a new career with the establishment? Last month, the Khandarken military was his bitterest enemy. His old boss, Makulski, ran a tight syndicate for gamblers and games players. The race track was just one of his hangouts. Damian had worked for Makulski for more than a few years and had become his number one enforcer. If a man made a bet, he paid his debt, and if he didn't Damian came after him.

No one knew the extent of what he had done, working for the gambling syndicate and collecting money owed from those who couldn't pay. It had been a desperate way to live, but these were desperate times. As Makulski's head man, nothing happened that Damian didn't know about. That's why leaving the syndicate was both very hard and extremely easy. He knew too much for Makulski to try to stop him. Damian just had to watch his back every step of the way.

Thank the gods he was alone in the room after that nightmare. Although there were four pallets stacked against the bare wooden wall, all were empty save his. Shuddering, he reached for his shirt on the rubber plastic rack where he'd discarded it the night before, and wiped at the sweat that stood out on his forehead and ran down his temples into his hair.

He hadn't had that nightmare in a while. Being a prisoner of the Empire on the Helmcken Trail during the Last War had left a permanent imprint on a lot of men, and he was no exception. Damian had only been fifteen when he ran away to join up, full of fire and anxious to do his share to defeat Emperor Aqatain and his army. He hadn't waited to train, had simply jumped into the fray.

His father did medical work on behalf of the Emperor's troops at the beginning of the war. He was an Empire man. But as the corruption and obscenities grew, he'd been forced to reconsider his position. After much agonizing self-scrutiny, and as the evidence mounted of the vicious attacks on civilians, Dr Stuke had taken the staggering step of changing sides in the midst of the fight.

At fifteen, Damian had been overwhelmed by that single event. If his own father, a principled, hardworking, thoughtful man and a good doctor, could no longer justify the Emperor's position, he couldn't either.

He was captured on his sixteenth birthday. The troops he'd joined were a roughly organized lot who conducted a kind of secret war against the Emperor's men, attacking out of the shadows, dealing a telling blow and swiftly retreating. They were often effective but poorly equipped, and with no discipline or training to speak of. Damian was one of the youngest fighting with them and the first to be caught.

He wiped his chest with a swipe of the shirt and threw the plain military blanket aside. He was still struggling with the fact that he was here in Deep Creek. Having a brother by marriage who was the Chief Constable of Khandarken had somehow changed things for everyone in the family. Cownden Lanser seemed to be the kind of man who arranged matters to suit his own vision, and Damian had been swept up in that process. Thus, his trip to the fighting arts centre.

Cownden had turned him over to the military to be trained. The plan was to meet with Abe Farmer today, sort out the programme he'd signed up for and get his stay here organized. He'd only met Farmer once, and that was at his sister Selanna's wedding to Cownden. It seemed odd that his path should cross with Farmer's again so quickly. The nuptials had taken place to the south in Sommerset, the capital of Adar Silva, the same place that had harboured Emperor Aqatain for so many years before he was driven back into the hills and beaten at his own war.

Damian grunted and grabbed his sack, stalking down the empty hall to the open garderobe. As he tossed his gear on a bench and turned on the tap of the nearest shower, he saw there were already a couple of men here in the early morning light. The water wasn't warm but it was tolerable.

Maybe he'd get himself private quarters in the town of Deep Creek, because it would be embarrassing to wake up screaming like a baby from his nightmares when he was surrounded by other military men and dispossessed who were here training to create a new life for themselves. What kind of impression would that make? Not a good one, by the graves.

He shucked his uniform shorts and watched the nearest guy carefully navigate a razor around the long sideburns decorating his jaw. He was wearing a towel wrapped at the waist, and Damian immediately noticed the replacement foot that had been installed on his damaged left leg. The man must have been wealthy or of some value to the military that they'd invested in such a device. His father had tried to send several men from his country practice at Bereford into the capital of Khandarken for replacement parts, but didn't often meet with success.

The guy caught his glance in the mirror. "Army or reserves?" he asked.

Damian nodded. "Army, but just joined." This fellow didn't need to know why he was here or who he worked for. It was supposed to be highly confidential.

The man drew the sharp razor carefully across his chin. "Yeah, this is where a lot of them start, if they're lucky. Good training to have, and Farmer is the best at the fighting arts that I've seen."

Damian nodded an acknowledgement of the comment and stepped under the stream of water, beginning to soap up. That's what he'd heard too. Farmer was the best, not just at the fighting but at the training. His brother by marriage, Cownden Lanser, had persuaded him to agree to this task. And judging from what he knew of the plan for where he was headed, he'd need every fighting advantage he could get.

CHAPTER SEVEN

Abe Farmer, owner of the fighting arts studio, arrived mid-morning. He took Damian into his private office, which amounted to no more than a tabletop made from a discarded door with a few chairs ranged around it, one with a broken leg. The room was small, a narrow set of shelves fitted tightly into the corner under the clerestory window. It was obvious that most of the space in the building was given over to the fighting arena in the centre.

"Sit there." Abe pointed to what appeared to be the best chair, upholstered in plush fabric with a high back and wheels under the feet, while he hitched one with no arms up to the edge of the makeshift desk.

Damian raised his brows but gingerly sat. The chair creaked ominously.

Abe grinned as he pulled a stack of onion skin forward. "Don't worry, it won't give out. At least I don't think it will." His face was tanned a light brown. It contrasted sharply with his white-blond hair sitting in tight curls around his head and down the sideburns that lined his jaw.

Damian's own hair needed a trim but he hadn't yet taken the time since he arrived in Deep Creek to attend to such personal details. He would soon, along with finding his own room. "Do you know why I'm here?" he asked curiously.

Abe nodded and glanced up. "Yes, and no." He stroked his chin. "Men are sent to me at different times for different reasons, by different people. A lot of the guys training here right now are the dispossessed who need some kind of structure and formality to their lives. They then hire out as bodyguards or personal protection."

He eyed Damian for a minute, then looked down at the onion skin under his hand. "I know Cownden Lanser pretty well. He's been quite precise about your training."

Damian shrugged. "In what way?"

Farmer sat back and tapped the plank thoughtfully with his fingertips. "I'd say he has something specific in mind for you, because the main emphasis is on self-defence rather than offence. He obviously wants to keep you safe. He also says you've fought in the military before, during the Last War, which would have been eight or ten years ago. You seem pretty young to have been involved in that battle."

Damian laughed. "Yah, I was. Fifteen when I signed up and sixteen when I was captured." The memory of his nightmare from the early morning burst full bloom behind his eyelids and he pressed a thumb to his temple to contain the headache that had been dogging him since he woke.

"Ah." Abe scrutinised the page again. "Along the Helmcken Trail, perhaps."

Damian nodded. "Yah, that's right."

"How's your head?"

He glanced up in surprise. "Huh? I've got a bit of a headache actually."

"Yah, I can see that." Abe stood and reached for the door. "Sprinter! Two teas." When the tea arrived, he rummaged on the shelves for a folded paper and sprinkled a powder into one of the bowls, passing it across the plank to him. "This should help."

Damian sniffed it suspiciously, then drank it down and as they talked he found the headache had receded to a dull throb.

"You'll have to deal with those memories at some point," Abe said casually. "Ignoring them doesn't make them go away. There's medication for that."

Damian shook his head. "Yah, I've had the medication, my Da is a doctor. But I don't like the way it makes me feel. I have another method of dealing with the problem."

"Have you?" Abe stared at him. "I'd like to hear about it. You're not the only one dealing with difficult events from the past. But if you're considering alcohol or phang as a solution, I don't recommend it."

"I've tried both of those, with limited success." Damian grinned, then cleared his throat awkwardly. "My sister's a sookie."

Abe nodded as light dawned on his face. "Ah, Selanna Nettles, Cownden's wife."

He grimaced. "Hard to stay under the radar with the Chief Constable of Khandarken for a brother by marriage."

Abe laughed. "All right, so how does having a sookie in the family help your nightmares? Because they are nightmares, aren't they?"

His mouth tightened for a moment. "She knows how to deal with them. It's just been a while since she gave me a treatment. If I have time this week, I'll make an appointment with her for a session."

"Sounds good." Abe shuffled the onion skins into a pile and set them aside.

Damian's shoulders relaxed and he stood. "Who's going to work with me on this training?"

Abe waved him toward the door. "I'm going to start you with Sprinter and we'll go from there. I'll work with you when I can but we're going to take it easy for the first bit. There's no rush."

~ * * * ~

Damian threw a kick and his opponent stepped out of reach just as he put his full weight behind it. He lost his balance and fell forward on the mat in a spectacular sprawl of limbs. As he lay there waiting to regain his breath, he heard a sound, like a giggle that was quickly muffled. Turning his head toward the open back door, he caught a glimpse of small legs powering out of sight, a long-legged hound bounding after.

35

It wasn't the first time he'd heard someone out there. Rolling to his feet, he stepped through the doorway, only to see the pair fleeing around the far corner of the fighting arts building.

Moving back inside, he wiped the sweat from his brow with a cloth from the bench and stalked toward the centre of the mats, getting ready to have another try.

"It's just a couple of kids," Sprinter said. "They hang around now and then. Like to watch the training, I guess." Sprinter was older, in his mid-fifties, his head completely bald, but the gray sideburns were long and full down his cheeks. He seemed to be a man of great patience, if their training so far was anything to measure it by.

"Is everyone as slow to learn as I am?" Damian muttered as he positioned his feet again.

Sprinter gave a guffaw of laughter. "You're doing fine. Most can't manage this much in their first sessions. Don't give up yet. I'm just getting started with you. We'll take a break now and come back at it in a bit."

As Sprinter loped off down the hall, Damian grabbed two apples from a bowl near the front entry and headed to the back door where he'd seen the child. Stepping outside, he narrowed his eyes against the glare of the sun.

There they were, a small boy hunkered down in the dry brown grass by the corner of the building, the dog lounging at his feet. The little fellow couldn't be more than four or five and small for his age at that. His face was thin, his skinny shoulders crammed into a too-small shirt. His shoes were worn through on one toe, the other one swaddled with binding tape. The hound was an elegant Penrhy, long-legged and rangy, with the notable elongated snout and drooping ears. Everyone knew they originated from Jiran and were from the dominant Penrhy tribe, raised by the nobles. What was such a hound doing in the company of this young ragamuffin?

When the boy saw Damian he jumped up and readied to run. Damian held his hand out with an apple balanced on the palm. "There's one for each of us," he called. Then he sat on the bench by the walkway and took a huge bite. The child hesitated, his eyes big and focussed closely on the fruit, but he didn't approach.

When Damian was finished, he rose and went back to work, leaving the second apple on the bench behind him. Even as he stepped inside, he caught a glimpse of a small body creeping toward the bait.

CHAPTER EIGHT

In the village of Discovery, just inside the north Khandarken border, Emperor Carlton smoothed wavy black hair back from his face and ran a hand down his long, neatly trimmed sideburns. By the gods, he was ready.

He stepped through the door of the crowded village hall which had been commandeered, along with every other building in the town, when they took it by storm months ago. He was followed closely by General Elkon, the leader of his troops. They waited expectantly in the entry as the noise of many voices rose and then abruptly subsided at the sight of him.

When there was total silence, Carlton paraded slowly between the tables to the front of the large room. Elkon waved at a chair situated there for his use. It wasn't much of a throne, more of an armchair that had been confiscated, hastily covered with a red throw, and placed on a raised platform.

Carlton reined in his impatience. These things would happen all in good time. For some years after the end of the Last War his father, Emperor Aqatain, had held a small province in the south of Legitamia as his stronghold. Carlton had assumed control at his father's death and managed to add more land to his holdings, including this village in Khandarken. Things were finally moving in the right direction.

General Elkon took up position at his elbow as Carlton adjusted the fit of his tailored black jacket and assumed his rather uncomfortable seat on the raised chair, scanning the attentive faces in the packed room. Everyone was standing, waiting for some signal from him. When he nodded, he saw from the corner of his eye as Elkon waved his arm and the men near the front found their chairs. First were the Counsellors, men who advised and planned strategy, working on theory and tactics. Next were the generals and section leaders of his army, the men who would make his empire rise once again from the bitter ashes of the Last War. At the back of the crowded hall stood troops who had pressed in to find a spot against the wall in order to hear what was said. He knew there were throngs of men outside, awaiting word of everything that was discussed.

His Advisor, Judson Lanser, was at the front. He would leave tomorrow morning on a diplomatic mission to Legitamia. It was hoped, but uncertain, that General Barrington would see him in Gilsigg. But the goal was to try to soothe feelings and calm nerves in the capital.

There had been a weighty conference in Gilsigg last month to which Carlton had not been invited, with leaders from all the surrounding countries in attendance. The purpose had been to demand Barrington put a rein on the Emperor's activities with regard to cross-border raids out of his Legitamia location. As a consequence, Carlton felt less secure about his holding of a small southern province in that country. He didn't want one step forward and two steps back, seizing a new village only to lose the ones he already held. He wouldn't stand for it.

Carlton raised a hand. "Greetings, gentlemen of the Empire." There was a low murmur of sound in response.

He tried again. "Greetings, gentlemen of the Empire." The reply was much louder, especially rising from the horde at the back of the hall. Carlton laughed and stood from the chair as it wobbled on the platform. He was more comfortable on his feet, the jacket tugged snugly across his chest. He'd gained muscle since his father's death and it showed in the fit of his clothes.

"We have taken the first step in Khandarken toward a new empire. You must be very proud because the town of Discovery is now *ours*." The crowd roared. Personally, he didn't think much of this step. Discovery was tiny, no more than a couple dozen houses and a few shops. But there was a sparse forest that gave them cover from attack by air, and a place for his troops to camp. And every inch closer to recovering the lost Empire was an inch closer to justice.

The howl of approval from the crowd drowned out his next words and he grinned, waiting for calm once more. If these men were pleased with their progress, then it was all to the good. Keep them moving, keep them fed. He hadn't always gotten along with his father, but he'd learned a lot from the late Emperor Aqatain.

He raised his hands for silence and began again. "Now that we have a foothold in Khandarken, we can take the next step. That would be to cement this place to our holding just across the border in Legitamia. Slowly we grow. Slowly we move forward. Who can question our claim when we occupy this land?"

The excited noise drowned out further words and he sat again, pleased with the reaction. The Counsellors weren't as vocal but most of them looked satisfied at the response. He waved General Elkon over. "Who's going next?" he asked.

"Your Advisor, Sir. He wanted the first words."

Of course he did. Judson Lanser had been a stalwart in support of Emperor Aqatain, even in defeat after the Last War. He'd managed to organize a retreat north, leaving Adar Silva where the Emperor had held court in the glory days. They'd moved through the mountains and eventually into the small province in the south of what became Legitamia that they now called home. When Aqatain died suddenly, Lanser had been just as quick to support Carlton's position as successor to the Empire.

Carlton nodded and Lanser rose from his seat at the first table to stride forward. He stood tall, his iron gray hair long on his shoulders and combed straight back from a high forehead. He preferred robes to the military uniforms most of the men wore. The one he had on tonight was tan-coloured and decorated with the old Empire crest embroidered across the back and down the sleeves, the collar encrusted with jewels.

"Gentlemen," he declared. "Give me your attention. I will be brief. We have taken the first steps in a long journey to power. There is no doubt of our right and ability to resurrect the Empire. It will take stamina, it will take persuasion, it will take…"

Carlton had heard it all before. Lanser was good at this and liked to seize the opportunity when some of the rank and file were present to send his message once again.

"But we need planning," Advisor continued, "and tonight we present our next plan. General Elkon, do you have the map?"

Elkon produced an onion skin map and spread it over the table at the front of the hall. There was a low murmur as chairs shifted and men rose to get a better look.

Lanser held up his hands. "Hold on. We'll all have a chance to examine it. Just listen for the moment. We have a foothold in Khandarken, here in the village of Discovery. But remember, of all the countries that have risen from the Old Empire and taken a stand against us, Khandarken is the most formidable. They are better organized, they have military and constabulary forces throughout their territories. Because of their government structure, they have the resources for military transports, aircarts, drones and bom carts.

"Why, you ask yourself, have they not taken us out for seizing Discovery? The answer must be that they are not sure of the loyalty of their citizens. Why else would they leave us here unmolested as we take secure possession of their land?"

Carlton heard murmuring and laughter amongst the men. Lanser was asking some good questions, but he didn't think his answers would measure up. Khandarken had hesitated to bom their own people and were using caution rather than indiscriminate force. It didn't mean they weren't taking steps to secure their land. Elkon had informed him privately that no one could safely set foot outside the perimeter of the village and the nearby forest. They were picked off one by one if they did. General Paulo Regiment knew exactly what he was doing. That's why Carlton needed a new plan.

Lanser spoke again. "On the other hand, we don't want to give them more reason to come after us. Discovery is ours and will remain ours. With this offensive, we have a foothold in Legitamia *and* Khandarken. These are big steps forward. Now we move again on a different front." There was an expectant pause in the room as all the men seemed to hold their breath. *What now?*

Carlton grinned to himself. What now, indeed. He hoped this was the right move. But he, Lanser and the Counsellors had gone over it from front to back and left to right. It appeared to be the best plan they'd devised so far. Of course, nothing was foolproof, but even Elkon had been impressed.

When he brought in all his generals and they'd gone over the proposal with tactical precision, it seemed very clear. This was the way forward, the next step toward restoring the Empire.

CHAPTER NINE

Fanny hurried down the street. The transit yard was at the end of the next block, but it was already getting dark and she was worried about Boulter. Usually she was back before now, but Ms Hawker had offered her a bonus if she got that rug done, so she'd stayed and finished the job. It looked beautiful, if she said so herself. She was proud of her work.

But Boulter was just young. He wouldn't understand that she didn't have a choice, that the work had to be completed before she could come for him. When she finally left Ms Hawker's home, she'd rushed to buy food before the shops all closed. Now she had three eggs, tea and some day-old bread in her bag and couldn't wait to get the little boy home.

As she reached the cross street, the precious bundle of groceries under one arm, she spotted his small figure dashing across the barren field from the playground, a swing moving wildly in his wake. The hound ran beside him, but they weren't heading her way. The pair reached the side of the large building she'd observed earlier and disappeared around the back.

She picked up her pace. In the dusk, he shouldn't be going anywhere near there, and the small crowd of dispossessed clustered at the entrance wasn't a good recommendation for the place. What was he doing?

As she drew near, a few of the men glanced over and one of them gave a low whistle. She almost laughed aloud. What would prompt him to do that? She was wearing her only dress, the hem uneven and nearly reaching her ankles. The garment hadn't fit when she first found it, and she'd lost weight in the interim. It must hang on her like a sack, not that she would know. There was no mirror in her abode.

She knew her hair had slipped out of its knot on the back of her head during the long work day, and was now hanging over her left ear. She glanced at the men, pushed her hair back self-consciously with one hand and stepped around the corner of the building.

Boulter was sitting on a bench near the open back door, where light fell onto the pathway. He was eating something he held with both hands. Mickens lay on the ground at his feet and seemed to be gnawing on his own meal. A tall figure stood before the bench, hands clasped behind his back. He was big and broad shouldered but lean, wearing only a pair of knee shorts belted at the waist. In the light spilling from the back entry, the muscles on his chest flexed and moved as he paced the path. He was speaking in a low voice and although she couldn't hear what he said, Boulter was paying close attention. When he finally turned and nodded toward where Fanny stood, the boy's head swivelled quickly around.

He spied her. "Mum," he cried and slid from the bench to dart forward. Mickens quickly clamped his jaw around his dinner and trotted along behind.

Fanny bent to wrap an arm around his shoulders as he bumped into her leg. "What have you got there?"

"See?" He showed her the pané sandwich he was munching, filled with some kind of meat paste. The dog whimpered softly around the bone clenched in his teeth. "He fed both of us."

She glanced over at the man still standing in the light of the open door. His hair was brown and curled back from a broad forehead. His sideburns were long but neatly trimmed. "Did he give this to you?" she asked suspiciously.

Boulter grinned gleefully. "Yah, it's really good. And he give us an apple before."

"Yes," she corrected automatically, keeping her eyes on the stranger. "Only grown men say 'yah'. We've talked about this before, Boulter."

The man nodded at her and she gave a grudging jerk of her head in reply, knowing good manners dictated she acknowledge him. Turning, she herded her little crew back around the corner toward the street. *What was he doing, feeding Boulter and Mickens? Was he after something?* She didn't know and that's what frightened her.

Perhaps he'd discovered who she was. Her heart beat triple time. *Was he just waiting to find out more before he turned her in to claim the reward from the government authorities? Then would she be safe or would she be in a more desperate situation than she was now?* Her father had been travelling with his elected officials in the company of a team of Constables when his aircart exploded.

She and her mother had been under government protection when the next *accident* occurred. There had been bodyguards in the transport ahead of them when they'd been sideswiped by the armoured vehicle and knocked clean into the Violetta River.

Hitching the bag of groceries higher under her arm, she grabbed Boutler's hand in hers and walked faster out of town.

~ * * * ~

Damian watched the woman leave, leading the child securely by the hand and followed closely by the Penrhy hound. He had a strange feeling in his chest. And yet it was so powerful, the emotion roiled in his gut. Who was this woman that had just wandered into the transit yard? Why would she leave her child in the field all day? If she cared about the boy, it would have to be desperation that would force her to take that step.

He shook his shoulders and felt a tingle run up his spine. *Would he see her again?* He hoped he would, throwing a prayer to the gods that she'd show up once more. Moving quietly, he rounded the corner of the sprawling building and watched as the little party headed toward the trail out of town leading uphill into the woods where they soon disappeared from sight.

~ * * * ~

The mother is confused again. But she doesn't need to be. The hound strode silently along the steep trail, now and then falling back to nudge the boy with his head as he began to lag on the long walk home.

I can tell when someone means us harm, and that man meant well. He had a kind heart, even as he tried to hide it behind his gruff manner. He even brought me a bone to chew. I haven't had a good bone in a long time. These days it's just a bit of food here and there that Boulter sneaks me. Otherwise I catch my own, mostly rabbit and olinguito. They're tasty but there are no big joints to gnaw.

He paused to cock his head. There was a sound far behind them and he froze for a moment, waiting. But soon he realized it was the man from the building, the man who gave them food.

The walk up the hill will be tough tonight because Boulter has had a long day and she's carrying a load of something in that sack. I wish she understood that I can help. Perhaps the man wants to know where we're going. Perhaps he'll become an ally.

CHAPTER TEN

Damian started back down the trail in the pitch dark. He had no idea where the woman and boy had disappeared. He didn't understand this yet, however it shouldn't take long to figure out what was going on.

The boy was quick and clever, if underfed. He'd listened carefully to Damian as he told him the sandwich was his reward for looking after his hound. The little face had shone with pride while the dog lounged at his feet, a very loyal animal.

When the woman arrived, her expression showed immediate alarm when she saw him talking to the boy. He was clearly too young for school. But even the school children were long gone from the playground by the time she had appeared.

He'd heard one of the dispossessed whistle low and had expected a woman to appear. Just not that type of woman. He'd been watching for a female of the street, or even a Clone, although they were seldom out at night on their own.

In spite of her dowdy clothes, this woman gleamed like a polished jewel in the dim light. Light gold hair glowed where it waved back either side of her face. She had pale skin, with large dark blue eyes shadowed by long lashes. Her mouth was wide and full, yet she looked like a woman of society the way she held her head and moved with such grace.

His whole body had stiffened with interest. Why was she there? Of course, the boy. And yet it didn't seem right. She was as thin as the little guy, almost frail as she stood there in her sagging dress and mended shoes, a heavy parcel anchored under one arm. He wanted to reach out and take the bundle, seize her hand and seat her on the worn bench by the back door of the fighting arts building. Feed her a pané sandwich or whatever he could search out in the canteen inside the building.

Instead, he read her guarded look and body language and held back, directing the boy to her presence. The little fellow had leapt up and run in delight to wrap his arms around her. Damian's heart did a dip in his chest. She must be a good mother if the boy loved her so openly.

They were a vulnerable sight – the three of them. As they walked out to the street and headed away from the tangle of tracks in the transit yard, he'd grabbed a shirt and slid it over his shoulders. He didn't know why, but he felt compelled to follow. Now, he puzzled it over in his mind but found no immediate answers.

Back at the building, Damian had a shower and headed for bed. The training was sapping his energy, but he felt like he was making progress. He wasn't ignorant of hand-to-hand combat, but the emphasis here was on coming out alive as well as being prepared to inflict a deadly blow, and he was grateful for both perspectives.

Cownden Lanser might not totally approve of his wife's brother, but he seemed to be doing his best to keep Damian alive, if for no other reason than he was Selanna's family. And he'd see his sister tomorrow, begin the treatments needed for the nightmares. He prayed he didn't have another one tonight.

~ * * * ~

Fanny slid the shuttle smoothly through the strands of wool-synth blend. The yarn was thicker and less flexible than wool alone. The bedspread had woven up relatively fast and she'd have time after work to make a quick call at the women's dress shop in Deep Creek this afternoon. It had been some weeks with no news and she was anxious to hear about any developments with the Constables. Spending her life in hiding was difficult and dangerous.

Tasha worked at the dress shop most days and saved bits of information to tell her when she was able to drop by. The two girls had been at school together in the City. Tasha's family moved to Deep Creek when her father opened his clothing shop. Unfortunately, the venture had failed and the family went broke. Now Tasha worked for someone else.

Swiftly Fanny tied off the threads and, using a fine needle, wove them into the fabric until they became invisible. There. It looked remarkably good for having been manufactured so quickly.

Ms Hawker was watching with interest and rose to have a closer look. "Very good, Fanny. I like it, but that didn't take you very long. Perhaps I'm paying too much for these."

Fanny's mouth turned down. Another tug of war about her pay must be looming just over the horizon. "I worked very fast on this, Ms Hawker," she responded, her tone crisp. "Don't penalize me for it or I'll have to dawdle over the weaving in the future."

Her employer huffed loud enough that Fanny's hair wafted in the passing breeze, but she resumed her seat without another word. Fanny gathered her things. "I'm leaving, and I'll see you in two days."

"Yes, that's fine, leave early if you must. Off you go," Ms Hawker waved her toward the door. "Don't be late next time."

Fanny pressed her lips together but refused to rise to the bait, letting herself out through the entry past the stacks of bags in the hallway. Standing on the top step, she took a deep breath of the brisk air and glanced up the strand. It had been a lovely day, although she'd only seen it through the plexi from inside the studio as she worked. But it was a comfort to know that Boulter wasn't shivering in the wet somewhere, or looking for shelter from a cold wind.

Moving hastily down the stairs, Fanny headed a few blocks over to where the downtown shops were located. The Femme Dress and Robe shop was situated in the middle of a trendy row of establishments, the plexi window jammed with fancy robes and stylish blouses. The finer garments and delicate underwear would never be shown to the public, but were hung in the inner chamber, Fanny knew.

As she entered, the owner glanced up and then frowned before returning to her customer. Fanny's dress was old and a bit shabby, not fitting into the rarified atmosphere the businesswoman was aiming for. "May I help you?" she called from across the floor, her voice impatient and slightly imperious.

"Just looking, thank you, Ms," Fanny replied. The girl hanging garments in the window turned and grinned before climbing carefully out with an armful of gowns.

"Fanny," she whispered, her fiery hair falling half out of the bun on top of her head. "How are you? I haven't seen you in ages. I'd begun to wonder if you were all right."

"I'm doing fine, Tasha. I just haven't been able to get over here to see you. Show me a gown or two so your boss doesn't get too irate."

Tasha laughed, her dark eyes twinkling, and hung some robes on a hook near the display window.

"There is one you should look at, actually. It was sold but returned by the customer. Madam did some alterations on it, so now it can't be put back on the floor. She told me to just get rid of it, but then I thought of you…"

She measured Fanny's frame with her gaze. "Not sure it will fit, but why don't you try it on?"

Leading her toward the back past racks of filmy slips and stacks of transparent undergarments to the fitting rooms, Tasha picked out a hanger and hung it on the door. "What do you think? It might be a bit big… I think you've lost weight again, Fanny." The girl frowned disapprovingly. "You can't afford to lose any more weight."

Fanny looked at the garment. It was a day dress of good cloth in a chestnut colour, probably a linen and wool mix, cut on the bias with glitters stitched into the collar and along the lines of the bodice. The colour wasn't something she would have picked a year ago, given in those days to choosing light girlish tones. But Fanny suddenly realized she was no longer a young woman on the verge of adult life.

She'd been thrust into chaos and loss up to her neck within weeks of her father's death. Everything in her life had changed from that day of turmoil and the disastrous events that followed. This dress reflected the new sober Fanny, the grown woman, the one who looked after herself. "How much will it cost, Tasha? I really can't…"

"That's the thing. Madam said to throw it out. That means it goes into the giveaway box. It won't cost you a dime. Now try it on." Tasha closed the dressing room door with a decisive thud.

"You didn't tell me if you'd heard anything," Fanny called softly.

"We'll go for tea and I'll fill you in," Tasha whispered through the door. "I'll get my break shortly."

Surprisingly, the dress looked good. It was a bit big, but Fanny knew with a regular diet she'd fill it out. The colour made her skin look pale and her hair darker gold, and it flattered her already slender frame. What a difference between this and the hack of a dress she was wearing when she entered the shop. That one had come from the free box at the Ladies Guild Mission House, donated by a woman obviously much larger than herself. Well, it did the job. But it would be so nice to have something decent to wear.

She smoothed her hand down the fabric as she gazed at herself in the mirror. The dress was warm but not too warm, the bias-cut moulding itself to her body. Would that fellow from the fighting arts building notice how it looked? She grew flustered at the idea.

What was that man doing with Boulter and Mickens? *Had he figured out who she was?* The thought made her shiver. She wished Boulter would steer clear of that place and all the dispossessed hanging around it.

"Well," Tasha called. "How does it look?"

"I like it." Fanny pushed the door open and peered out cautiously.

Her friend was standing on the other side and

stuck her head through the gap, nodding decisively. "Excellent. I knew it would look good, it's exactly the right colour. Let me have it and I'll wrap it to go. Quickly. I have my break now and we'll just have time for tea in the shop up the street."

CHAPTER ELEVEN

A few minutes later the two women settled across the table from each other at the nearby tea shop, hot bowls placed before them. The establishment was crowded with businessmen in huddled meetings around pots of stronger drink. A group of Clones sat at one of the window tables silently drinking tea while their minder waited patiently by the door. Four men were at a table in the back playing with a deck of cards.

Fanny had ordered spice caf tea while her friend bought Chilean. "Chilean?" Fanny demanded with amusement. "Quoting my father, that Chilean tea is so damn strong, it'll strip the hair off a dog." She started to laugh, but it changed midway to a choking sound, as if something were caught in her throat. It was a grief that never left her at the way her family had been torn apart. Tears popped into her eyes and she lowered her head to stare at the bowl in her hands.

Tasha leaned forward and covered her suddenly cold fingers with her own. "It's all right, Fanny. I'm right here with you."

Fanny nodded and took a deep breath. Somewhat calmer, she sipped the tea. "Ah, that's better." She sat back. "I'm fine now, really. It just caught me by surprise."

"I know. But it *was* funny. Chilean can be too strong sometimes, depends on where you get it. Your father was right about that."

Fanny laughed tiredly. "He had such a great sense of humour. He'd come home from meetings with the Board of Representatives and tell us all the funny stories. Mother loved hearing them."

"He was a great man, Fanny. He was a great Leader. And now we have this election campaign going on to choose a new one, and half the men who put their names up for election should be ruled ineligible."

Fanny sat forward in sudden interest. "How do you mean? Everyone is supposed to be eligible to put their name forward. Father was adamant about that issue, first and foremost."

Her friend stared at her. "Well, you know FitzGibbon is running."

Fanny shook her head. "He was Deputy Leader, so he's standing in as Leader on a temporary basis until the election can be held. He agreed he'd step aside when the Chief Constable's name was put forward to run. Mother told me about the arrangement."

Tasha shrugged. "That might have been the agreement at first. But now FitzGibbon says he's running because no one has more experience than he does."

She nodded in frustration. "That's true of course. I mean, Father's dead, and FitzGibbon had to step in to act as Leader, so he will have some experience by the time the election is held. But he's not a good candidate and surely his brief experience will not be enough to sway the electorate..." Fanny waved her hand in front of her face in sudden agitation. "I just wish the election was over. I know this whole situation I'm in stems from the race for Leader. Why else would we be under attack?"

She became light-headed just talking about it, and took another bracing swallow of her tea as Tasha continued, "There's also the man from the north who's running for Leader."

"Who is that? I don't hear any news where I live." Fanny's smile was derisive.

Her friend shrugged. "His name is DuSatoy and he says he has a gold mine, but no one seems to know anything about him. He looks kind of rough and sounds quite frightening. My mother is afraid he's got enough money to buy the vote."

Fanny squinted. "Wasn't that nice hotel owner campaigning?"

Tasha laughed. "You mean Jack Learmonth, from Learmonth Industries. He runs for election every time, my father says."

Fanny waved encouragement at her friend. "Tell me what you've heard about my family. There has to be some finding from the Constables as to who attacked the Master transport that day. Were there witnesses who saw them knock it through the railing on the bridge?" She bit her lip anxiously. "Mother didn't survive that, but I did and I want to know who's after me." If only she felt as brave as she was trying to sound.

Tasha looked quickly around, then leaned forward to whisper across the table. "There's no news on the infolink about who was involved, Fanny. They've played the events over endlessly, holographs of pulling the car out of the Violetta River with the dead driver still behind the frontboard. When your mother's body was found in the river, there was all kinds of speculation about your whereabouts. After all, you were never seen again, but many people have decided you were swept away by the water." She patted Fanny's hand. "Some others speculate that it's possible you were just carried out to sea. But the Violetta Harbour Authority swears that if you fell in the water, your body would have been caught by the weir near the mouth of the river and they would have found you."

The sinking feeling in her stomach left Fanny feeling nauseous. Surely they weren't still looking for her, whoever these people were? *Would she never be safe?* She glanced around the tea shop and spotted a fellow watching them from his table in the window. He looked familiar, with his erect bearing and powerful shoulders, the watchful eyes and strong straight nose. But he wasn't in uniform and she couldn't place him. Quickly she lowered her head in panic and took the last swallow of tea from her bowl.

When she looked again, he was waving to the waiter for a refill. Perhaps it was just her imagination that he'd been watching. Turning back to her friend, she whispered, "Tasha, has anyone been arrested for the accident? Surely they have some idea of who rammed our transport. Have they caught the men in the hydro-truck who attacked us?"

"Not that I've heard. No arrests, just lots of talk from the Chief Constable's office about pulling out all the stops to find the culprits and bring them to justice. But no comment about who it might have been."

"They did it on purpose." Her tone sharpened as she felt her stomach clench in despair. "There's no doubt in my mind. They came right at us and hit the transport broadside. Our driver yelled but it happened so fast, and the vehicle simply skidded into the barrier and broke straight through as if it weren't even there. I couldn't believe it, it was so…" Now she was dizzy. She slapped her hand to her damp forehead, sending her tea bowl spinning to the floor with a loud crash.

There was the sound of heavy footsteps approaching across the floor. "Is there a problem here? Can I help?" The deep voice seemed to come down a hollow tube to Fanny's ears, echoing along the way. She swayed in her chair.

Suddenly Tasha was beside her, blocking her view of the man. "No thanks. We're fine, we don't need any help."

Her friend spoke softly in her ear. "Fanny, hold on. Drink this."

Tasha pushed her own tea bowl into her hand. "Take a big drink, the Chilean is strong today."

Fanny took a sip and held it in her mouth for a moment as the spinning in her head stopped. "Sorry. I shouldn't talk about it. It's too upsetting. Tasha, you've been very good to me. I'm so grateful."

Her friend sat again and just looked at her. "You know what your father did for us when we lost everything. I can never repay that. But there's something else you should know." She grabbed Fanny's hand and held it tightly to get her attention. "There's another price on your head. You already know about the reward posted by government officials for information as to your whereabouts. Well, I saw a new announcement on the infolink last night. I don't know who has posted it, but it's a large amount. So if someone recognizes you, they're going to be very tempted to turn you in."

Fanny gripped the table and waited for another dizzy spell to pass.

CHAPTER TWELVE

Damian walked up the strand to the next block and turned left as he rolled the scene in the tea shop over in his mind. That was definitely the same woman who had picked up the little boy in the field outside the fighting arts building the other day. He'd recognized her the moment he laid eyes on her as he said goodbye to his buddy, Nikesh, and took a moment to finish his tea.

Nikesh was a good man, and clever. He knew how to make things happen. Damian had just recruited him for this new mission that Cownden Lanser was setting up for him. To his surprise, Nikesh had jumped at the chance to leave the gambling establishment and join undercover work. Makulski wasn't going to be happy, but then he was already irate about Damian leaving. It wasn't a new problem, just one to keep an eye on.

The woman had looked particularly vulnerable today. She didn't cry, but had made soft sounds of distress that caused the hairs to rise on the back of his neck. At one point, he was afraid she was going to faint. Although she wasn't looking his way, he'd been aware that her face went pale and she swayed in the chair, keeping a desperate grip on the edge of the table.

Adding what he'd already discovered, that she and the boy lived up a footpath through the bush on the hill behind the transit yards, it was even more alarming. There had been no track in to their abode that he could find that night. In fact, if he hadn't been following so closely, he wouldn't have any idea where they went. They'd been walking uphill and then simply disappeared from view. Returning in daylight, he'd been unable to find a trail.

Something was definitely wrong. And Damian didn't like it. Women, children – they should be protected not exposed to danger. They should be cared for.

He shut that thought down. It was obvious this woman came from some well-off or noble family. She wouldn't welcome the help of a wounded fighter who had acted as an enforcer for a territory strongman, even if he had left Makulski's employ now. He was still an unknown guy from the far reaches of the territory. Luckily he'd had a couple of treatments from Selanna and was feeling much more relaxed. The tension in his shoulders was gone and there'd been no nightmare last night.

Damian reached the Governor's offices just in time for his meeting. Chief Constable Cownden Lanser had requested he be here today.

Governor Francis Maude welcomed him into the sparsely furnished upstairs office. Maude had been in the military during the Last War, fighting first for Emperor Aqatain but changing sides as the battles grew more brutal. He'd joined the freedom fighters and helped organize them into a victorious army. It was the same story of switching allegiance for many men his age who'd started out with Aqatain.

Maude was tall and lean, had been injured several times during the conflict and wore an eye-patch, yet his sight seemed good and his gaze razor sharp. He ruled the Southern Territory as Governor with a firm hand and was well loved in his district, for good reason. He held the citizens' interests at heart.

Cownden was already there, seated in a chair to one side of the large oval desk. His build was so similar to that of his half-brother Emperor Carlton, it was a miracle he'd stayed disguised for so long. His skin was just as pale and his jet black hair seemed longer than usual, his sideburns bushy.

Damian raised his brows. "Been busy, brother?"

Cownden's grin was wry. "Do you mean have I had time to shave since the Gilsigg conference? Just barely. Your sister might be ready to annul our marriage if I don't soon find more time to spend with her. We haven't even secured a place to live, I've been so booked. We're still residing in the suite at the Constabulary Building in the City."

Damian shook his head. "She'll never leave you for something like that. And she's a patient woman. On the other hand, she also likes to take charge. So if you don't make a decision, she might just choose a place herself and when you get back you'll find yourself already moved in."

Cownden snickered. His aide Anatoliy muffled a snort and arranged his tomo on the corner of the desk for note-taking. Damian turned and greeted Maude. In a roomful of men in uniform, he was the only one wearing civilian clothes. Maude waved them all to seats and took a place behind his desk. "Let's get down to business," he began. "Since the conference in Gilsigg, things have taken a bad turn. The aircart bom was a devastating blow to Khandarken. Leader Harold Master wasn't the only one to die that day. His advisors and assistants all went up in flames as well. It's been a struggle for the government to pull itself together and the in-fighting amongst the politicians has been, shall we say, less than fruitful."

Cownden frowned. "Don't mince your words, Frank."

Maude grinned. "With Cownden starting his election campaign in the near future and the Head Ball Games about to begin here at Deep Creek in the Southern Territory, there's a lot to do." He glanced at Damian. "I've been talking with the Chief Constable, and we agreed that it would be better if you don't work directly for him. Family conflicts and all that."

There were a few laughs around the room. Damian relaxed back in his chair. "We try to avoid those if at all possible."

Maude's face went red. Damian had already heard about the Governor's son, Sable Maude, who had turned his back on the family to set himself up across the northern border in Legitamia as a strongman. He ran brothels from his holding there. Maude obviously found it a family embarrassment.

"I was thinking of my father," Damian added by way of explanation. "We've had our ups and downs."

"Ah," Maude nodded. "At least he survived the war. So many died in the conflict."

I know what you mean. Sometimes I feel like I died in the war too, Damian thought. *I've just been existing since then, not living. Selanna's treatments are all that keep me human.*

Maude continued. "In this territory, I already run the Constables of course, and several men who work under cover for the military. We think you should join me in that function. The men work independently, a sort of special force, and that's what we have in mind for you, Damian. You're used to being independent so it should suit, and these men sometimes have to cross the borders doing this type of pursuit. They can't do that if they're connected to the Constables, so this is probably the best solution."

"Does that mean I would report to the Governor of whichever territory I'm in?"

The men exchanged a glance and Maude shook his head. "This is a very closely held activity. We'll keep it between ourselves. So although I will introduce you to Rutman, my lead Constable here in the South, he won't know about your true role with us. But he'll be able to extend whatever help you need in his capacity as local department head."

Rutman. Damian filed the name away. He'd been aware of Rutman before when working for Makulski and had done his best to avoid drawing the Constable's attention. He was reputed to be a difficult man to deal with, even when on the right side of the law, and that had seldom been Damian's situation in the recent past.

But the military and Constable resources would prove invaluable. Maybe he could dig up some information on the woman and young boy using such access. They stuck in his mind, the boy so skinny and uncared for, the woman protective but frightened and vulnerable. It didn't make sense to him.

Maude spoke again. "These up-coming games are our first priority. I know you and Cownden have other issues to deal with, but having sports teams coming in from countries all over the continent is going to be a real challenge for us."

"You're talking about the Annual International Head-Ball Games," Damian interjected.

Maude snorted. "Annual, my foot. This is only the second time they've been held, and the first was three years ago in Adar Silva."

Cownden smiled. "True, but you have to acknowledge that it's been more like two years, and they would have been held last year but Jiran was to host and they backed out at the last minute. The wild fires sweeping over the plains were too fierce to take the risk of holding the games."

"Maybe," Maude muttered.

"I think the Games are a good idea," the Chief interjected. "Any excuse to host peaceful events that bring the countries together is a good thing. Even Barrington the Benevolent is getting behind it. He'll attend this year, I'm told, which just adds to the idea that he's cooperating with us over the Emperor issue. But I understand your point, Maude. With four countries involved, it's going to be difficult to tackle security."

Maude nodded. "That's why I'm glad to have Damian Stuke, just coming onboard at a time when no one knows him but he'll be well into his training and very useful in the crowd."

"I was starting to wonder why I was here," Damian admitted. "But if I can help, then by all means…"

"Oh, you can help." Maude rose from behind his desk and slapped him on the back. "I'm looking forward to working with you."

"If only we could solve what happened to Fanny Master," Cownden muttered. "It's a huge issue still outstanding. We haven't found a body, let alone the hydro-truck and driver that caused the crash in the first place."

Damian's ears perked up. "That was the incident on the Violetta Bridge, wasn't it? Our Leader's wife and daughter were in the transport.

Maude paused and glanced meaningfully at Cownden. "You can't solve them all, I've learned that the hard way."

The Chief shrugged. "I know that, but this happened right under our noses with Constables present in both vehicles. We still have no information."

Damian felt his interest peak. "Did she have a child with her?"

Both men turned to him. "No," replied Cownden. "She wasn't married. Just her mother and her in the vehicle."

Damian nodded to himself. *So probably not the same woman, although she was about the right age and certainly her accent spoke of the City, or perhaps somewhere near Sommerset in Adar Silva.*

"On the other hand," Cownden added, "there's been a new reward posted for information on her whereabouts. The government already had one up, of course. Any information to help us find her would be welcome. But this one is rather large, should bring the people out of the forest looking to collect."

"Who has posted it?" Maude said. "Surely it must be family, but I thought her family was wiped out."

"That's the thing." Cownden shifted in his chair. "We can't seem to find out who's behind it, can we Anatoliy?" His assistant shook his head, and he continued. "The question is, are they concerned for her safety, or are they after her? It's a headache and a huge concern."

As the meeting broke up, Damian walked out of the entry with Cownden at his side. He turned to his sister's husband, "You know Selanna's in town, right?"

Cownden chuckled. "I'd better know. Yah, I'm meeting her for dinner. Would you care to join us?"

Damian laughed. "Thank you for the invitation, but she already asked me. I'll see you at the hotel, I have something to attend to first."

By the time he reached the field outside the fighting arts building, the sun was low in the sky and there was no sign of the hound or the little boy.

CHAPTER THIRTEEN

DuSatoy stood on the platform of the transit station in Martonosha. He smirked as a woman approached, leading two children by the hand. She wanted to know what he was selling. Men understood politics but the women always thought he was a peddler. Whose idea was it to allow women to vote in the first place? It was something he intended to remedy once the election was won.

"I'm DuSatoy, Ms," he said. "I'm running for Leader of Khandarken. Do you vote?" He gazed down at the children who were staring at him, mouths open, one with drool on his chin.

"Of course I vote," the woman snapped, and his gaze popped back to her flushed face. "Why wouldn't I? It's my right." She marched off in high dudgeon, to his amusement. One vote he definitely didn't need.

He was here looking for the businessmen and dispossessed who travelled through this territory capital. Here in the north was where he would find his support. The politicians of the south and the City didn't understand what it was like living in the outlying territories. But DuSatoy did, he had made a career of surviving where it was toughest to survive. This is where he'd find the votes that would win this election.

A fellow in a leather vest approached, followed by five or six workers hauling heavy cases on handcarts. Now there was someone he needed on his team. As he made ready to greet the man, his voicelink buzzed insistently. That would be Rutman, reporting in at last.

"DuSatoy," he barked, turning away from the approaching men. "What can you tell me?"

"Well, you said there are rumours that she's been seen in the south. Nothing confirmed yet."

He thought for a moment. "That's not good enough. This lies with you, so get your shorts on and start work."

"Yes, sir, I understand. I just don't think she's down here." Rutman's voice faded and then came in stronger again. "...left the City and likely went north, or even into the interior to hide. Why come here to the Southern Territory when the Head Ball Games are bringing visitors flooding into the region?"

DuSatoy gritted his teeth. "Don't question me. Just do your job. And Rutman?" There was silence from the other end. "When you find her, don't blow it this time. I won't put up with it twice."

He clicked down and replaced the link in his pocket. Heading off the platform, he waved to his driver to get moving. It was time to travel south. With so much happening in Deep Creek, he needed to be there.

Finding Fanny Master was the most important item on his list. Her father had been a very popular man in Khandarken, and his family was well-loved. All Cownden Lanser or some other fool candidate had to do was get her on the campaign trail with them and DuSatoy would have a lost cause on his hands. The mother was dead, but Fanny was still out there like a secret weapon. He could feel it. And it was an issue that lay right in Rutman's lap to solve.

~ * * * ~

"How was your day, Boulter?" Fanny tugged his hand as he clambered over a rock in the path. "Did you have fun?"

"Um hmm." His little fingers were sweaty and slipped from her grip as he fell onto one knee on the rough path.

Fanny set her parcels down and hooked him under the arms to swing him back onto his feet. "There you go. We're almost home."

If that's what you want to call it. But it was the most stable residence she'd had since tumbling into the Violetta River from the transport those many weeks ago.

Mickens whined as she left her parcel where it lay on the ground and carried Boulter the last few yards to their shelter. Propping him up, she wrestled with the sand coloured flytarp covering the doorway and waited while the hound snuffled around to root out any unwanted visitors before she helped the boy inside. Their lair was not much more than a transit box sitting at an angle between the trunks of two trees. She never would have seen it herself if Mickens hadn't come in here chasing a rabbit and she'd run after, anxious to claim it for their dinner if the hound managed to catch the animal.

The space wasn't perfect, but it finally gave them a base from which to operate. Mickens had flushed out a couple of families of olinguitos, much to their disgruntlement. Then she'd swept it out the best she could with a branch and surveyed the area. It would work. The floor had rotted away but there was a pile of dried grasses that she'd pulled into place to form the makings of a bed.

She didn't cook much. During the day, the smoke would attract attention. But at night, sometimes, she started a small fire at the far end sheltered from sight of anyone on the trail by the walls of the box, and put a pot of water to boil for tea. It was a comfort, almost like home. She shuddered at the thought.

Today she had fish for their dinner. Boulter loved fish, they would share. None for Mickens. She glared toward the doorway and spied the hound dragging her parcel in, his teeth gingerly sunk into the outer layers of the wrapping.

Impatiently, she took it from the animal, then dropped a begrudging pat on his head. He sometimes seemed remarkably intelligent, for a dog. But he was so big! And where did he come from, just appearing out of nowhere and attaching himself to them?

Probably just as lost as they were. And really, he was good company for Boulter, especially on the days she had to leave him on his own while she worked.

She urged the child toward their bedding, a small pile of covers and rags she'd scrounged. "Lie down and rest, Boulter, while I start the fire. I've got fish and a bit of pané. And we'll have tea afterward."

By the time the fire was started and she'd balanced her small pot over the heat, Boulter was fast asleep. These were long days and he was just small. How old was he? She wasn't even sure, and nor was he. But there must be records somewhere. If she were back in the City, all she'd have to do is contact Father's assistant and ask some questions. The answers would quickly appear.

Tears of loss dripped down her cheeks as she added the fish to a pan over the small flame. If she was lucky, the water for tea would be ready at the same time.

Fanny roused the little boy when the food was cooked and propped him up on the stump while she cut his portion in a bowl along with fire toasted pané. He downed it eagerly, slipping a bit to Mickens when he thought she wasn't looking. She ate her own fish, poured the tea, and pulled the child onto her lap. They sat there in front of the dying fire and shared the bowl, the aroma of spice-caf rising to her nostrils.

Boulter leaned against her breast, his head lolling in sleepy surrender. "You're a good boy," she said. "Any mother would be proud to have you for her son. We'll sleep well tonight."

Straightening the sheets on the matted grass in the corner, she tucked him in and crawled over to cuddle beside him. Yes, it would be harder for others to find her now that she had a small child with her. But she was so comforted by his presence, it was difficult to think of being alone again. Wrapping an arm around his shoulders, she fell asleep, always knowing the hunter was still out there searching for her.

CHAPTER FOURTEEN

The Annual International Head Ball tournament began to ramp up. The Adar Silva team arrived first. They were already booked into one wing of the military barracks on the other side of Deep Creek nearest the ball fields, and the hustle and bustle of organizing baggage and assigning the players and coaches to their quarters took up the better part of a day.

Collier True-May, Leader of Adar Silva, had been eager to attend. Officials from Khandarken, led by Acting Leader FitzGibbon himself, descended on Deep Creek to meet his entourage as they arrived and settled into the Learmonth Hotel. Aircarts flew in a steady stream to the airfield as they dropped their passengers.

Damian Stuke had no fixed assignment. As promised, he'd been introduced to Constable Rutman by Governor Maude. Rutman was told Damian worked on call for Maude, but the Constable seemed unimpressed, although later mentioned in an undertone that he'd seen Damian before in the Western Territory and he'd better have cleaned up his act if he intended to stay out of trouble in Deep Creek.

Damian stared at him like he had two heads and walked off to consult with Nikesh who was there as his accomplice to watch the games.

When the Jirani delegation arrived the following day, they began to erect tents in the dry field beside the fighting arts building. It looked like organized chaos. The team itself was to be housed in the military barracks with the other players, but leaders of the Penrhy and Shafoneur tribes established a tent city sprawled across the space. Penrhy hounds roamed in packs, keeping intruders at bay.

Everyone knew the country of Jiran consisted of a confusing arrangement of five or six tribes, most related by blood in some fashion. Damian had been in contact with the dominant people, the Penrhys, over the years, and had even done business with the Shafoneurs to the south. But he soon discovered that the team players were at least half from the northern Moiselle tribe which he'd never encountered before. They were shorter, heavy-set and darker in skin tone which distinguished them from the other Jiranis walking the grounds.

With the difficulties keeping track of where the delegates were settling and who belonged to which group, he hadn't had a chance to notice if the woman and her boy were anywhere around. On the one hand, he was glad not to see them. Boulter would be unsafe wandering the fields around the fighting arts building with the influx of foreigners arriving. But he felt an uncertainty in his chest when he thought of them out in the woods in some isolated place.

Late that afternoon, with Nikesh off on his own errands, Damian headed up the trail he'd seen them walk several times before. Not sure where they went, or how far they travelled, he went several miles without finding anything of interest besides a camp of dispossessed in the hills, which raised the hackles on the back of his neck. The dispossessed were unpredictable at best, and at worst could be relied on to cause trouble for those around them. Trouble for the Games and trouble for the woman and child if they were to stumble across the vulnerable pair.

There were a couple of spots he'd passed that were obviously used from time to time by travellers passing through but nothing he could identify as a permanent abode. With the influx of visitors, he would bet more dispossessed would begin to arrive. As he walked slowly back down the trail, he was startled to see a Penrhy hound appear from the bush to stand stock still in his path. Was this one of the dogs that had recently arrived with the Jiranis and strayed into the woods? Or was Boulter nearby?

The hound watched him for a moment, then emitted a clicking noise in his throat and headed back through the trees. A couple of dispossessed came quietly down the trail, their clothes rough and worn, their beards bushy. As Damian stood in indecision, they continued on down toward Deep Creek and the Games.

Then the hound reappeared, its head turned as it watched Damian approach. The dog led him to a huge balsam tree, widely forked at the base. Stepping around it onto a flat stone, he discovered a faint path and readily followed the animal through the bush and into a small clearing.

CHAPTER FIFTEEN

There was a dwelling of some kind on the far side, its top and sides covered with branches and daubed a dull tan colour that made it almost invisible amidst the tangled vegetation. Boulter played on the ground with a set of sticks in front of the open flytarp.

The hound trotted forward, slowed near the boy and nudged his arm with the pronounced snout. The child laughed and patted its ear before returning to the game of stacking twigs to form some kind of tower.

When Damian cleared his throat, Boulter jumped in alarm. Then he blinked and squinted in his direction. "Damian," he said. "Why are you here?"

He walked forward and squatted before the child, gesturing toward the leaning tower. "What are you making?"

Boulter beamed. "This will be the house for the mother and her boy. And over here…" He pointed to a small hole he'd dug in the ground, framed by more sticks. "That will be the lake. They're going to learn how to swim." His little teeth gleamed in a grin. "Wouldn't you like to swim?"

Damian nodded. "I sure would. This looks like a great place you're building." In the bright sunlight, the boy's eyes were yellow-brown, but his pupils had narrowed to a slit like the eyes of a cat against the strength of the sun's rays. He'd never seen anything like it. When Boulter blinked, his eyes appeared normal again.

Damian shook his head to clear it and stood. What he thought he saw could have been a trick of the light. "Where's your mother? Is she here?"

"Yup." The boy nodded toward the sagging door. "She's making my lunch. Come on." Boulter grabbed his hand and dragged him toward the makeshift home.

Ducking under the tarp, the boy called out excitedly. "Mummy, he's here. He came just to see us."

It was dim inside the box, the only light coming from the entry where Damian stood and a gash in the canvas on the other side of the space. Dressed in the same sagging dress she'd worn in the tea shop with her friend, Fanny sat on a stump knitting, a strand of bright wool leading down into a sack at her feet. She jumped at the noise and quickly laid the needles on her stool, stepping forward to peer up at him.

"Hello?" Her face showed both alarm and confusion. "What are you doing here? How did you find us? Boulter, did you tell him?"

"No," Damian shook his head. "Boulter didn't tell me. I was walking the trail and the dog came out to greet me. He led the way back here."

"Oh, by all the angels!" Her breathing became shallow. "That hound... we won't be safe if he doesn't stick close by."

He shrugged. "I've never seen him approach anyone when Boulter and the dog are in the field during the day. I think he just recognized me."

Damian gazed into those dark blue eyes and saw naked fear. "No one followed me here," he assured her. He took her hand and looked at the rough skin on the knuckles, rubbing it with his thumb. "You've done a good job, hiding your tracks, Ms. I realized that's why I couldn't find your place, you have to slide behind that big tree and the trail takes up on the other side. You're well hidden."

Now, if I only knew who you're afraid of. He didn't say it. The expression on her face told him she didn't trust anyone, certainly not him. He could live with that. For now. At some point, he hoped she'd change her mind enough to divulge the secrets that kept her hiding from the world.

Her face showed shock. "You've been looking for us? Why?" She glanced with confusion at her son, and back at him. "Have you been following us?"

Damian shook his head, then nodded guardedly. "I followed you one night. It was dark and I thought it was dangerous for you to be heading up the trail alone," he said. "I've spoken to your boy several times and seen you come to pick him up from the field." He gestured at Boulter and smiled "My name is Damian Stuke. Can I know yours?"

She paled and glanced away, then seemed to have second thoughts and reached into her pocket. He spotted the ident in her hand and was tempted to grin.

"You don't have to show me your ident. I'm not a Constable or a banker. I just wanted to introduce myself," he managed. "Boulter knows my name but I haven't heard yours." He glanced down at the rubber-plastic document. It was ragged and worn with a Martonosha insignia, and he could barely make out the name – F. Winthrop. "Your name is F?" he inquired, a smile hovering.

She blushed prettily and he grinned at her. "It's Fanny," she said after a minute.

"Ahh. Lovely name." Immediately the conversation with Maude and Cownden leaped to mind. *Was it just a coincidence, a woman with the same name?* But the ident looked genuine and her last name was Winthrop. The boy was listed there as well. That didn't fit with what he knew of the Fanny Master story.

Boulter impatiently pulled him by the hand over to a corner of the hut. "This is where we sleep," he pronounced importantly. "Mummy and me, and Mickens over there." Someone had pushed some boards together to make a platform on the ground and covered it with dried grass. There was bedding – sheets and a makeshift blanket shoved to the side, and a well-worn spot in the dirt at the foot where the dog must curl up.

How do they get water? How do they stay warm?

The expression on her face seemed a mix of embarrassment and confusion that pulled at his heartstrings. "You manage very well," he said, pressing the boy's hand. Then he looked back at the mother. "I wondered if you would like to join me for dinner one night when you're in town. Tomorrow is fine for me."

"Oh, boy." Boulter jumped up and down. "Could we eat at the place by the transit yards? We can smell the food at night when we walk by. Can we, Mum?"

He watched Fanny's face for her reaction. "You mean the Legitamia Palace," he offered. "The food is tasty there. I think we could. If your mother agrees, that is."

Fanny seemed caught with indecision. Finally, she nodded uncomfortably. "Tomorrow would be fine," she said. "We'll be in town tomorrow."

"Will Boulter be in the playground?"

Her cheeks went pink. "Yes." Her nod was abrupt. "He can't come to work with me."

"I understand." He stared at her. "I'm afraid the field has been invaded. The Jirani delegation for the Games has taken over most of the space."

She looked blindsided. "The Games?"

He nodded. "The International Head Ball Games. They're being hosted in Deep Creek. The advance guard is already starting to arrive and the Jiranis brought their tents."

She blinked, then gazed at the boy in indecision. "Oh, dear. I'm not sure… Perhaps we had better stay home. I won't work tomorrow."

He shifted his feet and watched the hound snuffle in the corner. "Boulter could spend the day with me," he offered. He shrugged uncomfortably. *When had he decided to be the childminder?* That was hardly his role, especially given his job for Governor Frank Maude and the Head Ball tournament about to begin. But Selanna was here in town and her husband Cownden was very involved in policing the influx of guests. He relaxed. Perhaps she could help.

Fanny looked even more uncertain. "I'm sorry, I don't really know you. I've seen you at the training building in the transit yard, but otherwise…"

He nodded. Of course she would be careful. Given she was a woman of the upper-class, she'd have great hesitation in allowing her son to be looked after by a man with no visible means of support. He wore no uniform, she wouldn't have any idea what he did.

On the other hand, as he gazed around the shelter, he wondered how such a woman had fallen so far. What had happened to drive her to this place, and where was her man – the father of the child?

He reached for his brand new ident with the military insignia freshly embossed in the centre.

CHAPTER SIXTEEN

Damian rounded the corner and found Nikesh patiently squatting on his heels by the back door of the fighting arts building. Fanny had arrived with Boulter this morning as planned and, after a hurried meeting, carried on to her work. He'd managed to promptly pass the boy off to his sister. Selanna would spend the day with him, then return to the field later in the afternoon.

Nikesh rose to his full height, almost even with the building's doorframe and stretched his broad back. He was from lands far beyond Jiran, and his skin was jet black, as was his thick kinky hair. He had been Damian's sidekick in the Helmcken Trail battles during the Last War until Damian was captured and held in the Emperor's prison camp.

When Damian escaped and finally returned home, he'd spent months putting himself back together. Those had been difficult times but he'd come out in one piece – not whole, but a lot better than when he'd returned a broken youth. And Nikesh had been there when he emerged.

Damian was unsure why Nikesh even became involved in the War. The lands he came from, far west of Jiran, were untamed, and the Empire had never stretched that far in its influence. Perhaps he'd been like Damian – a wild youth anxious to fight, wanting to believe that he was on the right side of the battle.

The two men clasped arms and walked away from the doorway for privacy. "I've been right around the camp," Nikesh reported. "There are a lot of them, alright. The guy to talk to is someone called Shandro Penrhy, they tell me. He seems to be a prince or something."

Damian huffed out a laugh. "I think there are a lot of them in Jiran. There are about five or six tribes so it's hard to figure out who is who. Let's go talk to him."

Nikesh moved off toward the city of tents clustered in the middle of the field, aiming for one of the largest standing to the side with pennants flying from the centre post. Most of the structures seemed to be simply made of canvas sheets fastened at the corners and laid over a system of poles. But the one that Nikesh was zeroing in on had an elaborate overlay of decorative black and brown wildcat skins attached to the outside walls. The entry flytarp was pulled back, framed by heavy mammoth horns.

"Yah," Damian muttered. "I see what you mean about *seems to be a prince*. I've never seen anything like it."

Nikesh nodded and scratched at the flytarp. "Greetings," he called. "Is Prince Penrhy here?"

There was a moment of silence and a brown-skinned young man appeared from the dark interior to peer out at them. "Uh, no," he said. "But he should be back shortly." His accent was thick and it took Damian a moment to decipher what he'd said.

"Thanks," He bowed in acknowledgement and looked around. "Do you mind if we wait?"

The young fellow looked nervous, then his expression cleared. "Here he comes now."

Damian glanced into the field behind them. Prince Penrhy hove into view between the tents. He was no more than Damian's age, and walked like a military man. He was lean and muscled, with the handsome brown skin of most Jiranis and he wore what looked like an army uniform with loose pants tucked into high leather boots and a fitted jacket, unbuttoned in the afternoon heat.

"Gentlemen," he said, and stopped at the doorway of the tent. "What can I do for you? Nikesh, you were here earlier, I believe." He put out his hand and Nikesh gripped it in his large-knuckled black one.

Turning, he indicated Damian with a wave of his hand. "This is my overseer, Damian Stuke."

Damian shook hands. "I'm not sure if I need to bother you with my questions, Prince Penrhy. I just need to find the man who's organizing your entourage. We're trying to ensure there's room for everyone, and that the teams, when they arrive, are directed to the military barracks on the other side of town."

Penrhy nodded. "Well, that would be me and my men. Our ball team arrives tomorrow, as does Sovereign Penrhy. We'll work with you any way we can, of course. I'm very much looking forward to the Games." His grin was infectious.

Damian relaxed. "Good. It will be Nikesh who directs traffic. We'll see you again soon. Good luck in the competition."

Returning to the building on the edge of the field, Damian pulled a folded onion skin from his breast pocket. "Here's the plan, Nikesh." It was a map of the town of Deep Creek and the surrounding lands. "Jiran is occupying this area." He traced the field with his finger. "Adar Silva has taken over the whole of the Learmonth Hotel, here. Most of their people have already arrived, including Leader True-May, and their team comes this afternoon. The Legitamians arrive soon. They've booked two of the smaller hotels near the military barracks."

The men contemplated the map, studying the layout of the playing fields near the barracks where the teams would billet. Nikesh was silent for a moment. Without looking up, he muttered low, "Will Makulski be active in the midst of all this?"

Damian had been thinking about the same issue. Their eyes met and he shrugged. "I imagine he'll take whatever opportunity presents itself. Gambling is his business. Betting on the Games would be a huge opportunity for someone like him. Of course he'll be here."

"We'll need to watch our backs."

Damian frowned. "You know we do. But don't forget how much we have on him. He knows what evidence I took with me when I left his organization, and who will receive it if anything happens to us. He'd be a fool to try something."

Nikesh nodded. "Hope that's enough to keep him in line."

Damian shrugged. "I think it is, I haven't heard a word from him or his men."

Nikesh held his gaze for a long moment, then turned to walk away. "I know you've got some training on right now," he called over his shoulder. "I'll be checking the military barracks."

CHAPTER SEVENTEEN

anny put away her shuttle and arranged her loom against the wall. Ms Hawker had fallen asleep on the couch and seemed poised to topple over face first onto the cushions. Fanny grabbed her bag and stepped into the garderobe near the front door. Quickly she slipped her dress off her shoulders and let it drop to the floor.

She took the new dress out of her sack, the one Tasha had found for her from the Femme Dress and Robe shop. Pulling it over her head, she watched in the mirror as it settled on her shoulders and draped across her breast. The colour was perfect. Funny that a few months ago she wouldn't have looked twice at it, still given to choose light girlish tones. She fastened the small clips under her arm and across the shoulder, then closed the belt. The effect was lovely and she had to grin with surprised approval at her reflection in the plexi mirror.

Imagine, going out for dinner. It was so exciting, she'd been suppressing a smile all afternoon. Tugging the pins from her hair, she combed it out before twisting it up again on the back of her head. Pinching her pale cheeks, she gave her skirt a shake and opened the garderobe door.

Ms Hawker was just stirring from her nap, and there was a sudden banging on the front door. Fanny poked her head into the back room. "Do you want me to get that for you, Ms Hawker?"

The woman shook her head. "No, it's fine. I'll manage."

As Fanny gathered her things, she heard a low male voice. Then footsteps followed Ms Hawker's shuffling slippers into the kitchen off the hallway. Fanny walked down the hall to the front door and paused. Should she just leave, or stop in the kitchen to say goodbye? She didn't want to intrude. Neither did she want to be accused of sneaking out or taking something with her that wasn't hers. Ms Hawker did not trust anyone.

She stepped into the doorway. A tall lean man with white-blond tightly curled hair was seated at the small table, as Ms Hawker set a pot on the heatsurface.

Fanny knocked on the door frame. "Good bye, Ms Hawker. I'm leaving now. I'll see you again in a few days."

The fellow turned and grinned at her, his pale blue eyes striking in his tanned face. Ms Hawker waved her away without looking up. "Off you go, Fanny. We're finished for the day."

Fanny turned and left, moving carefully past the piles of sacks in the great entry to ease out the front door. She stood on the step to shift her bag higher on her shoulder.

That man had looked so familiar. She'd seen him somewhere before, she was certain. Then she remembered. He was often at the fighting arts building where Damian trained. She'd seen him coming and going at different times of the day.

So what was he doing here with Ms Hawker? *Was he spying on her? Had he seen her go by the building with Boulter and followed her to work?* She shuddered. The suspense was exhausting. How long could she continue to function with the dread of discovery hanging over her head at every turn, and now Boulter to worry about as well?

Suddenly she sensed she needed Damian's help. She couldn't manage alone, and hoped she could trust him. He seemed to be her only possible source of support at the moment.

~ * * * ~

Damian clipped his shirt closed and ran a comb through his damp hair. Fanny would be here soon and he wasn't sure where Selanna was with the kid. He grabbed an astrofruit and stepped out the back door just as Boulter rounded the corner, his hound galloping ahead of him.

Damian grinned. The boy was high-spirited, he couldn't help but be caught up in it. A few moments later Selanna appeared, moving sedately down the path behind the child.

The hound arrived first and stopped to watch over his shoulder as Boulter dashed up and stood panting before him. Damian clapped him on the shoulder in greeting and passed the astrofruit over, watching as the boy promptly sat on the bench by the back door and began to munch. He seemed to have an insatiable appetite.

Selanna drew close, smiled and leaned in to give him a kiss on the cheek. He draped a brotherly arm around her shoulders. "How did the day go?"

She nodded. "It went well, didn't it Boulter?" The little boy grinned, small white teeth showing and juice running down his chin. She reached in her bag for a wet cloth and wiped his face.

"So?" Damian prompted.

"So, we spent the morning with Da." She gave him a meaningful glance. "He did his game with the heart monitor."

"Ah." Damian glanced over at the child and pulled his sister a few steps away from the bench. "What did he find?"

She lowered her voice. "He said four and half years, not quite five. Fairly good health but too thin. And there was something about his eyes. He got quiet when he noticed them. Said he'd seen it before but it's been a long time and he wasn't sure."

Damian nodded. "Yah, the eyes. They're unique, all right. I've never seen any like that. I wonder where the trait comes from?"

Selanna frowned and gazed at Boulter thoughtfully. "He didn't seem worried, more in awe, I think. I'll try to get him to remember what it means."

"Thank you for the treatments." He found he couldn't look her in the eye, so gazed out over the field of tents. "They make a world of difference. They make me human again."

She rubbed his arm. "You're always human, Damian. You're a wonderful man, you just care too much. The treatments help you get in touch with your real self."

He shrugged awkwardly. "Whatever, they do help. I'm feeling a lot better, no nightmares."

"I'm glad," she said softly. "Any time. You know that. You don't have to ask."

Just then Fanny appeared at the corner of the fighting arts building. Damian's mouth dropped open, and he scrambled to close it again. She was wearing a different dress, one with glitters around the collar and in a pattern over the bodice. She looked stunning. For a moment, he was speechless.

Boulter spied her at the same time and leaped up with the forgotten astrofruit hanging half-eaten from his fingers. He skipped toward her, the hound at his heels and Damian belatedly lunged to grab the boy by the back of his shirt before he touched that dress.

"Hold it, hold on," he said. "Hi, Fanny. Boulter's a bit of a mess, give us a minute." He motioned impatiently to Selanna and she pulled the wet cloth out again and handed it to him with a bemused smile on her face.

He sponged the boy off and took the mangled fruit from his hand. "Fanny," he said. "This is Selanna. Selanna, meet Fanny." The women eyed each other over Boulter's head as if they were sworn adversaries. He'd never seen that expression on his sister's face. Glancing at Fanny, he was surprised at the suspicious look she gave him.

He frowned. "Fanny, Selanna is my sister." He motioned with his hand and added, "This is Boulter's mum." Surely that would clear things up. Fanny looked less antagonistic, but his sister's smile was definitely forced.

He gave an internal shrug at the illogic of women. "Well, are we ready to go? Selanna, we can walk you partway back to your rooms."

She finally turned and the pitying look she gave him was almost comical. "Thank you, but I'm meeting Cownden here. He's got a session with Abe Farmer."

"Yah, that works." He pointed to the door of the fighting arts building. "You can't go in there, though. What are you going to do?"

She laughed. "They're almost finished, Damian. I'll wait in the office." Turning, she waved at Fanny and Boulter. "Nice meeting you, Fanny. Bye, Boulter. Thank you for spending time with me."

Selanna disappeared into the building and Fanny turned to him with a small frown. "I thought *you* were going to look after him."

He pressed his lips together. "I was, but I had

other work where I couldn't take him. So my sister helped out. She's good with kids." Not that Damian would know.

CHAPTER EIGHTEEN

Damian held the door as they stepped into the crowded Legitamia Palace on the street above the transit yards. They were immediately shown to a booth in the back of the eating establishment, benches upholstered with purple velvet cushions on either side of the table. The place was packed and the noise almost deafening.

Fanny helped Boulter onto the bench and then sat beside him, so Damian took the one on the other side. It made sense. He was a big man and he needed space. But he'd kind of imagined her sitting beside him, rubbing elbows as they ate. He might put his hand on her shoulder as he helped her with a dish or while deciding what to order. He crushed that thought until it was a small inkling at the back of his mind. He had just recently risen from the status of dispossessed, Fanny was from the establishment. No more need be said.

"I don't think I've had Legitamian food before, although it does smell good in here." She eagerly eyed the sheet the waiter laid before them. Boulter was kicking the leg of the table in his excitement, and Damian grinned. It was like taking two kids out to eat. He grabbed the sheet and turned it to face her.

Running his finger down the list, he stopped at various items. "These are good. They're rolls with prawns and sprouts in them and they come with a cashew sauce. Boulter will especially like those." He moved his finger down the sheet. "This is great. It's a bowl full of thin noodles covered with a layer of sliced roasted olinguito, and shredded vegetables. There's a tasty red sauce to pour over it. That's usually what I get."

Fanny gazed at the menu and then gave a mesmerizing smile that stopped his breath in his throat. "You order," she said. "That would be best, right Boulter?" When she glanced down at the boy, Damian finally got his lungs working again. *What was going on?* She was like a witch or something in that dress, she had him hypnotised.

Fanny helped the child kneel up on the seat while Damian waved the waiter over.

Two glasses of Legitamian beer arrived, and a bowl of coco milk for the boy. Boulter huffed in excitement and was still as a statue when his drink was set before him. Fanny shoved it closer to the edge of the table so he could reach and he leaned forward to take a sip from the lip of the bowl. Then he took another. With the bowl half empty, Fanny nudged it toward the centre of the table. "Let's save some for the meal," she laughed.

"He can have more when he finishes that one," Damian said and was rewarded with a huge grin from the child.

He took a long swallow of beer. That felt better. He watched Fanny over the rim of the glass. She picked hers up in both hands and held it to the light as she examined the colour of the ale, then took a delicate sip.

"My, that's lovely," she said.

He stared down into his glass. When was the last time he'd sat in a restaurant with someone who said things like *lovely*? He couldn't remember, perhaps never. He demolished his meal as Fanny picked at the noodles in her bowl, then laid the three-pronged wooden fork aside. Boulter had waded into his rolls and had cashew sauce all over his face, but Fanny had eaten little.

"Don't you like it?"

She nodded. "Oh, yes. But I can take the rest home and we'll have it tomorrow."

Damian frowned into his golden tea, then waved at the waiter. "We'll have another order of the same to take with us when we're finished here." He gestured to the food on the table. "Bring it wrapped up."

Fanny's eyes widened as the waiter walked away.

"You can take it with you," Damian added as he picked at the last vegetable slice in the bottom of his dish.

Fanny stared for a moment, then glanced down. Slowly she lifted the fork and began to twirl some noodles around the prongs. By the time the packaged food arrived at the table, bound in an onion skin bag, she had just finished the last piece of roasted meat and Boulter had given up on the rest of his rolls. Laying down her fork, she gave a small burp and her face flushed a rosy pink as the boy giggled. Damian couldn't resist a smile.

"You can't stay in the woods, you know," he said. "It's not safe. With the Games beginning, the dispossessed are pouring into town and once they find you, they won't leave you alone."

She glanced sideways at the child playing with his second bowl of coco milk, and looked up at him. "We don't have other options at this time, if you understand my meaning."

"Well, actually you do." He felt his lips compress into a thin line. *Why should she trust him?* Perhaps because she had no one else to lend a hand. He leaned forward and took her fingers in his. "I have a room in the Transit Hotel. It's not fancy, but it would work for the two of you."

She went pale. "And where would you stay?"

In affront, he released her hand and sat back against the bench. *Did she think he was making a play for her, or trying to put her at his mercy?* "I can stay at the fighting arts building," he replied stiffly. "I won't impose myself upon you."

"No, Damian, please. I apologize. I just..." She glanced at the child again and then stared at the tabletop. "I have no resources at the moment, and

I'm having trouble deciding what's safe and what is not."

Something eased in his chest. "I mean you no harm," he said. "Only to help. And it's too dangerous where you are." He took her hand again and turned it so the palm faced up, rubbing his thumb in the hollow. "You must know that."

She nodded. "What of Mickens?"

"Take him with you. He's a smart animal and good to have at your side for protection."

CHAPTER NINETEEN

The waiter brought more tea and another bowl of coco milk for the boy. He removed the man's dish and fork, wiping the table clean. When he glanced at the woman he stalled for a moment, then casually rearranged the spice jars as he studied her face. Returning to the kitchen, he stood in indecision. Did he just have an over-active imagination?

He dumped the dirty dishes in the deep sink and went back out to the front. The two businessmen at his first booth were nearly finished their meal. He brought more beers and then their chit for the dinner. They paid him by link, which was slow tonight because of such heavy traffic in the Deep Creek area. At the next booth, the three Clones and their guide had just been seated, so he waited but they weren't ready to order. Clones always dithered on any decision and took forever to make up their minds.

Then he angled past the other booth again. The boy had stopped eating a few minutes ago, and was being cleaned up by his mother. Her face was averted and he couldn't get a good look. He pretended to pick up a napkin from the floor and moved down the aisle. It took several sweeps past but eventually his patience was rewarded. As he walked slowly by, the woman glanced across at her companion who was speaking to her in a low tone. Click. He caught the holograph images on his wristlink and headed straight for the kitchen.

Easing out the back door into the jumbled alley behind, he pulled a voicelink from his shirt pocket and punched in the particulars. His brother answered immediately. "Herd," he said, "It's me. Listen carefully. Check the infolink for the reward contact details on a woman named Master and get hold of the sponsors. Because I've just located her."

He paused to listen. "Yah, I know these guys are tough and they'll be hard to deal with, but I've got proof. They won't be able to deny us the reward because I took a clear holograph." His brother's laugh came through and he had to grin. "And Herd?" he said. "The reward is huge. When we get paid we'll never have to work another day in our lives!"

~ * * * ~

In the end, Fanny agreed to take Damian's room but insisted on returning to their hut to fetch the few things they'd left there. He walked the trail with her, impatient to get them moved to somewhere safe. Boulter was flagging, and he hoisted the boy into his arms where he promptly laid his head down and slept on Damian's shoulder as they walked, the woman carefully cradling the package of food in her arms.

Something stirred in his chest, a feeling of belonging, of family. He glanced down at Fanny's shape beside him. She was taller then he'd thought. It must be her underfed condition that made him think her so small and frail, but she came almost to his shoulder. He imagined her by his side as they walked home after an evening out with their child. Except she wouldn't want to walk home with her husband, she'd expect to be driven in a transport. He quashed the thought the best he could.

Stepping behind the forked tree he used his handlight to show the path into the small makeshift house. He lifted the flytarp and Mikkens sniffed every corner, then lay down at the foot of the improvised bed.

Fanny straightened the covers and he settled the boy into the blanket as Boulter sighed and rolled to his side. The mother drew the sheet up to cover him.

When Damian lowered the handlight, she lit a small candle on the corner of her tilting table, then gazed at him uncertainly.

"There's golden tea in the bag," he offered.

Finding two chipped bowls, she poured the tea and offered one to him, then settled on the stump. Damian took a spot on the ground beside her. He clicked his bowl lightly against hers.

"It's not safe here," he remarked as he sipped, keeping his voice low so as not to disturb the child. "You have no protection if you're found. And I don't doubt you'll be found by someone. The dispossessed are appearing in larger and larger numbers as the Games approach. I met some the other day heading down that same trail that you travel."

"I understand." She bowed her head in acknowledgement of his comment. "I'll pack our things and be ready to leave in the morning."

"You'll need help carrying everything." He made it a statement and saw her head pop back up as she stared at him.

"If I stay the night, I can help with the move."

Her gaze darted to the crude bed and back to his face but she made no sound.

"I'll sleep on the ground," he added. "It won't be the first time."

She seemed to study him for a moment as she relaxed at his words. "You've lived an adventurous life," she finally observed.

He laughed softly and she smiled in response. "You could say that. Eventful, at any rate."

"I lived a very ordinary life," she said wistfully. "But that changed a while ago. Now it's my job just to survive."

He nodded and touched the hem of her dress where it draped on the ground by his knee, rubbing the material gently between his fingers. "That's all any of us can do. Survive. It's our only job sometimes."

She leaned toward him and spoke low. "You understand, don't you? Boulter isn't my child. Did you know?"

He stared for a moment then shot a gaze at the sleeping boy. "How so? You're his mother."

"Yes, I'm his mother. But it's because his mother died and Boulter needed me. I found him along the road. So although he's not my son, he is. Do you see what I mean?"

Damian felt the tension in her pose and moved his hand to lightly touch her worn shoe. "I understand completely, Fanny. You've met my sister, Selanna."

She looked confused. "Yes, of course."

"Well, Selanna isn't my sister. My mother died when I was Boulter's age. My father married Selanna's mother when I was about ten. She was five and I loved her at first sight. So she's not my sister, but she is. No one can take her away from me."

He heard her sigh and a tear glistened on her cheek in the dim light. "Yes," she said. "Yes."

~ * * * ~

Mickens stirred. Boulter had grown restless and woken from his slumber while the man shared tea with the woman. *When she said he wasn't her son, the boy got worried and began to fret and stir under the blanket. He needs her and thinks of her as his mother.*

The dog stretched his limbs and moved delicately so the child's feet rested in the thick fur along his back. *As soon as she acknowledged him, he went back to sleep. The woman knows in her heart that he's her son. And that man just confirmed it. I knew he'd be good for us.*

The hound gusted out a long breath and relaxed patiently at the foot of the bed.

~ * * * ~

Fanny lay stiffly on the makeshift bed, Boulter pressed up against one side. She heard Mickens shift on the ground near her feet and sighed inwardly. That hound was a blessing and a curse. He ate so much, she was stretched to the limit just to feed them all. But it was still a comfort to have him there, especially as a companion to the boy. Otherwise, many days Boulter would be completely on his own while she worked.

Damian lay on the other side of her. She hadn't been able to let him bed down in the dirt, when they had the cushion of crushed hay beneath their bodies and a blanket to cover them. It wasn't much but it was more than she'd had on the road and she could share. On the other hand, having a near-stranger lying on the pallet beside her was distinctly uncomfortable.

She almost laughed aloud at how things were for her now. Fanny Master, daughter of the nation's Leader, sleeping in an abandoned box with a small boy, a strange man and a Penrhy hound.

She must have fallen asleep because light was just coming through the rip in the canvas when she woke. She could tell, even though she didn't open her eyes, that it was early morning. She felt warm and safe for the first time in forever. Boulter had curled against her, his head cushioned on her arm and his little knee pressed up against her stomach. And there was a reassuring steady heat all down her back. She stretched and the heat immediately withdrew. Lifting her head, she glanced behind to see Damian rising to his feet, boots in hand.

He seated himself on the stump and clipped them on his feet. When he spotted her eyes on him, he put a finger to his lips and walked softly outside. Even then she knew he wasn't leaving them and the comfort was immeasurable. She dozed.

CHAPTER TWENTY

Before the first competition of the Head Ball Games began, chaos erupted at the military barracks near the playing field. When it was announced that Adar Silva and Jiran would play the first game, and Legitamia would not play until the second day, the riot that broke out was a brawl from one end of the main building to the other. The Constables were called to restore order.

Several rooms had been demolished, doors ripped off, bed frames broken and pallets pulled apart. A hospital had been set up on the playing fields to service the Games and the injured men were transported there for treatment. Most were suffering only minor cuts and bruises, although one had a shattered nose and another a broken arm.

Damian was dispatched to find out what had triggered the disturbance and who was involved. He moved amongst the men, observing and asking questions, when a dark-haired tough-looking man pulled up in a private transport with a driver and several guards. The vehicle was heavily armoured, darkened plexi at the frontboard and huge signs attached to the doors announcing *DuSatoy for Leader*.

DuSatoy's suit looked like it was made of silk, his shirt linen and the boots on his feet were a masterpiece of hand-crafted leather. He stood outside with his men ranged behind him as the reporters milled looking for information on the riot. Then bracing his feet, he smiled and raised his hand to gain attention. Damian stepped closer to hear what he had to say.

"You've probably heard of me. My name is DuSatoy and I'm running for Leader of Khandarken in this election. When I am Leader," he announced, his voice strident, "this kind of activity will not be tolerated. We are a nation of law and order. We don't allow ruffians from foreign countries to arrive and start a war in our territories. Because that's what this is, a war. And there is no doubt, Khandarken will win this war."

Men who'd been milling about began to mutter amongst themselves and move closer to hear his next words. "I will be Leader, mark my words. And when that day comes, this type of action won't occur because the punishment will be too great. You won't want to take me on." His smile had disappeared to be replaced by a simple baring of teeth. "I'm strong and I'll make sure our country is strong."

"What if Chief Constable Lanser wins?" someone bellowed from the mob. "What will you do then?"

DuSatoy turned to stare into the crowd searching for the speaker, just as Rutman appeared at the edge of the gathering. Damian faded back amongst the men to avoid tangling with Maude's lead Constable. But Rutman seemed unaware of him, as he, too, searched for the fellow who'd yelled his comment. Then he waded into the throng and soon emerged on the far side with a man in tow who struggled to escape his grip. Rutman nodded to the politician and marched off with his captive while the speech continued.

So this was DuSatoy, the strongman no one seemed to know much about. What Damian had heard in the past always seemed to turn into mere myth upon closer scrutiny. He glanced around. People were listening, although the Jirani team had pulled away and drifted off to their rooms. Most of the Legitamian players and coaches were still being held by the Constables in an enclosure until everyone cooled down.

The politician didn't stay long, but Damian was unsettled by his speech. Not by the over-confidence, all politicians spoke like that, but the facial expression, body language and threatening stance of his guards reminded him too strongly of Makulski and his enforcer mentality. Surely this man would not be the next Leader, coming right after Master – a man of learning and integrity, of patience and pride in his country. And what business was it of Rutman, that he should arrest someone because he shouted a comment? People shouted out all the time, and no one gave it a second thought. The Constable must be particularly anxious to keep the crowds under control for the duration of the Games.

Damian didn't feel he was in any position to judge who would make a better Leader. Cownden Lanser was family now so he might be prejudiced, and at first he'd been distinctly unimpressed with the man. But as he got to know him, he had changed his mind. Lanser as Leader might be the best thing that could happen to Khandarken.

His next thought was of Fanny. Who was she and why was she hiding? If Boulter wasn't her child, she was a young single woman on the run. A woman from the elite in the City, he'd gleaned that much from her accent and the few things she'd said about her past. He turned and headed to Maude's office.

An hour later, having been served spice-caf tea and biscuits by the Governor's secretary, Ms Balcomb, and given the daily password to access the Constabulary data, he had spread before him several holographs of Fanny, daughter of Leader Master. He was almost certain now who she was, but there still lingered a tiny doubt. A much younger Fanny Master looked happy, plump and relaxed in her environment. In one holograph she was posed beside her mother as Master stood at the podium, ready with his acceptance speech as newly elected Leader. Her hair was pinned high on her head in curls and the earrings and necklace she wore would have paid for a small house in Bereford.

The Fanny he knew didn't wear her hair that way. It was either in a knot on the back of her head, or down on her shoulders. So he couldn't be absolutely sure.

In another holograph, she danced with Cownden Lanser in a crowded ballroom in the City. He figured from the drapery on the walls and windows it must be the Learmonth Hotel, decorated in similar style to the one here in Deep Creek. His chest tightened at the sight of Lanser smiling down into her eyes, his hand placed possessively on the small of her back. She beamed up at him in the image and he could only see the side of her face.

Damian loosened his collar and took a deep breath. Lanser had married Selanna and he'd had to work pretty hard to get her attention, so things probably weren't quite how they looked in the holograph he was fixated on. Printing off the one of Master with wife and daughter, he stuck it inside his shirt and searched further.

The reports of the accident where her transport was knocked into the Violetta River were devastating to read. If she survived that, how had she managed since then? As his conviction grew, his respect for Fanny increased even further. He would ask her. The one question, is this you? Then he'd know. Because if she trusted him, she'd tell the truth. And if she didn't, then what was he doing walking alongside the two of them as their personal bodyguard?

He shook his head. He knew why he was doing it. Because he had no choice. He couldn't leave her on her own with no protection, he couldn't leave the boy without help. Something ground in his chest and he stood and stretched to ease the pressure.

Time to get going. Boulter was staying in the hotel room today with Mickens, Fanny had gone to work and Damian had arranged dinner to be sent to them in the room when she returned. Nikesh would meet him at the fighting arts building for a training session and then patrol the Jirani tent city that evening.

CHAPTER TWENTY ONE

Inside the Legitamian border, General Elkon dismounted and handed the reins of his horse to the young dispossessed standing guard outside Emperor Carlton's building. The beast was sweating and breathing hard. It needed to be walked to cool down.

He turned and tugged at the door. It was a warehouse, no more and no less. But it was the best they had, and soon, by the gods, they would be moving forward with the plans for change.

Carlton was seated in the main room on a tall carved chair covered with bison fur. He had his feet on a stool and held a tankard of local ale in one hand. Advisor Judson bowed before him, he had obviously just arrived. A couple of the Counsellors were seated at the table already and three men were working quickly in the dim interior, putting together food and drink for the upcoming meeting.

Someone had arranged chairs at the small table near Carlton's elbow and Advisor sank down with obvious relief. Elkon bowed to the Emperor before assuming his own chair on the other side of the table.

"Good, we're all here." Carlton waved the servers forward with small bowls of tea and tankards of ale. One of the Counsellors pulled out a tomo and readied to take notes. Elkon understood the need for notes, but he had no use for them personally. He never forgot anything, remembered each word, how and where it was said and who spoke. It was both a curse and a blessing. He had never wavered in his loyalty to Emperor Carlton but there were times when words spoken rose up to haunt him and his dedication to the cause.

The Emperor pointed to Judson Lanser. "Tell us how it went."

Lanser nodded and drank deeply from his glass. "Barrington agreed to see me," he began, "but it turned out to be a very brief meeting. He and his whole delegation were leaving for the International Head Ball Games in south Khandarken, and he had very little time to spare."

Carlton grimaced at that news. "Did he commit to support us? That's all that matters."

Judson Lanser shook his head. "Not entirely. We weren't alone, Zhang, his chief of police was in attendance. I asked for a private meeting but Barrington just shrugged and told me to go ahead. I mentioned I had three issues to discuss and that I had your full support and authority to represent you. He accepted that. My first issue, I said, was about his men patrolling the entire Legitamia—Khandarken border. I told him it interferes with our need for autonomy in our small province."

Lanser took another swallow and Elkon's gut clenched. That was probably not the best way to present the issue to Barrington the Benevolent. A dictator would always take the position that no one but he had autonomy in his own country.

Advisor wiped his wrist across his mouth. "Barrington's reply was that he has a committed agreement with Khandarken to keep the border clear of the strongmen and raiders that operate on either side. It's his part to patrol the north side as it is Khandarken's to patrol the south."

Carlton's face grew dark. "Is he saying we constitute a group of strongmen? Is he equating us with border thugs?" His voice rose as he slowly stood from his chair. "Is that what he's saying?" he roared.

Lanser waved a weary hand. "No, no. Just that as part of the Gilsigg Conference, they came to an agreement to control the border raids. I knew that going into the meeting, but just wanted to push him on it."

Carlton paced across the floor, then back again and motioned with his hand. "Go ahead. What did you gain from your time with him?" His frown looked like a storm about to unleash.

Elkon glanced at Lanser. If the Advisor didn't have some good news to report, this meeting was going to deteriorate rather quickly. It wouldn't be the first time Emperor Carlton lost control, but better here in front of a few Counsellors than a whole troop of his men. That didn't inspire confidence in anyone.

Lanser's face was pale. "Barrington then announced I would only have time for one more request. That's what he called it – a request. So I gave him our declaration as a province of Legitamia. I promised our support for him in any altercations with the surrounding nations. And asked for his support for our interim occupation."

Carlton huffed a sigh and waved his arms at the waiters, who brought forward dishes of sablefish pasta and root salad. The mustard dressing leant a strong tang to the air. The men dove in, Advisor first. He polished off most of his pasta before he lifted his head and continued with his tale.

He seemed tired and defeated. "Emperor Carlton, Barrington took the document I presented him with and looked it over slowly. I'm unsure if he can even read our writing, I mean he speaks Legitamian. His accent when speaking Khandarken is so heavy I can't understand him. I hoped he would bring in a translator, or ask Zhang for clarification as his language skills seem somewhat better, but he didn't. So I tried to point out the main items in the document but he just waved his hand to shut me down and laid it on the table in front of him."

"Well, what was his response?" Carlton huffed impatiently.

"No response. He said—thank you for visit, time is up. He stood and Zhang showed me to the door."

Elkon seized the opportunity to finish his salad in the stark silence that followed. Emperor Carlton was visibly trying to hold back an explosion and for a moment it looked like a losing battle. But suddenly it morphed into something else entirely as he burst into gales of laughter. He bellowed, falling back to writhe in his chair until he had to hold his side. The Counsellors grinned and Lanser looked distinctly relieved at the hilarity.

Elkon smiled. This was better, much better than the rage he'd been expecting. This, he could work with.

CHAPTER TWENTY TWO

The first day of the International Head Ball Tournament dawned with bright blue skies and brilliant sun. The competition was set for noon to avoid either side being penalized by the rays of the sun in their eyes. The makeshift viewer stands were packed and teetered with the weight of all the people gathered to watch.

Damian had a group of seats marked off in reserve. Fanny had been persuaded to bring Boulter to see the opening game and he had them tucked up in the area he'd secured, while he roamed the field watching for problems.

His job was to scan the audience, and he needed to be able to see what was going on in the top seats as well as behind the stands. Nikesh was at the other end of the field. He didn't attract as much notice in the crowd as he had done, with his jet black skin and wiry hair. There were many with similar features here from out of country to watch the pending competition.

Immediately, Damian spotted his old boss. Makulski had a certain method to how he conducted business. For the moment, he was standing to the side in the shade of a locust tree, his short squat body relaxed against the trunk and his hands full of tickets. Four or five young men came and went, bringing money in and going off with more tickets in their pockets. Damian watched them work the crowd. It was relaxed, business was slow. In a while, after the game started and one team was pulling ahead, that's when trade would become brisk. And that's when Makulski worked his boys hard to bring in the bets.

Damian had located the whole Legitamia contingent of visitors, with a short bulky figure in the centre who had to be the renowned Barrington the Benevolent. His wife, even shorter, was seated beside him and they were surrounded by a horde of attendants. Cownden and Selanna were with a group of officials from Khandarken in the centre of the far stands. Damian had been invited to join them but he had a job to do.

Two blasts sounded as a warning for the players to get into position. The crowd roared as the men raced for their places. Seven on the field per side, two in goal and five to score. Adar Silva was the reigning champion of these games so far, although only one tournament had been played since the end of the Last

War. But this was an Empire game and Adar Silva played with force, focus and integrity.

The Jirani team seemed more relaxed. Extra players left the field for the sidelines and the goalies took up position. Damian moved fast, gaining his seat beside Boulter as the third blast sounded. The competition was on. Boulter bounced in excitement, probably not even understanding how the game was played but buoyed by the energy of the crowd. Fanny looked lovely. She wore a hat that she'd gotten from somewhere that shaded her face from the sun and made her look every inch a lady of the City. His heart thumped unevenly in his chest. *What was she doing with him? Would she ever be his?* The odds seemed strongly against him.

A noise from the crowd brought his attention back to the field. One man down already on the Adar Silva team. A halt was called while he limped off and another took his place. By the end of the first half, Adar Silva had two men injured, Jiran one and the score was three to two for the champions. The southern visitors roared their approval as the field cleared for the break. The Penrhys in their tribal robes trooped with dignity down to the field to consult with the coach, hounds running alongside.

"Look!" Boulter pointed. "Their dogs look just like Mickens."

Fanny turned her head to meet Damian's gaze. "Are all such hounds from Jiran?" she whispered. "How did Mickens find us?"

He shook his head. "I don't know how he found you. They're well-bred hounds, mostly owned by the

Penrhy tribe. Expensive to acquire, and they tend not to sell them anyway. Probably just as well you left him at the hotel. You don't want to lose him, or be accused of stealing a dog."

Fanny's hand found Boulter's and held tight as the blast sounded to begin the second half. The fight was fierce. Jiran was called out twice for cheating and Adar Silva managed one more goal. The game ended with a score of four to two for the champions.

The Jirani team stalked off the field to the jeers of the crowd and Damian saw Prince Shandro Penrhy with a few of his family in a heated discussion with the arbitrator of the game. Makulski had left with his men, a small horde of gamers following him into the trees on the far side behind the barracks. All bets would be settled up in private under the watchful supervision of his armed bodyguards.

Damian's job was almost done for the day. He would escort Fanny and Boulter back to the hotel room and find some dinner for them. With the town packed with people, it was hard to drum up meals of any quality. Once that was done, he'd return to his pallet in the back room of the fighting arts building. Not that he'd get much sleep. The Penrhy tribesmen were singularly noisy campers and the night before he'd been awake until well into the early hours of the morning.

Although, he couldn't really blame that entirely on the Penrhys. He was tied up in knots, wondering where he was going with Fanny. Was she the missing Master girl? He hadn't found the right moment to ask her. But if so, she was even further out of his reach than he'd first imagined.

CHAPTER TWENTY THREE

In the room of the Transit Hotel, Fanny set the dishes from their dinner aside and washed Boulter down at the small sink. He was a good boy, but the food did tend to spread out as he worked his way through a meal. He yawned mightily, and she gave him a hug and tucked him into the high bed where he promptly fell asleep. Mickens, faithful dog that he was, curled at the foot of the pallet and snored softly.

She couldn't wait to climb into it herself. It seemed so long since she'd been in a real bed with clean sheets and soft covers. What had been ordinary before had become a real luxury.

Washing Boulter's clothes out, she draped them around the room to dry and pealed her own clothes off to shower and wash her hair. It was a huge extravagance to not only have water but heated water, and she wouldn't pass up an opportunity to bathe.

Today the game they'd watched had been between Khandarken and Legitamia. Khandarken had won by one score but it had been a rough game and two players were out with broken bones. One of the Legitamia players had been knocked out and had to be carted off the field on a board.

Tomorrow Tasha was taking Boulter home with her for a few days. It would mean Fanny could work some long hours for Ms Hawker without having to leave him alone. Damian wanted to take her to another game, and the child was too young to stay out that late at night.

As she hung her dress up, she stalled. Was Damian courting her with his offer of the room and finding meals for them? It wasn't clear and she was in no position to entertain his suit – if that was what he was offering. On the other hand, why would he be interested in a woman with an adopted son, a suspicious Martonosha ident, and no past to speak of? None that she'd spoken of at any rate. Not that he'd asked, which should tell her something of his intentions. She just didn't know what.

Sighing, she sank onto the edge of the pallet. Boulter rolled toward her in his sleep and she propped him up and over onto the other side, then lay slowly back. Heaven. Pure heaven. She let her body relax and tugged the cover up. The plexi window was open to let a light breeze into the room, and the distant sound of music drifted through. That must be the celebration going on down at the transit field tonight. Perhaps the Jiranis were having a party, although they hadn't won anything yet.

The competitions had been thrilling to watch, the excitement mounting as the two southern teams pulled ahead, although it was still early in the Games. She'd been astounded at how often the Jirani team was penalized. Damian said it was because they were cheating, sending out too many players and using their hands against the other players or playing outside of bounds. Ridiculous, really, because there were three arbitrators and they hadn't let anything slip by without calling the infringement.

Rolling over, she nestled her face against the pillow. It smelled of Damian. She froze where she lay, then pressed her nose deep. Yes, there it was, that elusive spicy masculine scent that he carried on his body. As she fell asleep, she imagined him lying against her back just like that night up the trail in their hut, keeping her safe and warm.

~ * * * ~

Fanny stitched the edges of the table covering and cut the hanging threads. Then she smoothed it across her lap. It was a fine piece of work. She usually did her weaving with thicker material, wool or synth fibre, but this was made of the best linen. The result was a faint pattern in repeated circles that swirled and glowed in the body of the fabric.

It had been ordered from Ms Hawker by Cownden Lanser, Chief Constable of Khandarken, for his wife. Fanny had met Selanna, sister to Damian, and the connection was making her distinctly uncomfortable. She didn't remember knowing Selanna in the City but she certainly knew Cownden Lanser from her former life. She'd had a schoolgirl crush on him in the days before her father died.

Her hand tightened on the fabric until she realized she'd put a crease in the table covering and smoothed it flat on her knee. Cownden and Major Dante Regiment, son of the General, had been comrades at the social functions she'd attended in those days, and Julianne Adjudicator had been very attracted to Dante's older brother, Virgil. In fact, there had been some kind of family understanding regarding an arrangement to marry.

She stared out the plexi at the sunshine in the neglected garden in Ms Hawker's yard. And where had that agreement gotten Julianne? Virgil got sick and died and Julianne was left undefended. In the end, she married Abe Farmer of the fighting arts building and daily Fanny worried about meeting her on the street or in the field behind the building when she went to fetch Boulter. Maybe it was time to move on to another place, another town without so many dangerous connections to her old life.

Carefully she folded the cloth and laid it on the seat of her chair. Ms Hawker was deep asleep on the couch, snoring hoarsely. Fanny gathered her bag and walked down the hall just as a knock sounded at the door. She stopped and glanced back at her employer but Ms Hawker hadn't stirred. She hurried forward as a second rap resounded on the panel. Lifting the plexi she gazed out at the same fair-haired man she's seen here before. She opened the door.

"Hello Ms, is my mother home?" His pale blue eyes smiled into hers.

"Do you mean Ms Hawker?"

"Yes, that would be her." He gave a laugh. "She's hard to pin down, that woman."

Fanny nodded warily. "She's here but she's sleeping, I'm afraid." Hesitating, she asked the question she was desperate to ask. "Aren't you Mr Farmer that has the fighting arts building at the transit yards?"

His brows rose and he snickered. "Very observant of you, Ms. That's my cousin, Abe Farmer. I'm Loyal Hawker, at your service." He sketched a shallow bow.

"Oh." Her breath left her in a gust of relief. Abe Farmer's connection to Julianne Adjudicator was something that had been giving her nightmares. If she were to run into the two of them, there would be no way to hide her identity. "You do look rather alike."

"It's not the first time I've been taken for him."

There was a bang as something fell in the back room. "Fanny," Ms Hawker called, her voice cranky. "Where have you gotten to now?"

Fanny turned back as she beckoned Mr Hawker in. "I'm right here, Ms Hawker, and your son has come to visit." She plucked her shawl from the crowded coat hook and peeked into the weaving room. "The table cover is there, all finished, and I'm off. I'll see you in a few days."

But Ms Hawker had already disappeared into the kitchen, beckoning her son to follow and leaving Fanny standing alone at the door. She pulled it closed and heard it click shut behind her.

CHAPTER TWENTY FOUR

Damian put his full force into the kick and watched Sprinter reel backward onto the mat at his feet. Then he leaped forward and planted a foot at the trainer's throat, effectively pinning him where he lay. Sprinter pushed his foot away, taking Damian's hand to rise from the mat.

"Well done," he said, puffing as he stood with hands on hips. "I think it's time for you to move up to the fighters group. They can teach you a lot that I can't. They train most days, as some of them have work, so you can fit yourself into the schedule wherever it suits." His expression was kind. "I'm proud to have trained you, son. You'll make a good fighter, where and when needed."

Damian felt a smile well up and he stepped forward to give the older man a one-armed hug. "Thanks for the practice. Thanks for your patience."

As he showered, he pondered his next assignments. Likely Maude would be moving him out of Deep Creek to a new task soon. After all, the whole purpose of his training and placement was to work against Emperor Carlton and his schemes to invade further Khandarken territory.

What would happen with Fanny then? She could stay in his room at the hotel, he'd continue to pay for it even if he wasn't in town. But he wouldn't be here to see to her safety or that of Boulter. *What then?* They might only have a few more days together. He felt a tightness in his chest that had nothing to do with the battle he and Sprinter had just concluded.

Late that afternoon, he knocked on the door of his room at the Transit Hotel. Fanny opened it, a sunny smile on her face. He stepped inside and closed the door against the interested gaze of those roaming the corridor outside. When he looked around, he realized they were alone.

His mouth quirked. "Where's the boy?"

She waved him to the only chair and seated herself on the edge of the pallet. "My friend Tasha has taken him to her home. She has days off from her job and she's very fond of Boulter. This way he doesn't have to stay closed up in the room while I work." Her smile was open and his gut clenched as his gaze shifted sideways to the bed where she sat. *So close, so available.*

"Well," she continued, "are we watching another game tonight?" Her forehead wrinkled. "I'm not sure who is playing now, or who is leading in the tournament."

He tamped down his rising passion and pulled a rice paper card from his pocket, holding it out. "This will explain it. They print a new one every day." He pointed at the lowest line. "Tonight it's Adar Silva against Legitamia. It should be a good game because they both play pretty hard. Adar Silva is leading and so far, Legitamia is third in the ranking."

Fanny stared at the card in her hand as he pointed to the details of tonight's game. Her hair fell forward to hide her face, those honey-coloured strands that looked so soft and feminine. He wanted to bury his hands in it, just hold her against his chest. He left the card in her hand and stood abruptly.

She looked up at him in surprise and he gestured toward the door. "I have a reservation for dinner at the Legitamia Palace, but it's an early one so we should go. It's all I could get, very hard to make bookings with the crowd in town."

"Of course." She rose and picked up her shawl from the end of the bed. Damian stepped forward and took it from her, laying it around her shoulders. Her cheeks were a becoming pink as she thanked him and turned toward the door. He walked behind down the hallway, wondering at his gentleman's manners. *When had he ever done something like that for a woman?* But he'd seen Da with his mother, all the courtly gestures and caring acts that added up to a loving couple. Suddenly it was what he wanted with every filament of his being.

The Legitamia Palace was packed. They took a small side booth and had to move fast to secure it before the party behind them grabbed it for themselves. Their waiter brought golden tea and took their order, lingering at the table as he fiddled with his wristlink. Damian frowned. Wasn't this the same fellow who'd waited on them last time, when they had Boulter with them? What was the problem with his device that he had to adjust it while taking care of their table?

He watched suspiciously as the waiter walked back to the kitchens with their order. When he didn't immediately reappear, Damian excused himself and rose. He headed toward the facilities but at the last minute changed direction and entered the kitchen doorway. The waiter was nowhere to be seen.

He glanced around and pinned one of the cooks with a pointed gaze. "Where's the back door?"

The fellow shrugged as he formed a prawn roll and pointed with a greasy finger toward the hall at the rear. Damian stepped outside. The alley was crowded with trykes and scooters amid the cast-off junk that was piled in corners. Two men argued drunkenly over who should drive back to the barracks, and off in the shadows someone spoke low into a device, their back to the door. The white apron he wore stood out like a flag in the gloom.

As Damian drew near, he overheard his muttered words. "No, but I tell you, Herd, she's here again and no one has answered our claim for the reward. If we don't move fast, someone else will..." There was a pause. "All right, well send it in again. We need some action..."

Damian put his hand on the lad's shoulder and spun him around, looking down into the alarmed face of their waiter. "What's going on?"

The kid turned to run but Damian hooked a foot around his knee and threw him onto his back on the rough ground. The boy grunted and lay still, staring desperately up at him. "I said," he repeated, "what's going on?"

"Nothing. Honest, nothing is going on." There was a sputtering from his voicelink and he quickly clicked it down. "Listen, I need to get back inside or I'm going to lose my job. We're packed with customers tonight."

Damian reached for the kid's hand and hauled him to his feet. "Give me the link."

"What..." He looked at his hand as if he'd never seen the device before. "No, I can't. Who are you?" His tone was suspicious.

"I'm the man who's going to break both your legs unless you start working with me on this." Damian's expression must have been intense enough to convey his intentions, because the waiter slowly held out his hand with the voicelink lying on the palm.

"Thank you." Damian drew a curve on the surface and watched the particulars appear of the last contacts made. "I think I'll keep this for a bit. Now tell me who you were talking to."

The lad went paler, if that were possible. "Just my brother, all right? I was talking to my brother."

"And who is the reward on?"

He swung his head, obviously gauging his chances of escape. Damian locked one arm around his throat. "Don't even think it. Now, who was the reward for?"

The boy's voice came out in a strangled hiss. "It was on Ms Fanny Master, the Leader's daughter. She's been missing and there's a government reward, but a new one has been posted that's much larger." He struggled for breath and tried to pry Damian's arm away from his throat. "If my brother and I get that one, we'll be set for life."

Damian's face felt rock hard and his gut had clenched so tight, he was sure he'd never eat again. "And the woman will be dead."

"No!" The kid fought to escape. "No, they want to find her because she's missing. They aren't trying to kill her."

Damian loosened his hold slightly as he hurried to form a plan. "Where's your brother now?"

There was a pause. "He's at home. Why?"

"I think you better call him back and cancel the claim on the reward."

The waiter took a quick breath. "Cancel the claim? Why would we do that? Someone else will recognize her and take the money. This is our big chance!" Tears were leaking from the corners of his eyes and his legs kicked as Damian tightened his arm.

Damian leaned to speak in his ear. "Listen to me. This is your chance to die. Those men aren't going to pay that reward. They'll just take the information and make her disappear. Then you get to disappear as well. Call your brother and cancel the claim. Say you were mistaken."

Hand shaking, the waiter took the voicelink and punched in some particulars. But there was no answer from the other end, no matter how long he waited.

Out of time, Damian contacted Nikesh and got him to take the waiter home to check on his brother, while he went back inside the restaurant. Fanny was sitting nervously in their small booth, a plate of prawn rolls with cashew sauce untouched in front of her.

Her face brightened when she saw him approach, then alarm flared in her eyes at his fierce expression. "What is it? Is something wrong with Boulter? I'd better go and see..."

Damian shook his head to reassure her as he took his seat. "I'm sorry I was gone so long. I just had to deal with a problem back there but it's under control now. Nikesh is handling it."

"Oh." She cautiously pushed the plate toward him. "I ordered these to share for the first course, but didn't know..."

He managed a grin. "Great. I love these things. Let's order our dinner now before we get booted out by the next wave of guests." He motioned another waiter over who was looking after adjacent tables, because he already knew theirs wouldn't be back tonight.

CHAPTER TWENTY FIVE

Damian had a job to do at the Games, but he couldn't leave Fanny on her own. Before they were seated in the stands for the beginning of the event, Nikesh had already reported by beltlink that the young waiter from the Legitamia Palace had arrived home to find his brother dead in their entryway, his throat slashed. The thugs hadn't waited very long to silence him.

The waiter was devastated. Damian ordered him to be taken to the fighting arts building for now, and put in one of the rooms at the back for his own protection. They'd figure something else out later, but he sent a message to Abe Farmer to let him know about his new resident. Then he forwarded a confidential wristlink message to Governor Maude about finding Fanny Master.

The crowd was loud, packed into the stands and standing in ragged lines along the edges of the field.

Bright lamps shone down, flooding the field with light and the mournful Legitamian music blasting from the speakers drowned out any conversation. Damian took Fanny's hand in his, and she immediately turned her head to give him a smile. His breath was tight in his chest.

What was she doing with him? Well, it was obvious she was unsafe and had run from her attackers. What else could she have done? General Regiment had had her under his protection and that had been a dismal failure. A surge of resentment moved up his throat. Could Regiment not have kept her safe, especially after all the family had suffered with the loss of the father? *And who was after her anyway? Who had posted the reward?*

On the other hand, Damian would never have met her if she hadn't run. His admiration grew with each bit of information he gleaned. That she had managed to get here without help, after finding a child on the road and taking him under her care, was hard to imagine. It took a lot of determination and ingenuity to accomplish something like that. He tightened his grip on her fingers.

Two blasts sounded and the crowd went quiet. The players ran to their places on the field as the music ground to a halt. The third blast signalled the beginning of the game. The crowd surged to their feet to cheer as the arbitrator tossed the heavy ball onto the ground in the centre of the field. The game was on.

Right out of the gate, Legitamia played hard. They didn't cheat like Jiran, but they fought ferociously for possession of the ball. Within the first ten minutes, Adar Silva had two players out, one with a broken leg. The body slams were vicious. A third player had a concussion and lay unmoving on the field until they could carry him off.

The score was tied three to three at half time. Damian could just imagine what was going on between the Adar Silva coaches and their team. If they kept losing players it would be almost impossible to win.

He glanced at Fanny. "I'll get you a drink," he said and stood. "Now, I don't want to lose you in this mob, so don't leave your place. I'll be right back, and Nikesh is two seats up keeping an eye on everything. I'm concerned for your safety."

She gave him a veiled glance and turned her head to locate Nikesh in the crowd. "I'm fine here," she replied. "Yes, I'd love a drink."

"Good." With a feeling of satisfaction in his gut, he leaped a few seats and made his way to the lineup at a side booth. Flashing his military ident, he muscled his way to the front of the line and got three ales. Might as well look after Nikesh while he was at it. He didn't use his ident often, it was provided for emergencies, but his heart was beating double time in his chest and something told him this might be just such an emergency.

Turning to head back, he saw a rush of bodies as the loud spectators from the first two rows began a skirmish in the stands that quickly escalated. Nikesh pushed through from above to help the local

Constables as they barreled in to quell the disturbance and for a minute Damian couldn't see Fanny at all.

He ran, ale spilling over the edge of the glasses as he climbed the seats two at a time. There she was, face pale as stone, standing uncertainly where he'd left her.

"You weren't thinking of leaving, were you?" Damian tried for an easy grin but his breath was pumping in and out. "Have an ale."

She looked at him as if she had something to say, then pressed her lips together and took a glass. "Thank you." She glanced anxiously around. Damian sat beside her and waited for her to take a sip before he put the glass to his mouth.

Fanny didn't move, holding the ale awkwardly. Then she lowered her head as it trembled in her hand.

"What is it?" Damian put his hand to steady hers. "You don't have to drink it. I can get you something else if that would suit better."

"No." She shook her head. "No, it's fine. Thank you." She took an unsteady breath.

He touched her shoulder as his heart clenched. "What's wrong? Tell me. I can fix it." He was damned determined to fix anything and everything that affected her.

She had a desperate look on her face. "I have to tell you something, but it's secret." She waited for his nod. "Someone attacked my family, that's why I'm in hiding. They killed my mother but I managed to escape."

"I know some of that."

"You know?" She looked fearfully into his eyes.

"I figured," he said. "I have so much admiration for all you've done to survive."

Her expression softened and tears came to her eyes. "Thank you, Damian." She glanced around nervously. "The thing is, I think I saw the man who attacked us. I'm sure it's him."

Damian's heart stopped and he froze, carefully setting the glass down. "Where? Show me."

She shrank down on her seat and jerked her chin in the direction of the milling crowd as bodies shoved and shouts erupted. "He was in that crowd of people when the fight started." She didn't point, but her eyes burned down on the mob. "He didn't wear a uniform but acted as if he did, he was yanking the men to one side and yelling at them to move back."

Alarm built in his blood as he studied the crowd. *Someone from the military or police?* "Do you see him now?"

"No, I just had a brief glimpse."

"Did he see you?"

"Yes, that's the thing. He glanced up and his eyes locked on me. Then he kind of faded back into the crowd."

"By the graves." Damian sent a quick beltlink message and got one back almost immediately. Then Nikesh appeared on the stands a few seats above. Damian instructed him to stay close and provide backup. Someone was hunting Fanny.

CHAPTER TWENTY SIX

They stayed while the second half of the game began, which made Fanny even more nervous. Damian told her it was too dangerous to climb down the stands at half time, but the light was fading and it would soon be full dark. Then they could choose their moment to leave.

Who was the man? This felt like a nightmare. She'd given the best description she could but there was nothing that really stood out in his appearance. And yet she'd recognized him. That face had haunted her ever since she'd seen it through the plexi of their transport.

There was a screech of tires as she turned her head. Mother held her arm in a fierce grip as their Constable driver fought with the wheel to keep them from hitting the side railing of the bridge. Fanny looked straight into the eyes of the driver of the hydro-truck that was coming fast toward them. The driver's skin was tanned, he had brown hair and a tough mouth. And when he glanced back at her as the truck connected with the door of their vehicle, his grey eyes were piercing. They seemed to spear right through her.

She shuddered and suddenly felt cold.

The second half of the game was harder fought than the first. Legitamia quickly scored and was one point up when Adar Silva poured on their best men. One of their goalies seemed determined not to let another shot in and his attack on his opponent began with kicks and body slams and progressed to a head butt so forceful the Legitamian player lay dead on the field with a broken neck and the goalie had knocked himself out.

The game was stopped for a few minutes to carry the bodies off and bring in new players. Then the action began again. Fanny didn't even feel affected by the carnage. She was numb, fear having stopped up all her emotions. *What would she do now?* He was still after her, he hadn't given up.

It was pitch black away from the field lights when Damian finally helped her down the steps to the ground, Nikesh a pace behind. They headed through the moving line of spectators and out to the crowded street. Nikesh had managed to fade into the background, there was such a mass of people walking the strand and pouring out of the bars and restaurants. A group of Clones stood uncertainly on the corner with their jewelled robes and painted faces until their handler appeared and led them off.

Damian took her in a convoluted route to the back door of the Transit Hotel. He said he was giving

Nikesh the opportunity to locate anyone who might be following. Inside, they took the stairs. He told her the elevator display showed anyone watching what floor they got off.

Her whole body was shaking by the time Damian unlocked the door to his room and stood back to let her enter. She stepped inside and he closed the door, raking the area with his gaze.

"How does it look? As you left it, or is something different?"

It looked the same. She picked up Boulter's blocks and stacked them on the sill. Peering into the wardrobe she found her other dress hanging where she'd placed it.

"No, everything is as I left it." She tried not to seem desperate as she gazed up at him. *What would she do if he left her here alone?*

"Well, then." He shifted his shoulders and braced his legs. "I don't think it's safe for you here. But I don't have another solution, at least right now." His gaze was warm on her face. "I'm waiting for information from Governor Maude."

"I see." She looked toward the window and moved to pull the drapes, closing off the plexi from the street below. "I don't really want to be alone," she stammered, turning back toward him. "Boulter isn't here, which is probably better for his safety. But I'm nervous and I don't…"

Damian's face flushed a dull red. "I could stay here with you." His gaze shifted to the bed and then quickly away again. "I'll take the floor. At least then if someone comes I'll be here to protect you. If you don't mind, that is."

Pleasure flooded through her, followed by warmth. She stopped shivering. "No, I don't mind."

~ * * * ~

Moving away from the crowd, Rutman stood in the shadow of the barracks and pulled out his voicelink. He entered some particulars. There was no reply and after a lengthy wait he left a message.

Now what? He'd finally found her. Getting the request for the reward that told them Fanny Master was in Deep Creek had been a distinct advantage. DuSatoy was clever that way. Rutman just hadn't known at the time it was posted that the huge reward would never be paid, and it would be his job to take care of that end of things.

Seeing her here at the games had been fluke. But he knew that face well, he'd studied her holograph ever since she went missing from the hydro-truck incident. After the first call for the reward, he'd sent someone down to the Legitamia Palace restaurant, but she must have already moved on because no one saw her leaving the establishment. However, he was ready when the second call came.

The bigger surprise at seeing her during the games had been when he identified her companion. Damian Stuke kept showing up in unusual places and Rutman didn't like it. He'd known about the man when he worked for Makulski, although he'd never actually met him. But Stuke had seemed to be everywhere, enforcing and placing bets as Makulski instructed.

Rutman's relationship with the gamer was so secret only a few people knew about it. One of the reasons Makulski was successful was because, as lead Constable of the Southern Territory, Rutman left him alone to run his business. And in return, Rutman earned a pension that he couldn't get anywhere else.

But now Stuke was here at the heart of the territory and Rutman's nose was out of joint. Maude thought he didn't understand that these hand-picked men formed a special force to operate outside the purview of the Constables. He thought Rutman was too thick to figure it out. But everyone had their price, and it had been easy to uncover the activity Maude had put into process.

Now, why was Stuke in the midst of that? He was a small-time crook from the borderlands. Had the Governor taken leave of his senses? He wouldn't mind removing Stuke from action. It would be a distinct pleasure, and all in the line of duty.

His voicelink buzzed and when he pressed the button, DuSatoy's voice came through low and smooth. "How did it go? Have we brought in the last Master?" He gave a harsh laugh.

"Not yet," Rutman said.

There was silence.

"I took care of the fellow claiming the reward," he hastened to add. "So we won't hear from him again. I haven't yet figured out where the subject is hiding. But I saw her tonight at the games."

DuSatoy interrupted. "You're running out of time, Rutman. I can't let this carry on much longer. She's the only one left. If she comes out on the campaign trail with FitzGibbon or Lanser before the election, I lose. And believe me, I'm a sore loser."

Rutman felt a cold tingle run down his spine. "I'm not dragging my feet here. I just saw her. We're very close."

"Good, don't fail me." The voicelink went silent.

CHAPTER TWENTY SEVEN

In the bare room of the Transit Hotel, Damian watched Fanny bustle around heating water for tea. Her hands were shaky, she was obviously nervous. Rightly so. They were in a precarious situation. He glanced at the door. It was tightly locked and he knew Nikesh was out there watching for any unusual activity. The window was secure, the plexi strong and they were four floors up so it would be difficult to breach it from the outside. He had stashed his lasergun against the wall behind the door, knowing he could reach it from nearly anywhere in the room if needed.

Fanny hadn't been able to give much of a description of her attacker —he was average height she thought, muscular in the chest and arms, brown hair, piercing eyes and a tough mouth. *What did piercing eyes mean? A tough mouth?* A guy wouldn't recognize someone from that portrayal. For that matter, what did she think his mouth looked like?

The thought made him warm and he tried to refocus on the tea as it steeped in the pot. Right now his mouth probably looked pretty tough as well. Someone was hunting her and he needed to keep her safe. And that meant guarding her overnight in this hotel room until he could make another arrangement. *Am I an idiot, or what?*

He moved restlessly to the window and back, waiting for a reply to the message he'd sent to Governor Maude. He needed support and he needed it now.

How long did it take to brew tea? This could be the night from hell. He glanced sideways in time to see her pour the steaming liquid into bowls the hotel had provided. At last, something to do with his hands.

She sat on the edge of the bed, blowing across the surface of her bowl. He took the single chair. Then he stalled as she looked over at him, determination written on her face. *What now?*

"I don't think you know who I am," she said.

He waited. Her eyes looked darker in the light of the single lamp, her hair gleamed like polished gold.

"You know there's a reward on my head," she continued, "but there are dozens of those out there, probably hundreds if you search for them. I've escaped from the City and my father was Leader of Khandarken." There were tears in her voice.

He set his bowl aside and reached to take her trembling hand. "Your name is Fanny Master," he said.

"Oh." She gazed at him fearfully. "You do know."

"Yes." He smoothed her fingers. "That's why I was delayed during dinner last night, that's what I was trying to look after. Someone had contacted the service for your reward."

"That means they know where I am." She looked fearfully around. "What do I do now?" Her forehead wrinkled in alarm.

"We wait." Damian sipped his tea. "I've called it in and soon more men will arrive along with new instructions."

"Instructions?" She half rose from the bed but he motioned her back. "From whom?" Her voice wobbled.

"It's alright," he said. "We can trust this man."

She glanced down at her fingers twisting in her lap. "I'm sorry I didn't tell you. It just seemed... too risky."

Damian gritted his teeth. "Don't apologize. You did what you had to. You're a brave woman, Fanny. You've saved yourself and Boulter. That's more than many women could have done." A wave of emotion welled in his throat. Was she really apologizing to him – a dispossessed who had worked for an illegal gamer for years? *Someone who had killed a man?*

He wanted to gather her into his arms and rock her against his body. The urge was so strong, he stood and paced the short length between chair and door. It was suddenly too hot in here. He'd suffocate before morning at this rate. Bracing his back on the entry panel he jammed his hands in his pockets and tried to still his racing heart.

"Damian." He glanced back to find her gaze had followed him.

"What is it?" There was a limit, he didn't have nerves of steel any more, not since his capture. He didn't have the endurance for this.

"Let me." She rose and moved toward him, the tight focus of her gaze pinning him where he stood. Panic rose from his stomach. *What did she want? What if he couldn't control himself?*

She stopped before him and placed her hands on his belt. Rising on tiptoe, she laid her soft mouth over his. He froze in place.

~ * * * ~

At the door of his headquarters, Emperor Carlton grabbed the reins of his mount from the footman and heaved himself into the saddle. He signalled to Elkon, and the General lifted his arm for the bugle to sound. They were off to tour their Legitamian province and try to raise more men for the upcoming action.

Two outriders rode ahead to clear the way and Carlton's standard bearer followed carrying the banner of the Empire high, the staff resting in the mount on the side of his saddle. Carlton rode next, then his Advisor and two Counsellors. General Elkon came behind with his adjutant, leading some troops. It was a challenge to get enough mounts, whether horse or mule, and most of his men walked in file at the rear.

Elkon had put out the word. With a military action imminent, they would need more loyal and willing fighters. And more men meant more food, tents, horses and mules, weapons. Forget uniforms, he'd given up trying to provide them for anyone but the leaders.

Yet the numbers had not swelled as he'd expected, not like the last time he sent out a call. Carlton motioned the General forward and waited until they were riding side-by-side. "Where are the new troops?" he demanded through gritted teeth. "Where are the dispossessed? There should have been more arriving by now." He levelled a hard glare at Elkon but the General stared straight ahead.

"They'll come, my lord," he replied calmly. "The International Head Ball Games have become the current attraction, even for men from the north."

Carlton snorted. "The games should have been hosted by the Empire. Those games were our games, and now Adar Silva claims them. It's disgusting. Why can't the men see how senseless it is to hold them without our participation?"

"I understand your frustration, my lord." Elkon's voice remained even. "But until we have our own lands, we can't influence this. As it is, Adar Silva is in the lead in the competition, I hear. Perhaps that shows just how influential the Empire was."

"Was?" Carlton's voice was a low forceful demand as his hand tightened on the reins and yanked his mount's head up. The horse whickered and danced rapidly sideways in alarm, smashing into Elkon's mount. Soon both horses were thrashing together and the Counsellors coming behind got caught in the mêlée. Advisor Judson Lanser's horse went down, hooves grinding in the dirt. There was a shout and the animal scrambled to its feet and stood trembling, head down and reins dragging on the ground.

Lanser didn't move where he lay. His assistant leapt down to kneel beside him. "It's my leg," he muttered. "Can't move it. Get the medic, it'll have to be casted." He glanced toward where the Emperor impatiently sat his horse. "I'm sorry, my lord. I won't be able to go with you this trip. It will take some days to heal my leg."

"Yes, of course." Carlton felt the heat climb his throat. When would he learn to control his temper? This might be his fault that his Advisor was injured. On the other hand, he was the Emperor. It was his force, his rage that drove them forward. He would never regret what happened, never back off from his goal of recruiting men, training them, waging battles and reclaiming land until the Empire was a forceful entity again in its own right.

"Very well, three men stay with the Advisor, get him back to headquarters and tended to. We ride on." As Carlton turned his horse toward the trail, Elkon lifted his arm and the bugle sounded again

CHAPTER TWENTY EIGHT

Selanna opened the hotel room door to find Dr Harris Stuke in the corridor dressed for dinner. She waved him in. "Cownden's not here, Da," she said. "He sent a message that he'd be late and we should go ahead without him."

Da's mouth turned down at her expression. "He's a busy man, and these Head Ball Games don't make anything easier."

She frowned and shook her head. "He's not here, he's in the City with Anatoliy. He thought they would be able to come back tonight but now it's not certain. He had a security issue to deal with."

"Ah. A man on an important mission." Stuke nodded.

"It is important, Da." Her mouth tightened. "The result of the election will be very important for all Khandarken. And the result will depend on how well he does his job."

"I know, my girl. That's what I said. We've had a rocky year, and the ones before weren't smooth. I think Cownden is the best candidate to steer us through the threats and upheaval around us. It's important that he win." Da threw a lean arm around her shoulders and Selanna pressed her head against his bony chest.

"Thanks, Da. I needed that." She was perilously close to tears. Cownden was seldom here it seemed, but because of the Head Ball Games he was in Deep Creek more often than the City, so she'd settled at the hotel for the moment. Her father, Dr Stuke, had come to Deep Creek for the Games and would return to Bereford at the close.

Da waved her toward the entry. "Shall we go, then? Dinner awaits."

Seated in a corner booth of the restaurant in the Learmonth Hotel, they quickly ordered food and settled in over Da's ale and a bowl of wine for Selanna. "What has you so upset, child?" Da's long fingers gripped hers across the table top. "These Games are almost finished, just a few more days."

He took a sip. "With Jiran pulling out because they haven't won any competitions, it will wind up rather quickly. Tomorrow, Adar Silva faces Legitamia. Whoever wins that round will battle Khandarken the next day for first place and it will all be settled." He winked at her. "You have to admit, they've been a pretty exciting display. Jiran doesn't get any sympathy from me. Their team didn't try very hard and seemed to lack any kind of discipline."

"Well, Da. You've seen how Legitamia plays. Would you call that discipline?" The Legitamia team had been particularly fierce in their last game with

Jiran, and four Jirani players had to be carted off the field.

"Yes, of a sort. They won the meet fair and square. Can't argue with the score."

She sighed. "It must be a man-thing."

Da pulled in his chin. "How so?"

Selanna laughed. "Well, I don't know a woman who thought those games were fairly played. Julianne Adjudicator, Abe Farmer's wife, agrees with me."

"Well, that just goes to show." Da picked up a skewer of hard-boiled quail eggs and pulled one off with his implanted teeth. "It's not a man-thing, it's a woman-thing."

She made a face and he grinned as he chewed.

"Da, have you seen Damian lately?" Things were a bit out of whack with Cownden away so much and she was concerned about her brother.

"No, child, I haven't. But I know he's busy with his training and tasks that've been assigned."

"Aren't you worried?"

He raised his brows. "Worried?" he questioned mildly. "Why? I'd be more worried if he was still working for that Makulski bandit. That was a bad spot for Damian to be in and I'm ever so grateful to Cownden for flushing him out of it and into something much more suited."

She warmed with pleasure. Yes, it had been good of Cownden to look after her brother. Getting him out of gaming had been a big step, not just for him but for the whole family. They'd all worried about where that occupation would lead. "No, I'm talking about that woman he's seeing."

Da gave her an admonishing look. "You think your brother isn't worthy of such a woman, or doesn't deserve to find someone to make him happy?"

"That's just it, Da. You know I don't think that. But there's something strange going on there and I'm afraid he'll get hurt. He's never had a woman…" She stopped at the look in her father's eyes. "I don't mean like that."

Heat suffused her cheeks but she plowed on. "I'm sure he's been with a woman before, in spite of the shortage of females in Khandarken. Even a Clone, for heaven's sake. That's not my business… What I mean is, he's fallen for her. Fanny isn't the kind of woman who's going to stick around Bereford, and he'll be very hurt when she leaves. The treatments I give him keep him stable but… And there's that issue of her son and his strange eyes."

Harris Stuke shrugged and sawed on a piece of meat from his plate. "Yah, the eyes." He gnawed on a bone while Selanna cut a slice of fish from her dinner.

"Tell me about the eyes, Da."

He swallowed and dropped the bone on his plate, wiping his hands on the linen cloth by his elbow. "It's a strange story, child."

"Good, tell me. I'm ready for such a story." Her eyes were soft as she gazed at him. She loved his stories and sometimes it was hard to entice him to tell the tales. There were too many bad memories entangled with most of them.

"It was like this," he began. "We were on the Helmcken Trail and the fighting was bitter."

She nodded encouragingly. "You'd already changed sides by then, leaving the Emperor's army and joining the rebels."

"Yah, that's so. The injuries were brutal. There were so many boms planted either side of the Trail that it was almost impossible to get through unscathed. Every time we lost control of territory, it would be planted anew with detonations by the Empire forces before we won it back again."

He glared at his plate. "There were only a few medics with us, many had stayed with the Emperor. The tents were full of the wounded and more kept arriving, dragged up the trail by the freedom fighters looking for help. There was no end in sight. We were very tired, probably making mistakes even as we tried to staunch the flow of blood or amputate ruined limbs."

He looked into her eyes and the pain was evident. "I knew Damian was out there somewhere, but didn't know where. So I stayed with it, thinking any one of those young men could have been him, needing my help. I'm sure the others felt the same.

"One night, I noticed that the other two doctors were sleeping. It's not like they went off to bed. One had collapsed on a cot near the door, his boots still resting on the ground, the other had been looking after a young fellow's arm and he'd dropped asleep right in the middle of wrapping it. I stood there, not knowing what to do. I couldn't carry such a load on my own."

Selanna took his hand in hers and held on tight. Those gnarled fingers had done a lot of work and saved many lives. "What happened, Da?"

He seemed to be looking inward. "Three men walked in the door," he said. "They were tall, taller than I am, lean and sinewy, wearing plain serviceable robes. They moved without sound. I didn't hear the clump of their boots coming up the trail, or the swish of their robes as they entered the tent. I asked who they were looking for, because anyone coming in was usually looking for a loved one who'd gone down in the fight.

"The first man shook his head and said, *we've found him*. He just put his hand on my shoulder and I found myself lying on an empty cot beside the other medic. The three men began work. No talking, no sound. I watched them touch a wound and it stopped bleeding. They straightened limbs and the swelling went down, the bone healed. Amputations were mended. The crying and moaning of the injured slowly subsided till all I heard was the soft breathing of all the men in the tent as they slept. I slept too, I know. When I woke I was rested, for the first time in weeks, months. The three men were gone, the tent quiet.

"When I got up, the cooks had prepared breakfast and we sat to eat. No one else had seen anything. That was what was so remarkable. No one had seen a thing."

Selanna puzzled over that as she stared at him. "But who were they, Da? And what do they have to do with Boulter and his strange eyes?"

Da smiled. "I don't know who they were, child. But I know what they were. They were angels. They'd come to lift the load for us, just for a moment. They'd come to help in any way they could. Angels don't have names maybe, I'm not sure. But all three of them had yellow eyes, with the slit in the iris the way a cat does. Just like Boulter's."

"Oh, my goodness!" Selanna let go of his hand and half rose from her chair. "Da, aren't you afraid for that woman with Damian? She has a child who's an angel and she probably doesn't even know it! She treats him like her son. Why, she wouldn't know, would she? And what if the boy leaves? She'll be heartbroken."

"Sit, girl. Sit." Da looked around the crowded room and spoke softly. "We can't know what angels do or why. That isn't for us to understand. The woman will survive. If Boulter is one of them, then she's been granted the privilege of looking after him and that's not something anyone would wish away."

The pressure under her breast was painful and Selanna rubbed at her rib cage, hoping to ease it. Damian was in the middle of this and he didn't even know what he was dealing with. "Da, why would an angel show up with her?"

"I don't know, girl. But maybe they needed each other."

CHAPTER TWENTY NINE

Fanny watched Damian's wide expressive mouth. His lips were usually pressed firmly together, but sometimes when caught off guard they relaxed into a grin and the dimple in his chin deepened. He was a handsome man and it always gave her a little thrill she tried hard to suppress.

She felt safe, for the first time since Father died. But only with Damian. He didn't press his attentions on her, he wasn't highly directive, but when her safety was at stake he took charge without apology.

Now they were alone in the hotel room, it was her turn to take charge. "Damian, kiss me," she said and put her mouth to his. He hesitated, but when her hands rose to press against his chest, his mouth slanted to take her in. Warmth flooded her breasts. What a hard body, the wide straight shoulders and lean waist spoke of a strength that could support and defend her. His keen eyes noticed everything, yet his mouth seldom shared what he saw.

When he thrust his tongue between her lips, she opened up and he invaded as his hands rose to caress her back. Her heart caught fire and she panted against his chest as he devoured her. When he finally lifted his mouth away, she pressed her forehead to his breastbone in a desperate attempt to control her breathing. "Oh, my," she muttered.

He pressed fervent kisses to her temple, then tilted her head with a finger under her chin. "Kiss me again," he said.

It was long moments before she rose for air and Fanny feared her body would explode with need. Heat curled in her belly and between her legs. Her knees wobbled dangerously as she clutched urgently at his belt. These sensations were so new to her. They were alarming but at the same time, she was wound like a spring and ready for more.

"Fanny, what are you doing with me?" Damian's voice was ragged. "I'm not of your class. You don't belong with a man like me. I'm dispossessed."

She glanced up at his fierce grey gaze as her mind slowly cleared from the fog of passion. She frowned. "How do you mean? You aren't dispossessed. You have a home in Bereford where your father, the doctor, lives. Your sister is married to the Chief Constable. You have a position with Governor Maude."

"Yah, but that doesn't give me status. I've been working for a gamer on the border as an enforcer. It's what I do." He looked desperately down at her. "Don't play with me, Fanny."

"Play with you?" She stared straight into his eyes. "I'm deadly serious. My life has been in danger for months. Both my parents have been murdered and someone made an attempt on my life. Do I look like I'm playing?" Tears formed and she blinked rapidly to clear them. *Would she have to beg? If so, she didn't know how to even begin.* "I want you to make love to me."

The reaction was immediate. His arms tightened like iron bands around her waist and his mouth went straight to her throat, kissing the side of her neck and behind her ear, tugging on her earring. The heat began to rise again and she moaned against his chest. "Damian, I'm too hot."

He gave a rough laugh. "Yah, me too. It's because we have all our clothes on." He pulled her across the room and sat on the bed, tugging her onto his lap. Taking a deep breath, he slowly let it out, seeming to gain some control. "Fanny, you don't know what you're asking. If we do this, we can't turn back."

"No," she admitted. "I know that. I've not made love before, but I want to now, with you. There's a fire burning in me. You can't just leave me in this condition. Isn't there something you can do?" She squirmed on his knee. "Please, Damian."

His answer was a groan. He unlaced her blouse and put his hand inside. His rough palm slid across her breast and stroked the nipple. Delicious sensations slithered down her belly to centre between her thighs. She gazed at him in wonder as he lifted his head to kiss her again.

More clothes disappeared and Fanny found herself spread across the bed as Damian placed his mouth wherever he could reach. She tugged at his shirt and he ripped it over his head. His chest was broad and deeply muscled, a light sprinkling of hair decorating the centre. Muscles rippled down his belly, and when he stood to remove his trousers, Fanny's heart nearly stopped. He seemed very large down there. She should have expected it, he was a big man, but it still gave her pause. How was this going to work, after all?

Yet, when he lay down and began to kiss her again and caress with his hands, the fears slipped away to be replaced by anticipation and delight. She loved him. He'd stepped inside her boundaries as she fought to survive. He'd managed to insinuate himself into their lives in such a way that she leaned on him now, instead of having to stand alone.

She wanted to cement him to her. If she were to go home to the City, he would be with her, lending his support and security. It was what she had come to rely on.

She ran her hands across those thick shoulders and down his arms. The bed dipped as he raised himself over her and an inkling of alarm sounded beneath her breast. This was so new to her and he was a big man. When he settled between her legs, she braced her hands against his chest.

"Damian, I don't think this will work…"

He smiled, such a tender expression on his face. "I'll be careful," he said. "You'll see." His mouth claimed hers and slowly she relaxed against him, the fear replaced by anticipation. He gazed fiercely into her eyes. Oh… unbelievably the excitement mounted. "Damian," she whispered. "Thank you."

He seemed to hesitate as moisture ran down his temples, but then he pressed inward. She tensed, the pressure becoming uncomfortable. He plunged and she stiffened against the invasion. Yet he held and waited, kissing her gently on the mouth until she forgot about the fullness and weight as the delight built again within.

As he began to move inside her, she moved too, until she couldn't bear the rub and slide, couldn't stand the heaviness any longer, and rose against him as a huge release swept over her, spreading upward to her belly and breasts, outward to her fingers and toes. Damian groaned and plunged before collapsing over her and rolling to the side, taking her with him.

Nestled against his shoulder, feeling his arm around her back, Fanny laughed, for the first time since her transport plunged into the Violetta River.

~ * * * ~

Damian heaved a sigh and tightened his arm around her. "You were meant for a different kind of man," he murmured in the dim light as his fingers caressed her hair. "Someone from the upper class who would be awarded a political position in the country. Or a man who holds family assets like mines or property."

"Do you mean like DuSatoy?" Her look was deceptively innocent as her gaze rested on his face. "Someone like that?"

He grunted. "No, not like DuSatoy. More like the Learmonth family."

She scoffed. "Have you met the young Learmonth son? He's a buffoon, if ever I saw one. I don't know if his father, Jack, will ever be able to retire with an heir like that sitting in the wings."

Damian lifted his head to peer down at her. "That's just my point. You know these people. You belong in that society. What are you doing with me?"

Sudden uncertainty rushed up her throat. "Don't you want to be here?" Her voice wavered hesitantly.

Damian rolled to face her and his arms came around her in a locked grip. "I love you, Fanny," he growled. "There's nowhere else I'd rather be. I've wanted you from the moment I first saw you in the field by the transit yard, come to get Boulter that night. You looked so vulnerable and defenceless but you stood ramrod straight and stared me right in the eye. You didn't trust me a bit but you didn't back down. I've loved you from that moment. But I'm not the right man for you. I'm damaged." He shot her a desperate stare as his lips pressed firmly together.

Her heart warmed at his words of love and she immediately took issue with his claim. "How do you mean, damaged? I see the scars on your chest and back, is that what you mean? Why would you think I couldn't look at those?" She traced a finger across his belly where it looked like he'd sustained a slash, and watched his muscles twitch beneath her touch.

He grabbed her hand and held it firmly in his. "Not that. I mean in my mind. I've been damaged in my mind." He refused to look at her.

Fanny shook her head. "Tell me."

He glanced back at her. "It's not a nice story."

"Then tell me," she insisted. "Help me to understand."

"I was captured," he said, and lay back on the pallet to stare at the bed curtains hanging above them. "Along the Helmcken Trail. I was tortured." As he told the tale, he seemed to physically withdraw from her, from everything in the room. Fanny moved closer until she was glued to his side, her arms wrapped around his shoulders. When he finished, there was silence for a moment as she tried to understand what he'd told her.

"I am so sorry that happened," she murmured. "So sorry." They were both silent for a moment. "I'm damaged too, Damian. I don't trust anyone, not even General Paulo Regiment. He was in charge of our security. He promised Mother and I would be safe. But we weren't, were we? Not safe at all. Who can I trust now? Only you."

He turned his head to gaze into her eyes, but she continued. "I love you. And I think you're perfect for me. This is the first time I've felt safe since my father died. You make me warm, Damian. You make me whole again."

He groaned and pulled her up against him, pressing her head onto his shoulder and her breasts tight against his chest. One hand swept down to cup her bottom.

Just then his voicelink rumbled.

CHAPTER THIRTY

Rutman groaned and rolled over in bed. He grabbed his voicelink from the night stand before a second rumble could wake his wife. Pressing the *hold* button, he slid from the pallet and padded softly into the entry of his home.

"What is it now?" He knew who was contacting him, but why do it in the middle of the night? Surely whatever it was could wait until morning.

"Because you're supposed to be on top of this," DuSatoy snarled across the link. "I'm looking for Fanny Master and you're supposed to be the one to deliver her. What's the holdup?"

"There was a problem."

"What kind of problem?"

Rutman shuddered. He never should have given in that very first time in Wymark. Never should have betrayed his position as Constable. But the pay wasn't that high, and DuSatoy's men in the north just made things easier to manage if he worked with them. Those tentacles of cooperation had followed him as he left that city, stretched all the way to his new position in the Southern Territory. He hadn't been able to leave his history behind. DuSatoy saw to that, like he saw to everything.

Rutman lowered his voice and moved further into the entry. "I tried to find out more from the kid but he didn't seem to have any information. All he knew was his brother had seen her having dinner in the Legitamia Palace. She was with a small boy and a man."

He took a breath. "When I saw her at the games she was with a special forces man. Not someone I can take on alone."

DuSatoy growled into the voicelink. "Afraid, Rutman? Because I'm not. I'll take on anyone, even you."

"Now, now." Rutman stifled a shudder. "I'm not saying I won't take him on, I'm just saying that I'm more valuable in position here than I am in prison or dead. So we need to make a plan to handle this."

There was crash at the other end and DuSatoy swore long under his breath. Then he was back on the link. "Do you have anyone there who can help you? Someone you trust?"

"I don't trust anyone here. I've never divulged a thing in all the years we've worked together."

"All right, then we wait. When the time comes, I'll have my men ready to assist. I'll be back in Deep Creek campaigning, so won't be far away when we need to act. Someone else is bound to recognize her.

We'll get another call to collect the reward, and you better handle it differently this time. This time we get her, without fail. You have my word on it, Rutman."

Rutman paced his entry, voicelink quiet in his hand. That had sounded like a threat, but DuSatoy didn't bother with threats. He just told him what would happen, and it would be on Rutman's head if Ms Master escaped again.

He moved quietly into his bedroom, watching his wife sleeping peacefully on her side of the pallet, her long dark hair spread across the light-coloured bolster.

There were other issues right behind this one that were just waiting to explode in his face. He shrugged and climbed into bed. It had all been for her. Everything he'd done had been for her. Soon he might have to make the last sacrifice because there would be no other choice.

~ * * * ~

Damian stepped outside the hotel room and closed the door, listening for the sound of the lock as it engaged inside. He walked softly through the hallway, looking for Nikesh, and found him down in the lobby talking with a couple of Jirani military by the look of their clothing. He kept going, moving to the front staircase and heading back to the fourth floor outside the room where Fanny slept. Soon Nikesh appeared to join him.

Damian jammed his hands in his pockets. "What have you got?"

"Not much." Nikesh's voice was low. "The Jiranis are leaving tomorrow, disgusted with their performance at the games. The tents on the field behind the fighting arts building will be cleared out by nightfall, according to those men. Their aircarts are equipping to take them home."

He nodded. "Well, that will make it a little easier to patrol the crowd, given that only three teams remain."

Nikesh looked at him but didn't respond, obviously waiting for more.

"I've just received a strange message." Damian shifted his feet as he looked down the hall, watching an older man stagger to his room and fumble with the code to open the door. "I don't know what to believe at this point. But I guess we need to take it seriously until we know better."

He bent a stern gaze on his partner. "Makulski sent me a wristlink communication."

Nikesh pulled in his chin and looked at him sideways. "Makulski? You're sure it was him?" At Damian's nod, he muttered, "Was it friendly? I've been surprised we haven't had any encounters with him during the games, but he's more or less stayed off our path through this whole thing."

"Yah, that's surprised me too. I can't say the message was friendly, more cautionary. He said Rutman is not to be trusted."

Nikesh opened his mouth, then closed it. Finally, he put a hand to his jaw and rubbed his whiskers. "That was it? Not to be trusted?"

"Yah. I don't know what it means. But if it's true, we have to be very careful. If it isn't, Makulski is up to something." He shrugged. "It complicates things."

Nikesh nodded. "I've often wondered about Rutman. I ran into him a couple of times coming out of a bar in Bereford."

Damian eyed him dubiously. "That's not unusual."

"No, but Constables don't spend time in bars as a rule, and each time Makulski came out a few minutes later."

Damian frowned. "You never said."

"I wasn't really paying much attention at the time. But since we've come to Deep Creek and we're working for the other side, it's time to care about such details."

He grinned and Damian laughed. "True," he said.

"So what about the woman?" Nikesh prodded. "What's the plan? We have to keep her safe but I'm not sure who we're protecting her from."

Damian clamped a hand on his shoulder. "We only have to worry about tonight. Tomorrow, Chief Constable Cownden Lanser is taking her to secure quarters. That's the plan."

CHAPTER THIRTY ONE

Damian lifted the cover and slid back onto the pallet. Fanny lay curled on her side in a deep sleep, her face turned to the wall. He rolled slowly toward her, sliding one arm under the pillow and wrapping the other around her body. They would only have this one night before the Constables took her away, and it was tearing him apart.

It was right that they take her, he understood that. She couldn't continue to live in a broken hut up the trail with Boulter and the hound for company. But to lose her when he'd just found her was making his chest ache. His hands were desperate to touch, his mouth longed for another kiss.

Fanny sighed and turned her face to his shoulder as he gathered her in.

"Damian?"

"Yah, I'm here."

She sighed. "Oh. I wondered. I woke for a minute and couldn't find you."

"I had to talk to Nikesh, but I'm back now."

"That's good." Her breath wafted across his skin in the darkness and he shuddered.

"Are you awake?" he asked.

"Um hmm." She yawned and laid one hand in the middle of his chest. His muscles jumped in an involuntary spasm.

"I need to talk to you."

"All right." Pressing her lips to his neck, she cuddled closer.

He spoke through a tight throat. "Fanny, you'll be leaving in the morning."

She was still for a moment. "I will? How do you mean?"

He felt her lashes brush his skin as she blinked. "Chief Constable Lanser is coming to take you to safety. You can trust him, and you can't stay here. It isn't secure, not after that man saw your face."

"I can trust him? How can you be sure?" She was wide awake now, he felt the tension in her body.

"I know Cownden pretty well. He's married to my sister, remember."

She didn't respond.

He rolled toward her. "I know General Paulo Regiment was looking after you before, but no one understood the danger you were in. They do now. Cownden will ensure your safety."

"What about Boulter?"

Damian nodded. "I'll look after that. We'll get Boulter and he'll go with you."

She seemed to relax under his hand and he pressed his cheek against her hair. She moved her mouth to his neck and he lit on fire. Stroking his sideburn with her fingertips, she moved from there to trace a trail down the middle of his chest and nothing could stop him after that. He pulled her leg over his hip and laid his lips on hers as he nudged himself at the entrance to her secret opening. The sensation was transforming. He tried to hold her still as she writhed against him.

They would be coming to get her soon and he was running out of time. In the dim light she was beautiful, slender and soft, her skin like silk. Her golden hair was mussed and fell forward to cover one rounded breast. He used a finger to push it aside for his gaze, rubbing across the nipple until it peaked beneath his touch. Then he pulled her into his arms as he kissed her. The feel of her mouth on his was heaven. The sleek skin of her back seemed like satin.

"I miss you already," he said. He didn't know what the morning would bring, or what decision would be made about her future. All he knew was she was his for now, for tonight he could be with her.

Giving her almost no time to prepare, he slid home, catching her gasp with his mouth and beginning a slow seduction with his tongue. She wrapped her slender arms around his neck and his breath stopped in his chest. When it started again, he had to heave for air, then began moving his hips to the beat of his heart. She sighed unevenly, then held her breath as she began to close around him. It was more than he could bear. He moved at a frantic pace to catch up, to keep pace, to follow her down.

When he woke to his wristlink vibration, it was still dark out. Dressing silently, he pulled the door open to find Nikesh waiting on the other side as agreed, plasma gun by his side, and down the hall came his brother by marriage with six Constables trooping behind, all with their visors pulled down.

Then he took a last long look at the woman in the bed, her face a pale oval, one breast peeking forth, and tugged the cover up before he turned to meet her guards, pulling the door closed behind him.

~ * * * ~

Fanny woke in the pre-dawn hours and rolled over, reaching for Damian. The pallet was empty. She sighed and blinked at the window where light was just beginning to form. Perhaps he was meeting with Nikesh again. *Would he return before she left?*

A soft voice asked, "Fanny?"

She lifted her head in alarm and gazed toward the door. A woman was seated in the solitary chair, a bag at her feet. She wore a conservative robe, something Fanny would have chosen for travel in that other time, that time before her life fell apart.

"Fanny Master?" The woman rose and approached the bed. "It's me, Julianne Adjudicator. I hope you don't mind, but they wanted someone to be here when you woke and I knew you before..." She paused awkwardly.

"Julianne." Fanny's voice went faint with surprise. She pushed her hair behind her ear and unsteadily propped herself up in bed as her friend sat on the edge of the pallet. "I'm glad it's you," she said, voice wavering. "I was hoping I wouldn't be all alone again."

Julianne burst into tears and wrapped her arms around her, sobbing softly. "I wondered so often if you were alive. We just didn't know, none of us knew... And when Abe told me last night, I couldn't believe it."

Fanny wiped her eyes on the sheet as her friend sat back. "I couldn't tell anyone, Julianne. I didn't know who to trust. No one was above suspicion."

"That's so sad." Julianne pulled a hankie from her bag and blew her nose. "How did you manage? I want to know everything, but perhaps not everything, because it must have been very hard and lonely."

Fanny felt more tears gather. There was a knock on the door and Cownden Lanser stuck his head through the gap. "We have a visitor bearing gifts," he said and opened the portal wider.

Tasha stepped through, her work robe swishing about her legs as she entered. "Fanny, I have some things for you. Your guard came by the shop and asked me to gather what I could." She gave her a meaningful look and then glanced curiously at Julianne.

"Julianne, this is Tasha, a long-time friend who lives in Deep Creek now. What have you got for me, Tasha? How is Boulter?"

Fanny's eyes widened as Tasha laid filmy undergarments on the cover, then hung a dress and shawl in the wardrobe. "Boulter is fine," she said. "He's anxious to see you, but we need to take care of things here first."

Fanny rose on shaky limbs, gathered her nightdress around her and entered the garderobe, closing the door softly behind her. Her guard had asked for the clothes? That must have been Damian. How would he know about her friend at the dress shop? She thought back to that day she'd learned there was a new reward on her head, and how the man seated across from them in the tea shop seemed to know her, even came over to offer help. He must have discovered who she was with.

What a clever man. When would she see him again? There were all kinds of things to attend to— she understood that. They had to find out who was offering the reward. They had to find the man with the piercing eyes who drove the armoured hydro-truck that smashed them into the water.

But surely there were others who could work on that. Didn't Damian have more important tasks, like looking after her? She laughed weakly as the tears dripped down her cheeks. She just needed to get through today. She stepped into the shower and reached for the soap.

CHAPTER THIRTY TWO

The noise from the Games was deafening. Seated beside Governor Maude in the stands, Cownden raised his hand as his brother by marriage approached through the throng. "Damian, I thought you'd be here earlier."

Damian sat beside him and propped his elbows on his thighs. "I had some things to take care of, but I'm here now."

Maude looked tired but determined. The situation was obviously a high priority issue to get this level of attention. Damian knew, as low man in the group, his views would be the last to be considered and he wondered how it would work out.

Maude began. "This is my territory," he fumed, "and I'll be damned if I let anything further happen to that woman on my patch."

Damian bristled. "That's what Major Regiment

said. His father, General Paulo Regiment, guaranteed her safety, and look where that got her."

Cownden's face was red. "Those were my constables driving the transports for Ms Master and Fanny. This is my failure and I'm the one who's going to correct it."

Damian's gaze went from one flushed face to the other, then he stood and braced his feet, facing the others where they sat on the bench. "This isn't about you, any of you. This is about Fanny Master, her safety, her future. We have to find out who's after her and get them before she'll be safe anywhere. That has to be the first step. Then she can go home."

Maude stared for a moment, then relented. "Of course." He rose and nodded at Dante's assistant, Anatoliy. "Keep in touch and let me know what the plan is." He stalked from the field.

Cownden gazed at Damian. "Good. So, I want the Constables to be in charge of this in terms of sorting out the reward and who's behind it."

Damian shook his head adamantly. "No, absolutely not." His mouth was a grim line. "We can't do that, Cownden. You have to listen to me, I've told you why."

The Chief Constable looked frustrated. "What you're saying doesn't make any sense. Rutman has been a Constable for years. There's never been a hint that he isn't loyal."

"I can't help that." Damian glowered toward the field. "The message was clear, Rutman can't be trusted. So although I don't trust Makulski, I have to pay attention to the information."

"Well, why not ask Makulski? You know the man better than anyone, find out what he's referring to."

"I did, that's part of what I was taking care of this morning." Damian looked away uncomfortably. He'd cornered his old boss earlier in the day, finding him stationed at the start of the game under the huge lotus tree at the side of the playing field, sending his runners out with handfuls of tickets to sell.

Makulski looked surprised and then decidedly guarded at the sight of him, but motioned his runners away so they could talk. When Damian asked about the message, at first he denied any knowledge of it. But as he persisted, Makulski finally muttered, "I've had second thoughts about sending that, if you must know."

Damian nodded. "I can imagine. I was surprised as hell to get that information in the first place. Especially after the way we parted company."

The gamer gave a reluctant grin. "Don't think I've forgotten, because I haven't. I won't trust you again, Damian. But see, the thing is, you can't trust Rutman either and it's not so obvious with him." Makulski glanced cautiously around. "Watch your back, Stuke," he said. "He's been on the take for years."

"But from whom?" Frustration clawed at his throat. "How do we prove that?"

Makulski shook his head and motioned one of his runners forward. "You won't get any more out of me."

Now Damian braced his elbows on his knees as he and Dante sat on a bench of the stadium. The crowd roared and both men glanced up. Adar Silva had just scored and their fans at the other end of the field went wild. The teams were tied now, three all, and Legitamia was playing fiercely. One of their players had been carried off on a board during the first half, and Damian heard the man was dead by the time they got him to the hospital tent.

Cownden turned back to resume their conversation. "What do you suggest then? We have to catch these people, and it has to be fast. It's outrageous that Fanny Master has spent months fleeing for her life when we were supposed to have her safely under wraps as General Regiment ordered."

Damian's stomach knotted. Fanny was gone, had left Deep Creek almost the minute the Constables took her into their care. She would be arriving in the City and he'd never see her again. It was almost unbearable. He straightened and tried to wind the tension out of his shoulders.

"I think we have to make a claim on the reward. The fact that it's been posted and we can't find out who is behind it is just another warning flag." He glanced at Cownden. "I can't make the claim, I've been seen around here too much. If this is linked to either Makulski or Rutman, they both know me."

"I think I've resolved that issue." Cownden glanced at his wristlink as it buzzed. He read the screen, then clicked it off. "All right, Abe Farmer has a fellow who will do, we can work it through him.

"Abe Farmer?" Damian puzzled over that. "What does he have to do with this? He runs the fighting arts and has some land along the Adar Silva border."

Cownden looked amused. "Abe is a trained fighter, has been out with the reserves several times since Emperor Carlton invaded through the north, and he's a man of many contacts. His wife, Julianne Adjudicator, is a close friend of Ms Master. This fellow Thames works for Abe at Farmer Holdings and lives at Farmerville with the dispossessed. He's the perfect foil—older, rough around the edges, looks uncouth, and he's very clever and fearless. Let's go. They're waiting at the Transit Hotel."

Damian called Nikesh to get him over there, along with two other men they'd pulled from the Bereford teams they'd had previous dealings with.

Thames was everything Cownden had said, and more. His voice was hoarse, from smoking phang he claimed, and he was missing several front teeth. But he was a burly dispossessed who was totally loyal to Abe Farmer and willing to do whatever was needed to help. After much discussion, it was agreed among the men that Thames would make the call for the reward on his own voicelink. He'd claim he saw Fanny Master at the Games and followed her, that's how he knew where she was staying.

If pushed, he'd claim it was the room at the Transit Hotel where she'd been the day before, and they would keep a guard in the room in case there was any pre-emptive action. Meanwhile, the meeting would take place along the trail leading uphill from the transit yard on the edge of town.

"There's lots of cover," Damian said. "We can have men hidden either side of the trail around the meeting site. Don't forget, the last one to make a claim on this reward was murdered in his front entry."

Thames didn't seem daunted by that. His voice was gruff as he replied, "No problem. I've seen worse."

Damian huffed a laugh. So had he, by all the dogs of hell. So had he. And if being without Fanny was going to be as tough as it seemed, he obviously hadn't yet seen the worst life could hand out.

Cownden pulled on a sideburn. "If they have plasma guns or lasers, it could be more difficult than you think. How do we plan for that?"

"We have men planted up trail and down from the site. We'll see who's coming and what they're armed with." When Damian pulled out an onionskin sketch, the holograph of Fanny that he'd discovered while researching her fell on the floor. Hastily he scooped it up and crammed it back in his pocket.

With red face and thunder in his chest, he spread the map of the trail on the table and tried to look composed. Pointing to the shack where the meeting would take place, he identified the trees and hiding places they could occupy. There were plenty of spots for surveillance.

When everything was organized, Thames entered the particulars to make the call for the reward and they settled in to wait. Several hours passed with no response. Cownden left, asking to be kept informed and Damian slipped out to corner him in the hallway and reinforce his concerns. "You can't tell anyone, Cownden. Governor Maude trusts Rutman and works with him on a daily basis. Any of the Constables will report back to him. Only special forces, the few men in the room. With Nikesh, that will be enough."

Cownden gave him a piercing look. "You seem to be taking this assignment very seriously. I'm just not sure what's behind it."

Damian turned his head to glare down the hall. "Whatever it is, the most important thing would be to get this right and free up Ms Master to live her life in safety."

"True." Cownden placed a hand on his shoulder. "I trust you, so do it right this time, on my behalf. I'm responsible for this mess."

By the time Cownden left, the game between Adar Silva and Legitamia was over and Legitamia was the victor. The noise from down at the playing field could be heard all over this end of town, and a line of Constables went by at a fast pace in an attempt to keep the crowd under control.

That meant Adar Silva would hold third place while Khandarken and Legitamia would battle it out for first and second. A day off was called to give the teams a chance to recover from the fight, and the streets were full of rowdy spectators and wired head ball players. Damian expected a lively night in Deep Creek.

Just as he returned to the room where Thames waited, the voicelink in the middle of the table buzzed. Thames went to pick it up as Damian pointed to the list they'd set out to guide the conversation.

"Thames," he barked into the device. Everyone in the room froze as he scheduled the speaker to pick up.

A thin voice, obviously filtered through a synth, replied. "You put through a claim on the reward from Deep Creek."

"That's right," Thames boomed. "I did."

"Have you seen Fanny Master?" The voice squeaked and then flattened.

"Yah, so I have. That's why I called, you dumb mother." Thames looked around the room and shrugged at the looks he was getting from the other men. He bared his teeth in a grin.

"So where is she?" The voice had faded to a wisp of sound.

Thames bristled. "I'm not telling. Meet me with the reward and I'll give you everything I have."

"Look, I need something. Otherwise I can't tell if you know anything or not."

Thames pulled the device closer to his end of the table. "I wouldn't call if I didn't have information. I won't give you information, if you don't pay me. So, what do you want to do?"

"I think we should meet." The voice grew more firm. "There's a place behind the military barracks in Deep Creek, a small shed that's used for transport fuel. We can meet behind that."

"Nope." Thames took a deep breath and glared around the room. "I've decided where to meet. No fuel, no military guys, no constables. We go up the trail out of the transit yard travelling south-west about a mile. There's a shack there—been there for ages, and there's no one around. You bring the money. If I don't see some money, I don't tell you a thing."

There was silence from the other end and before he could respond, Thames added, "Tomorrow at noon. See you there." He clicked the device off.

Damian almost hit him, the reflex was so sharp. Yet once he calmed, he realized Thames had run the conversation from the start and that's exactly what they'd needed him to do.

"Noon gives us time to get everyone in place before daylight," he observed. "In fact, we can send a few men up there now and keep an eye on things."

Thames grinned, the gap in his teeth prominent. "That's what I thought," he said.

CHAPTER THIRTY THREE

Fanny strapped herself into the seat of the aircart and leaned over to make sure Boulter was secured. Mickens had been protected in a cage at the rear. Four men rode with them, all from Cowden Lanser's group, although none wore uniform. She was unsure if they were Constables or from some other force that he led. The pilot started the engine and the aircart vibrated rapidly.

Boulter flashed her a surprised grin. "I thought it would be loud," he whispered.

"No," she replied, "they're usually silent. When it takes off there's a bit more noise, then it smooths out and seems to fly in the clouds." She smiled at his look of delight and thought back to the many trips she'd taken with Father over the years. He'd started taking her with him when she turned ten. In those days, Harold Master taught at the Khandarken University, and most of his travels were back to Adar Silva for meetings to put together a cohesive education package that both countries could support. If she had a break from school, she was allowed to go.

Even under Emperor Aqatain, Adar Silva had been the centre of training and instruction. In the later years, it had spearheaded an education programme utilized in several countries.

Fanny shook her head and looked out the plexi. The town of Deep Creek was falling away fast beneath them. Soon they'd be on their way back to the City and home. *And what would she find there?*

Leader House would have been taken over by others – she'd heard FitzGibbon, as Acting Leader, had promptly moved in. Perhaps they had packed up the things belonging to the Master family and put them in storage somewhere. And after the election, the next man to live there would be the new Leader. Would that be DuSatoy or someone else? Perhaps Cownden Lanser or Jack Learmonth.

Where would she and Boulter live? Her mother's house near the university had been their home during the years before Father became Leader. Perhaps that's where she'd go. It wouldn't be as difficult for her. The memories triggered in that house would be from earlier happy times.

She fingered the brilliant blue of her dress. Tasha, with her excellent taste, had arrived with a shawl of darker hue and shoes to match. It picked up the colour of her eyes and flattered the gold of her hair. Even so, she knew her cheeks were pale under the strain of all she'd been through.

She heard Boulter's laughter and saw one of the guards was playing a hand game with him. Turning back to the plexi, she watched the forest pass below. The river came into view, with wide flat plains lining its banks, then a high waterfall before it fell into a canyon so deep she could no longer see the water. That must be the Violetta River, the largest in Khandarken as it travelled in the same direction as the aircart – toward the City.

She shuddered. Perhaps she'd never feel safe again, especially if Damian didn't join her. She could only hope that he would come.

~ * * * ~

Damian spent the night up the same trail where Fanny had lived in her small hut. He was restless, unable to sleep even when he was spelled off by one of the other men. What if they blew this effort at a trap? It was so important to catch these guys, whoever they were, not just for the safety of the country's citizens but for Fanny. If this didn't go well, and word got back to the man posting the reward that they were onto him, they might not get another chance to find out who it was. Fanny would never be safe.

His beltlink vibrated and he glanced down at the screen. The two men near the entry to the trail reported they were trading off as others came to relieve them. The sun was only moments from appearing, the sky lightening in the east and already tension was high amongst his crew.

With the arrangement to meet at noon, Thames had stayed the night in the Transit Hotel and should soon be appearing to walk the route to the shack they had chosen. Even now there was one man bedded down inside it, another in the brush behind and several across the trail in a tree. Damian had chosen to take up a position closer to Deep Creek. He was pretty sure the men would be coming from town and would likely arrive early.

But they were also crafty. They'd be aware of what Thames looked like by now, having almost certainly searched for his voicelink information. They would notice when he moved out of the hotel to head up the trail.

Sudden shafts of sunlight beamed through the trees to illuminate the path before him. He glanced around, spotting Nikesh a few yards away. It was quiet as a tomb. Then the first birds burst into song, a riot of sound that was near deafening and brought a reluctant grin to his mouth. The sheer joy of the noise caused hope to bloom in his chest alongside a feeling of defeat that was crushing. Even if they caught this man, Damian still couldn't be with Fanny. He was a damaged man who had ended any future opportunities on the Helmcken Trail during the Last War.

The birdsong ceased with alarming suddenness and Damian shifted position to glance down the path in time to see Thames lumbering rapidly into view, his big boots stumbling over stones that lay in his way. He was supposed to have sent a beltlink message to let them know he was on the move. Damian entered a quick note and Thames paused, then pulled the device out of his pocket and fumbled with it awkwardly, obviously not familiar with its use. Eventually a reply appeared and Thames disappeared around the bend up above.

Beltlink reports continued to flow in from his crew as Thames passed the rest of the men along the trail to finally arrive at the shack. Then they waited some more.

Time slowly passed as the sun rose higher till the rays shone straight down through the branches to illuminate the ground around them. A small family of olinguitos chittered by, alarmed by Damian's presence, and the birds settled down to steady calls back and forth. The heat of the day became oppressive.

Then silence descended once more. Damian's beltlink alerted him to a new message—*two men up the trail.* He sent back—*are they armed?*

Can't tell—came the reply. That wasn't good, but it was hot out so they likely weren't wearing jackets. If they were armed, it should become apparent relatively quickly.

Damian heard the sound of footsteps and voices as the men drew closer. Peering through the trees, he thought they looked like dispossessed, similar to those who had come down the trail in droves to attend the Games. The men walked on past, talking low between them. One shifted a long bundle in his arms and Damian felt a shot of alarm – that could be a lasergun, too short for a plasma. But they never paused, and as they continued past the shack and up the hill out of town the message went out—*false alarm.* Even so, Damian ordered two men to follow them partway and set up in stations along the path above the shack.

Crows began cawing in the trees ahead and within a few minutes, a second message arrived. They waited and two more men appeared. These guys looked different. They weren't in uniform but something about their body language spoke of military or police. Damian couldn't see their faces, both wore hats pulled low over the brow similar to the first two, but this time it seemed intentional.

He sent out an alert and moved softly through the trees parallel to the trail. These men didn't talk, they seemed tense and guarded. Within sight of the cabin they paused, then one moved forward and called out a greeting while the second stood back and cautiously pulled a long-barrelled pistol from a holster under his shirt.

Holding his breath, Damian pressed the silent alarm on his beltlink and took aim with his laser.

Thames bellowed a reply to their greeting from inside the shack and then action erupted—there was motion in the dimness of the shack where Thames lurked, the man with the pistol raised his weapon, pointing it at the interior of the shack, and then promptly dropped to the ground as Damian fired with a roar of his gun. The other fellow whirled and charged him as the first two men who'd gone up the trail appeared running fast downhill, weapons in hand. Damian's men tackled them out of the brush at the side of the trail. Shots sounded, the bushes caught fire and men screamed with pain from the laserflash.

When the flurry of activity was over, one man lay dead and three were pinned to the ground. One of them was Rutman, the Lead Constable of the Southern Territory. Two of Damian's men had laser burns, one serious.

Rutman raised his head and railed angrily. "Damian Stuke, release me at once," he bellowed. "I'm Lead Constable! Governor Maude will have you hanged for this."

Damian ignored the rant and motioned his men to tie the captives up as he sent a message for transport and Thames moved cautiously out of the shack to help with the injured.

"Stuke," Rutman screamed. "This is outrageous. Release me now. I knew you'd be trouble. Having the Chief Constable for a brother by marriage won't get you off this! I'll have you shot!"

Damian looked at him as he lay in the dirt and stones of the trail. Blood dripped from Rutman's nose where a random blow had landed, and one eye was rapidly swelling shut. Foam leaked from the side of his mouth.

"I doubt you'll have any say in what happens to me, Rutman," he said.

CHAPTER THIRTY FOUR

Governor Maude looked tired. The lines in his forehead drove deep and the brackets around his mouth were firmly fixed. He waved Damian to a chair and pointed at Cownden. "What did he say, have you questioned him yet?"

"Only a preliminary interview. He wants to bargain."

"Bargain?" Maude's voice was loud enough to be heard on the street below his office. "What bargain? He's never going to see the light of day." He limped to the window and glared out. "We won't bargain. Why would he do such a thing? He was my Lead Constable." His shoulders slumped.

Cownden shrugged. "He said it was for his wife. The wage of a Constable wasn't enough and he found a way to augment his income."

"Well, at least there's someone out there who cares about him. Not that it will do her any good, of course. He won't be released."

Damian glanced between the two men. "What we need to know is who is behind this, behind him. No way could Rutman post a reward that big, even if he is getting some income on the side. It has to be someone else, someone with deep pockets."

Cownden glanced at him. "We'll find the man. We haven't even started digging the information out of Rutman yet."

Damian ignored the tightness in his chest. "Time's running out. Fanny Master is in the City and thinks she's safe. But it won't be true until we catch this guy." With a purposely bland expression, he faced down the calculating look he got from the Chief Constable.

~ * * * ~

Fanny piled the weeds in the wagon and wiped a grimy wrist across her damp forehead, leaving a line of dirt in its wake. It was hot out again this morning, but the garden was a mess and she was determined to clean it up the best she could. She slashed at a thistle with her shears and only succeeded in crippling it.

"Mum."

She glanced toward the door leading to the garden. "What is it, Boulter?" He'd grown so much since they left Deep Creek just days ago. It was hard to believe how fast a child could develop but he was taller now, and his legs seemed much longer. Perhaps it was the result of having a home and steady meals.

He bounded down the garden and Mickens ran behind, tongue lolling to the side of his mouth. "I wondered where you were. Why didn't you ask me to help?" He gazed around at the patch of plants. "I can do this. You sit there and catch your breath. Ms Maya is bringing lemon water."

Ms Maya had been their housekeeper when Fanny was a child, and had stayed on when the Master family moved into Leader House. She was too old to look after a whole household by herself, but wouldn't listen when Fanny tried to retire her. Now she walked sedately down the lawn behind Boulter, a tray of bowls and a jug balanced precariously in her fragile-looking hands.

"Here, let me," Fanny said and moved swiftly to take the tray before it landed on the lawn, setting it on the picnic table near the potting shed. "Sit down, Ms Maya. We can all do with something cold to drink in this heat."

Fanny poured the lemon water into bowls and passed the first one to Ms Maya, then took a sip of her own. "Oh, that's lovely. I was thirsty."

Meanwhile Boulter dove into the garden. "This one, Mum? This one?" As he pointed, she guided and he began pulling the unwanted plants, the muscles in his back bunching as he worked. He didn't look like a small boy of four or five any longer, but an older child of eight, perhaps even ten. Fanny frowned. She should contact Leader House and get some help tracing the ident of F. Winthrop and locating the information on Boulter. It shouldn't be too hard to find out when he was born.

Mickens growled low and then emitted a clicking noise from his throat as he stared down the garden. Fanny glanced up to see Selanna Nettles and Julianne Adjudicator coming around the side path from the front of the house. Her heart stuttered, then took up a faster beat. Selanna might have news of Damian. She'd heard nothing since leaving Deep Creek, weeks ago. It was devastating not to know how he was.

She stood, wishing she wore a nicer robe. This one was old and only good for yard work. "Did you ring the doorbell?" she asked. "I'm sorry, but we're all out here. The garden has our total attention."

Selanna smiled and took her hand. "Fanny, you're looking much better. You've even gained a bit of weight, and lost that gaunt look."

"Thank you." Fanny nodded uncomfortably and turned to give Julianne a hug. "Welcome to my new home," she said. "Would you care for some lemon water?"

Ms Maya went back to the kitchen for extra bowls and Fanny turned at Boulter's shout for more information about the plants in the garden. When she glanced back, she caught the two women exchanging a guarded look and reached to place a hand on Julianne's shoulder. "What's wrong? Do you have news?"

Julianne nodded. "Some news, sit and I'll tell you." When they were all seated, she began. "I only know this because one of Abe's men, Thames, was involved in the operation. Thames called in a claim on the reward on your head, saying he had seen you and knew where you were, and he arranged to meet the men up the trail behind Deep Creek.

"Damian and his men set up a blind. Four men showed up, one died in the conflict but they captured three and are holding them in prison right now."

Fanny's head was spinning and she braced her hands on the table to hold herself steady, fearing for Damian's part in this. "Were any of our men hurt?"

"There were a couple of injuries, but nothing severe."

She gazed helplessly into her friend's eyes. "Who were they, these men? Do I know them?"

"We are not sure, but I have some holographs on my wristlink that you might want to look at." Julianne's face was kind as she peered into her eyes. "You don't have to, Fanny. Just if you want to look and see if it's the same men you saw when your transport was pushed into the water."

Fanny nodded, as bile rose in her throat. "Yes, I want to. Give me a minute." She glanced away, then rose unsteadily. "I'll be right back." She walked to the garden door and entered the house. It was cooler in here, she could hear the faint noise of pots banging in the kitchen where Ms Maya was probably working on dinner.

In the garderobe, she hung over the bowl. They had captured three men who were dealing with the reward on her head, and a fourth had died in the confrontation. What did that really mean in terms of her safety? *She wouldn't be sick. She was too strong to be sick over this, after everything she'd done to survive.* Washing her hands, she splashed her cheeks with cold water and patted them dry. She could do this.

When she emerged from the back entry, Boulter was in conversation with her visitors. "But will she want this plant left, or pulled out? Oh, there she is. Mum, which ones do you keep?" He gazed anxiously at her, and she realized she seldom noticed his unusual eyes any more. Those different-looking irises were just a part of him now, a beloved part.

She smiled. Boulter was very energetic, and once he began a project it moved along at a rapid pace. She'd already put out feelers for a tutor, it was time to get started on his schooling. "I keep those," she said. "They bloom in the fall, a lovely autumn flower."

Seating herself at the table again, she arranged her gardening robe around her legs, brushing at the dirt on the hem. "All right, Julianne. I think I'm ready."

Julianne took her wristlink and scrolled through the frames until she found what she was looking for. "Here they are. There are three holographs of each. Perhaps you can see if you recognize any of them."

Fanny laid the device on the table before her and paused over each frame. She swallowed heavily, a headache hovering behind her eyes. *She wouldn't be sick. She was past that now.*

"Yes, that's him." She pointed to a holograph. "I wasn't sure about the first two images, because his eyes are squinting against the light. But I recognize him. That's the man that drove the hydro-truck."

Her headache was escalating. "Mum." Boulter's voice seemed a long way off. "Mum, what about this plant?"

Then she was falling.

CHAPTER THIRTY FIVE

When Fanny woke she was lying on the daybed in the entry of her house and Julianne Adjudicator was seated beside her, holding her hand. The light seemed dim and she realized the blinds had been drawn to block the sun. Boulter leaned at her feet, anxiously patting her leg.

"There you are, Fanny." Julianne pressed her palm. "You're back with us now. That's good news." Her smile was sunny. "You have been so brave, I don't know how you've managed. This is just another example of how strong you are. You didn't have to look at those holographs."

Fanny struggled to sit up and her friend tucked some pillows behind her back. She noticed Selanna seated across the carpet from them in a high-backed chair.

Her voice weak, she soothed her son. "I'm fine now, Boulter, really. Don't worry, sweetheart. You go help Ms Maya in the kitchen. You know how she needs your support."

As the boy departed, she turned anxiously to Selanna. "What news do you have of Damian? Was he injured in the skirmish?"

Selanna frowned. "No, Damian's fine. A couple of his men have laser burns, but that's all." She leaned forward and clasped her hands together. "Cownden sends his greetings, Fanny. He thought it would be better if Julianne showed you the holographs, then you wouldn't feel pressured. You could look at them or not, as you wished."

She winced. "He also says to tell you this isn't over yet. He's appointed a Constable to stand guard at your door, of course. But what they're trying to do is get the information from these men as to who is behind the reward. Then they'll be arrested and we'll discover what they hoped to gain by it."

Fanny stared at her for a long moment. "Selanna, I know you've had a difficult time in the past. Damian told me some of what happened before you were married."

"He did?" The woman flushed a light pink, a look of surprise in her eyes. "Did he tell you he saved me?"

Fanny pinched her fingers together. "He told me he killed someone."

"Ah." Oddly, Selanna's eyes brightened. "Did he? Yes, that's exactly what he must have done. One of the men who worked for the gamer attacked me, and Damian caught him and banished him from Bereford.

208

He was gone for nearly a year, but one day he came back." She paused, her gaze far away. "He arrived at our house when I was the only one home. I opened the door and he pushed his way in."

Fanny shuddered. "By all the angels. What happened?"

Selanna's voice was low. "Damian arrived. He took the man away and I never saw him again. He hasn't told me what he did, but I knew the man was never coming back. I was sure he was dead."

Fanny frowned. "But wasn't that the best result?"

"Oh," Selanna's gaze cleared. "I would never be safe if he hadn't taken care of things."

Suddenly cold, Fanny pulled a wrap off the back of the daybed and draped it around her shoulders. "That's what I'm looking for," she said. "Someone to take care of things."

~ * * * ~

Selanna stepped out of the official transport, leaving the driver to carry on without her, and crossed the strand to the entry of the Constabulary Headquarters in the new part of the City. She wondered how long she and Cownden would live in the top floor suite, and when they might get a place of their own. They'd been married for months but things had not slowed down enough to take care of such details as finding a home.

She buzzed the suite but there was no answer. Cownden was undoubtedly still in his office. When she entered the particulars in her wristlink, Anatoliy answered immediately. Cownden's assistant was a shy, dear man with a huge brain and wonderful organizational abilities.

"He's with your brother and Chief Investigator Radha," he said. "He shouldn't be too long now."

"Thank you, Toll. I'll be right up."

As she entered the outer offices, her brother was just leaving. "Damian," she called. "Hold up a minute."

"Can't wait, sister," he replied. He looked deathly tired, the lines grim around his expressive mouth. "Got a deadline here."

"All right," she said. "I won't keep you long. Just two things."

Damian stopped and tapped his fingers impatiently on his thigh. "What is it, Selanna? I really have to get out of here."

"I understand. Come into the hallway." She dug her fingers into his bicep and half-dragged him with her.

"All right, two things." He glared down at her. "What things?"

She held a finger under his nose. "The first thing—did Da tell you about Boulter's eyes?"

He stalled, then slowly shook his head. "No. What about his eyes?"

Selanna told the story Dr Harris Stuke had related about the angels on the Helmcken Trail. Damian's eyelids fell to half mast but he didn't say a word until she'd finished with the tale.

"So Da thinks Boulter is an angel." It was a statement, not a question. "His eyes *are* very strange. The first time I noticed, I decided it must have been a trick of the light, but I saw it again afterward—the slit in the iris and the strange yellow-gold colour."

Selanna watched his expression go from impatient to considering, to soft. She twitched his shirtfront. "If he's an angel, what will happen to Fanny if he has to leave? She'll be devastated."

A veil seemed to descend over his gaze. "I think she'll be fine. She's back where she fits, with the upper class of Khandarken. That's where she's from, that's where her support is." He shook his head. "What was the second thing, or can I go now?"

She held up two fingers. "The second thing is—I saw Fanny today."

He focussed fiercely on her face. "And?"

"And she's struggling."

He blinked and his mouth flattened. "How do you mean?"

"I mean, she lives in a nice little house. Julianne told me it had belonged to her mother and that they lived there before her father was elected, when he was still teaching at the university."

"Yah, the university. What seems to be the problem?" He swung his head back and forth.

"She's afraid."

The air seemed to leave his lungs. He deflated in front of her. "She's smart, she knows this isn't over yet." He gazed over her head. "Does she have guards? Cownden said he'd send guards for her."

"Yes, but she's still afraid. "

He moved impatiently. "Of course she is. We don't know who posted the reward and tried to kill her."

Selanna shook her head. "Oh, we know who tried to kill her."

His eyes bore into hers. "What do you mean?"

Selanna took his hard hand and held it. "She identified the man who drove them off the bridge. It was Rutman."

"By the dogs of hell!"

CHAPTER THIRTY SIX

Selanna knocked on Cownden's door and Anatoliy pulled it open, giving her a shallow bow. "I told him you were on your way," he said, as he motioned her to a chair. Cownden rose from behind his desk, a smile curling slowly on his mouth.

"Come in," he said. He pointed to a small dark man with thin chin whiskers and weathered skin who was waving a drafting wand at the screen on the far wall. The screen showed what appeared to be an enlarged portion of the map of Khandarken.

"You know Radha, my investigator."

Selanna nodded and the man continued his discussion. "This is where Fanny Master travelled." He pointed from the Old Towne side of the City situated south of the Violetta River and along roads and back trails all the way to Deep Creek.

Selanna's breath caught in her throat. "How did she do it? It's amazing that she managed that without being caught."

Cownden nodded. "And in return, our job is to find these men who are after her. We can't fail this time."

He gave a meaningful look at Radha who was silent for a moment, tugging at his wispy beard. Then he stood. "I'll be in touch as soon as I have something from Rutman and the other prisoners. These other men are not Constables, so they must either be hired by Rutman or by his handler. We need to find out."

"Good." Chief Constable stood and shook Radha's hand. "Toll, make sure the links are open and secure. We want information the minute it becomes available."

Anatoliy nodded and followed Radha through the door, discretely closing it behind him.

Cownden turned to her and walked around his desk. "How are you, my dear?" He tugged her close and placed a kiss on her temple. "How was the visit with Ms Master?"

Selanna sighed. "It was heartbreaking. She's angry and frightened. She doesn't trust anyone now, I think."

"No doubt," he murmured. "I wouldn't either if I were in her shoes. How did Julianne deal with it? She had a hard time herself before she and Abe Farmer were married."

"Julianne was so good with her. They're close friends and it's obvious they have a strong connection between them."

"That's good."

She glanced up at him, one hand resting in the centre of his chest. "She said it was Rutman who drove the hydro-truck that knocked them into the river and killed her mother. She identified him from the holographs on Julianne's wristlink."

Cownden's face went dark with repressed fury. "By the graves," he muttered. "A Constable. It just tears my heart out, my soul bleeds." Letting her go, he paced to the giant plexi window behind his desk, then back again. "How can we have a force that pledges to uphold the law and in the next breath attacks our own citizens? It's like a plague among the police."

Selanna took his hand and led him to the couch against the far wall. "Sit here for a moment. I don't know what we can do about that right now. But I think I have an idea that might help a few people."

Her husband sank heavily on the cushions and pulled her down beside him. He put an arm around her waist, holding her close. "What is it, what do you want to tell me?" He ran his fingers lightly up her arm and she trembled from the tender impact.

"Cownden, you have to begin campaigning or you'll run out of time before the election."

He leaned his face against the side of her head, breathing out and ruffling the curls by her jaw. "I know that. I've just been busy. Someone has to take responsibility for what's going on, don't they? And that's my job."

"I know." Cuddling closer, she pressed her cheek to his chest. "And I have the perfect solution to get you going. It wasn't my idea, actually. It was Julianne Adjudicator's suggestion. I think you're going to love it."

~ * * * ~

DuSatoy left Deep Creek as soon as word reached him that his men, along with Rutman, had been captured up the trail outside of town. This was a mighty fiasco, and had been from the very start. How had Rutman failed at the task of eliminating Ms Master and her daughter in the first place? It was a straightforward job, just get it done.

But he hadn't managed to finish the task, only half completed because Fanny Master was tougher than he'd thought, and now it had come back to haunt him, haunt them all.

DuSatoy was still campaigning. If he suddenly stopped, it would look too much like he was fleeing rather than travelling the country looking for votes. But instead of heading for the City and the transit station there, the absolute hub of the country, he changed his plans and instructed his guards to take him by personal transport to Moreshead in the Coal Lick Territory. He could campaign, and board the transit for the north without raising any eyebrows.

He'd continue to stop at towns along the route, probably end up in Collaros Territory by the end of the week. From there he'd be poised to return to his stronghold near the northern border if things went decidedly wrong. Although it probably wasn't as safe there as it had seemed in the past, not if the Chief Constable had him directly in his sights.

Would he have to flee the country? He had to consider the possibility. If that were the case, Sable Maude immediately came to mind. The Monarch's base was right across the Legitamia border and no one was chasing him.

~ * * * ~

Sable Maude rode through the gates into the yard of his manorhouse. The sound of his horse's hooves echoed off the quarried stone of the new road. The noise brought the stable boy running to take the reins and lead his mount into the freshly completed stables behind. He always felt a little thrill coming home. He'd set out to establish a monarchy, and he drew closer every day to finishing the work.

Just inside the Legitamian border, his holding stretched for a couple of miles of flatland and forest. His manor was still under construction, but the gates and forecourt were magnificent and the main floors were finally finished. He was well on his way to becoming the Monarch of the Territories. Once Governor Francis Maude's son, the connection had become useless to him and he'd closed that link forever.

He strode through the great entry as his doorman hurried to open the door. Waite was expected this afternoon with his weekly reports, and nothing would make Sable happier than to hear the brothels were running smoothly and another batch of women was expected from the west.

By the time he'd been seated in his office off the great entry with a pitcher of ale and a cold deep bowl, he heard the approach of another horse. His doorman soon ushered in Sable's right hand man. Waite was in his mid-thirties, an ex-military from during and after the war and as reliable as anyone he'd ever known.

And unlike most men he encountered, Waite wasn't intimidated by Sable's appearance. Sable had been badly mauled by a mountain cat on the northern border some months ago. He knew that if he turned his head one way, Waite would see the old Sable Maude – good-looking, medium brown hair combed back from his forehead to just reach his shoulders, smile a bit sardonic, eyes clear. But when he turned his head the other way, the sight was vastly different.

His ear was completely gone, the skin on his head had been torn to tatters and the hair grew in uneven patches. His cheek had been ripped off, so that his teeth showed through the gap in the flesh. Not a pretty sight.

Sable sprayed his throat with lemon and honey and leaned his chair back on two legs. "Waite," he said. "Right on time. Have a seat." He poured a second bowl of ale and passed it across his desk.

Waite grinned tightly and took a long swallow. A medium height man, his shoulders and arms were heavy with muscle, his gaze flat. "It's hot out there," he remarked as he set the bowl down on the corner of Sable's desk. "Damned hot."

"So what's going on?" Sable allowed his chair to thump down on all four legs as he leaned to rest his elbows on the desk top. "How is business at the brothels?"

Waite nodded and pulled an onion skin from his breast pocket. "There are the numbers for last week. A bit down at Krimen, but they tell me it should pick up again when the travellers and dispossessed arrive back from their journey south to see the Head Ball Games."

Sable suppressed a sharp pang of longing. He'd actually wanted to go, be part of the crowd and watch the fierce combat that would only get more forceful as the play ensued, rather than being isolated in this northern hideout. But he couldn't go anywhere in Khandarken. His father, Frank Maude was Governor of the Southern Territory and he'd issued an ultimatum. Leave the country, or be arrested, there was nothing in between. Maybe if the games were held in Legitamia next time... "Khandarken is playing for gold," he said finally.

Waite gave a rare smile. "Yah, first time. And a big turn around with Adar Silva in third. It looks like Legitamia is the team to beat now. We'll have to keep our eye on the training to catch up with some of their tactics."

Sable looked at the numbers on the onion skin and frowned. "These aren't down just a bit, they're way down. What's going on?"

"The Constables." Waite eyed him guardedly. "There've been two raids on the establishment outside Martonosha. They managed to hide the women the first time, but someone must have been watching because the police returned when all the females were in the back room working. Arrests all round. Don't know if those women will be freed, but I doubt it. The bar owner is in jail at the moment."

Sable paced to the door and back. "We aren't making headway like this. I can't wait till this infernal election happens. With DuSatoy as Leader, we'll have some protection from the Constables."

Waite watched as Sable moved back behind his desk. "You haven't heard, I guess," he said.

Sable paused, then sat heavily in his plexi chair, the slides creaking loudly. "Heard what? This had better be good."

"I doubt it's good," said Waite. "DuSatoy is losing support around the country. It's not likely he'll ever be Leader."

"Losing support?" There was a clenching in Sable's gut. DuSatoy was the man who kept him and his workers safe as they brought the kidnapped women through the border regions. That was the basis of Sable's success so far.

"Yah," Waite pondered the top of the desk. "Something to do with his attitude, people tell me. Too high-handed maybe. Apparently DuSatoy thinks that kind of approach will work with the populace."

Sable's fists clenched. "By the dogs of hell, the stupid bastard. I can guess what that's about." He shuffled through the detritus on his desk and came up with a printed holograph. "See this?" It was a picture of Fanny Master with her father courting votes at the transit hub outside the City from a few years ago. She looked happy and confident and the people around her were all smiling just to be near her.

"DuSatoy was scared. If Fanny Master campaigned with one of the other candidates, they'd likely win the election and there'd be nothing he could do about it." He thought a moment. "I'll bet he's heading this way."

Rising, he turned to his right-hand man. "Find him, Waite. Find out where he is and get rid of him. He can't come back here, it will just draw the Constables down on me."

Waite stood too, his hands on his hips. "They can't come after you here, Monarch. You're outside the border. They can't touch you."

"You know what I mean. They can make life very difficult. Get rid of DuSatoy."

CHAPTER THIRTY SEVEN

Damian was mired in Deep Creek, back in training at the fighting arts building. Nikesh had signed up for the programme as well, and they had just spent a long hot morning sparring on the mats. Sprinter booked him in for tactical exercises, but he was having trouble concentrating. Fanny and Boulter occupied his every thought, their images impressed on the back of his brain like holographs.

What were they doing now? How were they getting along? Was Boulter really a messenger from afar, an angel as Da claimed? If so, he was here because he had a mission to carry out, and when it was over—*what then?* Fanny would be abandoned once more.

He threw a kick that sent Nikesh flying across the mats, fetching up hard against the far wall. Immediately guilt swamped him, and he walked across to offer a hand to his friend. "Sorry, bud. I wasn't paying attention."

Nikesh grunted and grabbed his hand to yank himself up. "No, I was the one who wasn't paying attention. Let's try it again. I doubt you can do that twice."

Damian coughed a laugh. "No, probably not." He was in limbo—going nowhere. Even this training seemed repetitive, designed to keep him occupied rather than help him move ahead.

At the break, he grabbed his wristlink and went outside. This is where he used to find Boulter darting around with his hound. The delight in his eyes when Damian gave them something to eat had warmed his heart. Now the field was empty. The Penrhy tents were gone, witness the holes in the ground and the garbage blowing across the trampled grass.

He entered the particulars for Cownden Lanser but it went to message. Next he tried Governor Maude but his secretary, Ms Balcomb, took the call. Frank was out and would be back later. He clicked off. *Who else could he contact?* Perhaps Anatoliy, Cownden's assistant. Anatoliy answered around a mouthful of lunch, relaying the information that there was no word yet from Rutman and the others.

The final competition of the Head Ball Games was to be held that afternoon. He and Nikesh were scheduled to patrol the grounds, so he took a shower and changed. The crowd was huge and it was loud. Every seat on the stadium benches was occupied, with more people bringing their own chairs and encroaching on the playing field. It was a madhouse.

Constables removed dozens of people who had taken up position too close to the play, and the loose horde roamed and milled restlessly as the first two warning shots were fired. The teams got into position, extra players leaving the field at a run, then the single shot sounded. Play was on.

The teams clashed head-on in the middle of the field. Immediately two players were removed—one with a damaged leg, one unconscious. They were quickly replaced and the game resumed. Damian knew a few of the Khandarken players and the kind of conditioning they endured to qualify for the team, yet it was still astonishing how fast and violent the game became.

The Legitamian players were shorter and heavyset, but many of the men on the Khandarken team were tall with rugged physiques. It was a battle of sheer physical power.

Half-time found Legitamia up by one point, and the roar from the stands was deafening. Vendors moved up and down the sidelines, dispensing ale and cider, nutmeg biscuits and pané sandwiches. Something stronger had definitely become available as well, because a growing number of men were drunk and staggered haphazardly across the grass as if acca drops had been added to their drink. The odour of latah smoke hung in the air.

Nikesh tried to herd the lurching fans off the field as the warning shots sounded. Damian and a Constable joined the struggle to clear the playing area as the commencement shot was fired and play began again. The teams roared into position and several of the drunks were mowed down as the game commenced. They were soon dragged to the side.

Khandarken scored immediately, tying the game, and Legitamia sent out their roughest players. Soon both sides had scored again and players were dragged off the field from body slams and head butts, broken collar bones and twisted limbs. Khandarken landed one more score and the crowd went wild. The play because more violent but when the final shot came, Khandarken had maintained their lead and won the tournament.

Barrington the Benevolent rose grandly from his seat at the end of the makeshift stadium and proceeded across the field to shake hands with his players, then carried on to meet FitzGibbon in the middle of the grass. He bowed and offered a salute to Khandarken's Leader, then swept from the field.

The hospital tent was swamped with bodies, and transports soon arrived to move the more seriously injured to the town hospital for treatment.

"Well, Nikesh. We won." Damian clapped his friend on the shoulder. "This is turning over a new leaf for our country. Adar Silva has fallen from top rank to number three. That's going to hurt."

They pushed through the crowd and were heading toward the fighting arts building when his voicelink beeped. It was Cownden's particulars and he clicked to answer.

"Damian, is the game finished?"

"Just now. We won."

"Yah, I've been watching the infolink, the feed is slow. It looked like we had a good chance at it, but those Legitamians are fierce players. I'm glad we won, there'll be a very positive reaction throughout the country, especially in the north. With Emperor Carlton still holding some land up there, it's been hard to keep things positive."

Damian waited for the real purpose of the call. His brother had better have some news for him—he was chomping at the bit.

There was a pause, then Cownden said, "Listen, I have something for you that should suit. I need you and your buddy Nikesh to come into the City tomorrow. Talk to Maude, he'll get you on an aircart. Bring your gear because you won't be going back there for a while."

Damian's heart beat faster. To the City? That's where Fanny was. *Would he see her?* "What's this about?"

Cownden chuckled. "You'll find out when you get here. I think it will work. See you tomorrow night for dinner with your sister and me." He clicked off.

~ * * * ~

Radha wiped his hands on a cloth and got up from where he'd been kneeling on the floor of the damp cell beside the prisoner. "Give him a drink of water." He pointed at the nearest Constable and moved across the room to his chair.

"Now, Rutman. You haven't told me everything. It's time to start talking."

Rutman scrambled to his hands and knees and teetered there a moment before he staggered to his feet, taking the proffered bowl of water. He drank deeply, emptying it, and held it out for more. One eye was swollen shut and his nose leaked blood in a steady stream. He hugged an arm close to his chest, the hand battered and red.

"I've told you what I can," he mumbled. He spat and part of a tooth clinked on the prison floor. "I can't tell you more."

"Yah, you can." Radha leaned forward and tugged at his wispy beard, motioning his man to refill the water bowl. "I don't need to beat it out of you. You need to tell me what you know."

He waited until Rutman had finished the second drink of water, and waved him to a chair opposite. "Let's start again. You say you were going up the trail to see who was claiming the reward—because it was illegal to post a reward and claim it like that. Now we both know it isn't illegal to either post or claim, and we also know there was no report to the Constables about the claim." He paused for effect and when Rutman glanced his way, he added, "Quit pissing around, because I'm losing patience."

Rutman squirmed on his chair. "I was there because we needed to know who was claiming the reward and what their information was about Fanny Master."

"Ah, now we're getting somewhere. Yah, so who is *we*? The two men with you who survived the ordeal are talking their heads off in the other room. Just so you know. I'll be going over there shortly to fit your story with theirs."

Rutman glanced down. "I'm hungry," he said.

Radha nodded. "We'll get to that. It's only been ten hours. Let's start again. Who told you to go there and find out where Fanny Master was?"

He hung his head. "I work for DuSatoy sometimes," he muttered.

Radha paused. *DuSatoy?* This was getting sticky real fast. He'd been expecting someone like Makulski, because Rutman had spent time in the Western Territory as a Constable. "Is that so?" he said. "I'll be right back."

Out in the hall he moved down to the next room and unlocked the door. Stepping inside he shielded his face from the bright light that was shining straight into the eyes of the men tied to two chairs. "What have we got so far, Anatoliy?"

"Not too much." Toll moved to the doorway to speak low. "They haven't really said who they work for, but I get the feeling the younger one on the end would talk if he was alone somewhere."

"Yah, good observation. Let's make that happen." The other man was quickly removed and the bright light turned down a notch.

Radha sat where the interrogator had been and offered the young fellow a bowl of water.

His hand shook as he took it and held it to his swollen mouth. "I'm hungry," he said.

"Yah, we'll get to that eventually. And if you cooperate with us, you'll still have some teeth left to eat your dinner."

The fellow's red face became pale and he glanced nervously at the investigator. Radha picked up the round metal pole from the floor and slapped it into his palm, drawing the man's attention to the weapon. Then he placed the tip on the prisoner's thigh perilously close to his groin. "I'm ready," Radha said. "Tell me who you work for."

The kid wet his lips and glanced pleadingly over at Anatoliy. "I've been with the Monarch for a few years now."

Radha dug the end of the pole into the muscle a little closer to the groin. "See, that's not the information I'm looking for. You'd better think this through. Your job is to tell me what I want to know."

The prisoner struggled against his bonds and tried to shift the chair backwards away from the pole. "Honest, I work for the Monarch. He's also called Sable Maude but he gets mad if you use that label. Apparently he's on bad terms with his family, or something."

Radha jabbed him hard between the legs and he doubled over in pain. "I'm out of patience. I heard you work for DuSatoy."

The kid raised his head, tear tracks shining on his cheeks. "That, too."

Radha sat back. "Why didn't you tell me?"

"I thought you wanted to know who I work for! I work for the Monarch and he loaned me to DuSatoy for the duration of the election campaign. DuSatoy told us to find out who had made the claim on the reward and what information they had."

"Then kill them," Radha spat.

The boy hung his head.

"Who posted the reward?"

He shook his head. "I don't know for sure, but DuSatoy was very interested in what claims came in and who they were from. He wanted to find Ms Master."

"I'll bet he did," Radha muttered.

CHAPTER THIRTY EIGHT

Fanny welcomed Julianne into her garden and arranged tea bowls on the tray. Ms Maya had made spice-caf but it was powerfully hot out and she didn't feel like serving it. "Perhaps some lemon water instead, Ms Maya," she said.

The housekeeper disappeared through the garden door and re-emerged a few minutes later bearing a jug of water, sliced lemons floating on the surface.

"Thanks for coming, Julianne." Fanny poured water into the bowls and set one before her friend, as protocol demanded, before raising hers to her lips and taking a sip. "I need to know what the Constables have found out."

"I know you do." Julianne placed a hand over hers from across the table. "I don't have much more news. The men who were caught are being questioned.

You'd be better to ask Selanna, her husband surely tells her what's going on."

Fanny thought about that. "Selanna isn't my friend. You are."

The two women smiled at each other and Julianne nodded. "Yes, for a long time now, since young school in the City. Your father was teaching history at the Khandarken University and there was so much controversy about the courses he taught. No one could agree on what our history was, what had really happened before and during the Last War. Remember the uproar?"

Fanny chuckled. "Mother always got a kick out of that too. She was very pragmatic and thought they should just get on with it." She choked up at the memory of those times and took a sip of lemon water to soothe her throat. "And your father, Julianne. He was a judge adjudicator then, newly appointed in the Supreme Court."

There was silence for a moment as they contemplated Little Harry's fate after he became Chief Adjudicator. Julianne wiped a tear from her cheek. "Now we're both crying," she said. "Well, enough of that. I've come on a mission."

Fanny stared. "A mission? What kind of mission? Are you here to save me?"

Her friend laughed. "Kind of, you could say so. It's a proposal. Cownden Lanser is beginning his election campaign this week, it's late because he's been so busy with Constabulary work for the Head Ball Games that he couldn't get away. And Selanna is going with him as his wife and helper. She's a lovely woman, Fanny, smart and caring. But she doesn't have your background."

Julianne took a sip of water as she let that sink in. "You and your mother worked with Harold Master through two election campaigns, very successful ones. You know all about how it's done, what works and what doesn't. And you're just sitting here wasting time in your house, hoping this monster that's been after you gets caught. What if you were to do something to actively help catch him? What if you put yourself out there on the campaign trail with Cownden? He could use your assistance."

Fanny stared at her helplessly. "Whose idea was this?"

"Mine." Julianne gave her a cheeky grin. "I know you'd be great at it, and you've been sitting here in mourning since you got back. That can't be good for you or for Boulter. Look how he's grown since you returned. I hardly recognized him when he answered the door this morning. He looks about twelve years old. But he's growing up and you need a reason to get out of bed besides helping Ms Maya manage the house."

Fanny laughed softly. "She won't accept any help from me. I've offered, and I've even tried to hire an assistant for her but she resists at every turn. I'm afraid she'll have a fall or hurt herself when I'm not here."

She gazed out over her garden, still weedy in patches. "I wouldn't mind having a job like that. But what would Cownden's response be?"

"Selanna already asked him. He's ecstatic. Politics isn't his strength."

Fanny turned back to her friend's mischievous expression. "You asked him before you asked me?"

She frowned and tapped the edge of her bowl against the table.

"Well, no point in getting you worked up if he wasn't going to accept the help. But he said he'd love it if you came to work on his campaign. Anatoliy is a good organizer but he's unfamiliar with this line of pursuit."

Fanny gave a faint laugh. "You're bad, Julianne. You're a manipulator, too."

Her friend leaned forward and took her hand. "Fanny, nothing that happens now will make what happened before any easier to bear. I know that. I've had my own times of hopelessness. But life gets better. It really does. On top of that, you have nothing to do right now and the country is in dire need of a good Leader. I think Lanser is the best in the running."

Fanny nodded at that.

"So let's do what we can to make it happen."

The garden door burst open and Boulter loped down the lawn toward them. He seemed taller than even a few days ago, and his smile was confident as he came up to them. "Hi, Mum. Ms Maya wants to know if Ms Julianne will stay for lunch as she's making her famous sablefish pasta and salad with mustard dressing."

"Thank you for the message, Boulter. Can you stay, Julianne? It would be nice to talk over lunch."

~ * * * ~

Damian ducked low to exit the aircart, Nikesh on his heels. He leaped to the ground and quickly moved out of the way of the wave of passengers heading up the ramp to take their place on board for the return journey back to the City.

Looking around, he was surprised by the barrenness of the landscape. Collaros Territory covered the north-west corner of Khandarken, and Discovery, where Emperor Carlton held sway, was as far north as it was possible to go, right up against the Legitamian border. Damian had landed just outside Martonosha, the territory capital.

The meeting with Cownden in the City held some surprises that he hadn't quite been prepared for. He must have imagined he'd be working there, because the anxiety to see Fanny had been at its height. But no, Cownden had other plans. So here they were going undercover in the northern reaches of the country.

His clothes provided by the special forces staff were old and worn, the clips gone from his shirt and replaced by uneven stitches to keep it closed. The boots on his feet had holes in the toe, one of them mended with binding tape. Nikesh didn't look any the better for wear. His hair had not been cut in weeks and stood out around his head like a dark halo. Both men had been slathered with a solution of stain to change their complexions to a weathered appearance.

A civilian in drab clothing approached and introduced himself as a helper for Frank Maude, although he failed to give his name. Waving them over to an old armoured transport that had clearly seen better days, he grabbed one of the doors to wrench it open. "Don't want to attract attention," he remarked with a wry smile. "Most transports up here are either military or Constable and in much better shape. The locals keep a close eye on them."

Climbing in, he pulled up a holograph map on the frontboard for them to look at. "I have orders as follows— you're to be dropped off here, east of Krimen." He placed a finger on the spot. "It's about fifteen miles to Discovery from there and you'll find a lot of dispossessed living in the hills and forests. It should be easy to fit in with one group or another, as they all tend to drift from place to place depending if there is work to be had, or food available."

He glanced back, lifting an eyebrow. "Are we on the same page?"

Damian nodded. "That was our understanding, too. What's the extraction plan?"

~ * * * ~

Emperor Carlton leaned over the map table and planted a blunt finger on the onion skin at the point where the borders for Legitamia, Khandarken and Jiran collided. "What about here?" he demanded.

Elkon took a look. "Yah, it should be possible to get through the mountains at that point, although there's nothing there to see."

Carlton nodded. "I know. But I'll be sending Advisor Judson in to talk with the Jiranis and we need to ensure there's secure passage for him."

Elkon raised his brows. "You know they pulled out of the Head Ball Games, don't you? I'm not sure what that means but perhaps it signifies a lack of determination. Could the Jirani tribal alliance be falling apart? Because that would be best for our purposes."

Carlton shrugged and stalked the length of the warehouse. "That's partly why I'm sending Judson in there. We need to know what's going on. Everything we hear is tainted with local politics."

A knock sounded at the door, just as it was pulled open and Judson appeared, his robe bunched around the walking wrap on his injured leg. He used his cane to tug the door closed behind him and limped forward. "Carlton," he said, bowing his head. "Elkon."

Elkon saluted and pointed at the map. "We're just discussing the best route for your trip to Jiran. When does that wrap come off your leg?"

Judson's jowls grew red. "Not long now, they tell me. I can't ride at the moment, but in a few weeks or a month it will be healed."

Carlton grunted and turned back to the map table. "Come and have a look. I think this is the best path through the mountains."

Judson limped closer, his fingers tight around the walking stick clutched in his grip. "Have you heard the news, Emperor?"

Carlton straightened and turned back, a heavy frown marking his brow. "Heard what?" he said.

"Yah, the Head Ball Games are over and Khandarken took the trophy."

Elkon held his breath. This wasn't good news, not from the point of view of the Empire. Carlton paused, then shrugged his heavy shoulders. "So now Adar Silva is in second place. Well, I'm not surprised, given we weren't present to ensure that it was properly played."

Judson shook his head. "Third place."

"What?" Carlton's voice was low and lethal. "What do you mean?"

"I mean, Legitamia is in second place, Adar Silva is in third."

Carlton stalked from the building, slamming the door in his wake.

CHAPTER THIRTY NINE

Anatoliy arrived at the grand entry to escort Fanny into the Constabulary Headquarters on the fourth floor. He led her down the hall and through security into the inner offices. She'd never been in this building before and gazed around curiously. One whole wall at this level consisted of plexi, so each office had entrancing views across the City and the Violetta River. Just the sight made her nervous, and she tried not to get too close to the windows, following Cownden's assistant as they entered the Chief's office.

Cownden rose to greet her, taking her hand and holding it. "Fanny, it's very good to see you. I know nothing I say will make things better, but I'm sorrowful over the failure of the military and the Constables to keep you safe. It's been a blow to the force and to me that this could happen."

He pointed to a chair by his desk. "Have a seat. You look well, better than when we brought you home. I take it things are going fine. How is the boy, Boulter?"

Fanny nodded and extracted her hand from his grip. "He's fine, thank you. Growing like a weed. I've just hired a tutor for him and he's begun his studies." She clasped her hands together and leaned forward. "You don't have to apologize, Cownden. You've done that already, when we met in Deep Creek, but please don't feel you need to. What's done is done."

Anatoliy placed a bowl of hot tea before her and took a seat, arranging two more tea bowls on the desk. He had his tomo and wand in hand.

Cownden nodded. "You're here about the election campaign."

"Yes. I want to help." The tension left her shoulders and she sat back, suddenly very comfortable with this decision

His eyes lit up. "You do? That's good news. Toll, here, is my organizer and even he doesn't have much of an idea how to go about this. Watching FitzGibbon just gives me the shudders."

Fanny laughed, a soft slightly confused sound. She hadn't laughed often since the attacks on her family, and it felt foreign, and at the same time freeing. "I know what you mean. I think it's partly because he looks like a little rooster strutting about. We can do much better than that, I'm sure."

Toll snickered and scanned his wand across the tomo. "I have a tentative schedule here, been working on it for a few days. What do you think?"

Fanny gave it a cursory glance, then looked back at Cownden. "The thing is, your goal is to cover the whole country. Perhaps there are more votes in the west and south, the City and its outskirts. But you have to represent everyone and you have to appear to represent everyone. It's very important to touch on as many towns and villages as you can in the time we have left."

She thought a moment. "When we travel, I'll need more security. The guards at my house would have to stay there, especially if Boulter doesn't come with me."

Cownden sobered immediately. "I've thought of that and put a tentative plan in place already. Toll will have a schedule for security and he'll ensure you're covered at all times."

Glancing at Toll, she lifted her brows. "How long do we have before the election takes place?"

"About a month," he said, checking something on his tomo. "A month and twelve days."

"Right." Fanny scanned the office. "We have to get moving. It's a lot of territory to cover in that short a time. Where would I work?"

Cownden grinned and stood. "What do you need in the way of space?"

~ * * * ~

"Radha!" Cownden's shout could be heard all the way down the hall where Anatoliy was just receiving the investigator into the offices.

"Right here, sir," Toll said, as Radha came through the doorway. "He's in a tearing hurry."

Cownden laughed to himself. He was seated by the time Radha put down his case and took a chair.

He looked up from the file on his infolink. "I gather DuSatoy is the one we're looking for in regards to the reward posted on Fanny Master. Why would he do that? What does he gain?"

"I haven't figured that out for sure." Radha fingered his sparse whiskers. "But it occurs to me that having her campaign for you is just what he's feared all along. The Masters were beloved all over the country. Ms Master was a force herself, with the Children's Corral and her other charities. Once DuSatoy decided to run for Leader, he might have known that whoever convinced Ms Master or the daughter to campaign would hold a distinct advantage over the other candidates."

Cownden took a deep breath. "We might be playing right into his hands. Perhaps we're putting Fanny in even greater danger than she was before she left the City."

Radha hitched the chair closer. "What if he was the one that put the bom on Leader Master's aircart? We still don't know who was responsible, do we? Given that DuSatoy declared he was running for Leader, as soon as the election was called right after the explosion…"

"But a bom in a foreign country?" Cownden looked skeptical.

"It's possible. Remember, Assistant Chief Constable Duncan was working with him, and his two bodyguards disappeared up there before we even left Gilsigg. Has to be suspicious."

Cownden's chest was tight. That such a thing could happen during his watch was galling. Yet, it almost made sense.

Radha continued, "We've put out a warrant to bring him in for questioning. DuSatoy was last reported in the Foothills area. Governor Phelong says he was campaigning through the small towns around Buckley the last few days. He's sent a couple of Constables to nab him before he takes transit out of there. I'm waiting to hear."

Cownden frowned.

Radha continued, "Not that I'm saying she's safe. We don't know that." Pursing his lips, he gazed out the plexi at the dirty flowing water of the Violetta below. "I just want him in my grasp. I want him in prison and secured before you head out."

"I can't wait." Cownden stood and paced the length of the room. "The campaign has a life of its own, it seems. Toll and Fanny have got me organized to the eyebrows. Selanna just supports what they tell me. If I'm going to be in the running, I have to get out there and earn the votes."

Radha was silent, calmly stroking his chin. Cownden's investigator had always been a man of few words, but this had to be some kind of record. Then he finally stirred himself. "I'll have another go at Rutman," he said.

~ * * * ~

DuSatoy finished his speech and stepped down from the box his assistant had placed for him on the sidewalk of this small place just across the territory line in Collaros. It had been a short talk, less than fifteen minutes. But there were only four men and a few women who had gathered to listen to him in front of the ale shop. What was the village called again? He couldn't remember and it didn't matter anyway.

He'd just caught a signal from his driver waiting by the transport. Time to go, something was happening. He shook a few hands and walked with purpose toward the vehicle waiting at the end of the block, the motor running. His driver pushed the door open as he approached and DuSatoy clambered behind the frontboard as his assistant grabbed the standing signs for the campaign and ran after him, dumping them in the back.

"What is it?" he barked.

His guard jumped in and the motor roared, giant wheels spinning in the dirt and rock of the road. "Constables, sir. Two of them, their vehicle just came around the corner back there."

The transport swerved as it struggled for traction, then rapidly gained speed as they left the tiny village behind and entered the woods on the far side. The road ahead was rough and pitted, and he didn't think they could outrun a Constable vehicle anyway. He needed another plan. They turned a corner and entered deeper forest. "See that spot, just ahead," he said to his driver. "Pull into the clearing right there."

Gathering case and coat, DuSatoy waited until the transport had nearly stopped, then threw the door open and fell out into the weeds beside the high wheels. "Drive," he yelled. "Just drive."

The transport pulled back onto the road in a flurry of dust and took off. He lay in the dirt, waiting to catch his breath, and heard a second vehicle approach. Raising his head a couple of inches, he watched the giant wheels of the Constable transport roar past.

No matter how hard his men tried to get away, they'd soon be caught. That vehicle was just too powerful. DuSatoy clambered to his feet and brushed the dead leaves from his pants. Then he moved off through the woods to head cross-country. He had to put as much distance as possible between himself and his men.

No point in heading to the transit hub, the Constables would be all over it, waiting for him to appear. But he had his case and his money. He'd find someone to take him north, to his own personal enclave. He'd hole up there and see what happened, because this campaign wasn't over yet.

CHAPTER FORTY

The first trip of Cownden's campaign was a rush of travel and meetings. Fanny wanted the entire Southern Territory covered before the grand gala that was to be held in the City at the end of this tour. The South was nearby and easy to organize. It also allowed a build-up of anticipation for when the officials and nobility gathered in the nation's capital to endorse Lanser for Leader.

Cownden dragged his feet a bit but Fanny just left that to Anatoliy to deal with. She set a simple schedule covering some of the tiny establishments such as the fishing village of Coronation and the trading town of Farmerville before heading to the territory capital.

Deep Creek, where the Head Ball Games had finally wound down and the foreign visitors departed, was settling back to normal business. She coordinated with Governor Frank Maude to hold a town meeting the day after their arrival. Hundreds of people turned out and with Maude as his backer, Cownden had a lot of support. It was thrilling, and only their first stop in this rushed crusade for votes.

In her room at the Learmonth Hotel, Fanny finished pinning up her hair. Immediately, Anatoliy arrived to escort her down to dinner. It was ironic she was no longer rooming at the Transit Hotel, let alone the abandoned box up the trail. Things had definitely changed. "How do you think that went?" she asked as they encountered two guards in the crowded hallway outside her door. The guards turned and followed them down the main staircase to the dining hall.

Toll grinned at her questions. "Couldn't have been better. The boss was surprised at the numbers who came out to hear him. Obviously they weren't all supporters, I heard some muttering from the crowd and catcalls when he talked about keeping Emperor Carlton outside our boundaries. Not surprising, given they're inside our boundaries as we speak." He held the door to the dining room and followed her in. The guards took up position, one at the door and the second against the far wall.

Fanny laughed. "Yes, we'd better refine that speech a bit, take out the parts that don't fit and get better talking points to add to it. I'll work on that tonight."

Toll led her to the table reserved for them, where Cownden and Selanna had yet to appear. "I'll help," he said. "Selanna's good with that kind of stuff, too."

Fanny stiffened, but reminded herself that Selanna was Cownden's wife and so had to be welcomed into every part of the campaign. She was also Damian's sister, but when they had first met in the field behind the fighting arts building, Fanny had noted a distinct lack of welcome in the woman's expression.

She bent her head over the menu. She had more things to worry about than if Damian's family would treat her with kindness. Perhaps Selanna could help polish the speech after all.

Cownden and his wife soon appeared, with Governor Maude in tow. They settled in for a light supper. Roasted olinguito, stewed vegetables in red sauce, fried lentils quickly appeared, followed by cinnamon rounds, glasses of ale and bowls of spice caf tea.

As the dishes were cleared away, Toll pulled out his tomo and they settled in to re-work Cownden's speech. It was the first of many times, she was sure, that they would adjust the plan. She remembered her parents working far into the night as they changed the speeches to address issues that were important to each area of the country as they travelled.

Nonetheless, this campaign had finally gotten underway.

~ * * * ~

Damian heard the grinding noise coming from the far wall and tried to raise his hands. They were already tied behind his back. He couldn't move. The noise grew louder, then the clicking started off to his left. He twisted his head wildly, trying to dislodge the blindfold but it was no use. He was bound so tightly his hands were numb.

He emerged from the dream and turned over on the pallet in the hunter's hut where he and Nikesh had holed up with three other dispossessed. The sound of snoring filled the air. Slowly he sank back beneath the surface of sleep and the dream returned, but it was different now.

The whirring commenced and seemed to draw closer. Then it hovered above him, yet when he looked down it was Fanny who lay on the table. It was Fanny who was about to become the next victim of torture.

Heart hammering in his chest, he flew at the machine, a metal wrench in his hand and began smashing it, knocking the elongated arms off and breaking the plexi face. Bits of debris flew around as he pulled on it, trying to yank the menace off its track.

He looked down to find Fanny lying on the table in a dress of lace. She opened her eyes and stared straight into his. He was transfixed. Then she rose and the bonds on her wrists and ankles fell away.

Confusion wrapped him in a web and he glanced around. They weren't in the torture room at all, it was the room they had shared at the Transit Hotel.

She placed her palm gently in the centre of his chest and his heart began a different beat, slow and heavy. Suddenly he knew where this was going, and he couldn't wait to get there.

Damian rolled over, as the excitement of his dream slowly faded. He stared around the unfamiliar space. Nikesh was on the dirty pallet beside him, and the other men had shared the space the best they could. The roof of the hut was sagging in one corner and the dried grass beneath them smelled of mouse droppings and mold.

But they were making progress. One of the men who had joined them last night, a dispossessed named Ollie, brought news that Emperor Carlton was recruiting for a new military offensive. All they had to do was get close enough to cross the Legitamian border and there were meals and jobs waiting for them.

"Nikesh?" he murmured. "You awake?"

His buddy rolled over and opened his eyes. "Right here," he said low.

"Today's the day." They both sat up and the other men began to stir. Damian pulled his pack closed and rose to step over bodies toward the warped door. Outside, he stood tall and stretched, then walked off the track to relieve himself against a bush. The men inside would know how it was possible to cross the border, but he wasn't as familiar with the terrain as he wished. They had to be watchful or this wouldn't work.

Hours later Damian and Nikesh, joined by Ollie and another man, stopped to rest beside a stream. They had been walking through the forest for a long time, not wanting to be observed on the roads and tracks used by the northern residents. There was a crackling sound in the bush nearby. Damian cranked his neck to look, but Ollie made a motion with his hand. "Hold still," he murmured. "They're just checking us out."

"Okay." He glanced at Nikesh and dug some strings of dried meat out of his pack to share. They all drank from the stream, then sat to rest.

"How far now?" Nikesh asked.

Just then two men approached out of the trees and came to a stop on the edge of the clearing. They were obviously dispossessed but seemed well fed and dressed with warm clothing. Each carried a raygun on a sling down his back.

"Whoa." Damian clambered to his feet and backed up a pace, watching as they approached. "Can we help you?" he called.

One of the men stepped forward, hand outstretched in friendship. "We're recruiting men for the New Emperor." He looked them over, noting the ragged clothes. "Any interest here?"

They exchanged glances. "What does that mean?" Damian asked. "Why is he recruiting?"

The men squatted on the grass. "You see, it's this way."

Late that night the two recruiters led them into the Emperor's makeshift camp along with a couple of other men they'd encountered along the way. They were now inside the borders of Legitamia.

CHAPTER FORTY ONE

Waite rode his horse hard, hoping to get off the trail before nightfall. It was dangerous in the north after dark, even for an enforcer like himself. Working for The Monarch of the Territories gave him some status when negotiating with the businesses they made arrangements with, but not much protection when he was out alone on the roads. And the work he did for Major Dante Regiment was so secret, even the Constables were unaware of it.

He was close to DuSatoy's establishment, so took the next cross track and soon rode into a corral at the side of the road. A few horses milled and a guard challenged him in the darkness. Waite identified himself and left his mount to be tended while he trod wearily up the path to the stone structure that consisted of DuSatoy's headquarters.

As the Monarch's right hand, he'd visited this place many times, bringing payments to the strongman or using it as a way station while smuggling women from the western reaches on the far side of Jiran. The smuggling was more difficult now, and fewer females were getting through, largely due to Waite's secret contacts with Major Regiment, but that was no one's business but his.

DuSatoy's staff seemed to have retired for the night. He pounded heavily on the door and eventually the footman came to open it for him. The place was unkempt, debris had blown into the corners and dirty dishes with dried food in them sat on the dining table. DuSatoy hadn't been here very often in the last few months due to his campaigning efforts, and it showed in the way the staff was caring for the place.

Waite had a quick bite to eat and bedded down in one of the bunks in the staff quarters at the back of the structure. All he needed was a good night's sleep.

It was early hours of the morning when he was wakened by a hammering at the front entry. He watched the footman lurch off his pallet and run down the hall to answer. Then Waite rolled over and went back to sleep. It wasn't his business who came calling.

When he woke again, refreshed, he found all the staff had left the room, so something was definitely afoot. Taking care of himself in the garderobe adjacent to the barracks, he made his way to the kitchens looking for a morning meal. Everything there appeared to be in chaos. The head cook was whipping up a concoction in a wide bowl as he threw orders at his minions. Meat was frying in one pan on the heatsurface, eggs bubbled in a pot at the back. Someone was toasting pané in the oven under the dire directions of the cook.

"Waite!" He turned to see DuSatoy weave into view from the direction of the dining hall. "Didn't know you were here. Join me for breakfast." He turned unsteadily to address the cook, "That'll be three of us," he declared loudly.

He pointed at Waite's chest. "This way. I've got a farmer joining me, he was kind enough to give me a ride here." DuSatoy staggered and the strong scent of whiskey wafted from his general direction.

Waite grinned to himself and followed down the hallway into the dining room. He nodded at the short, barrel-chested man in grungy overalls who was already seated at the table, as a boy brought tea bowls and water glasses from the sideboard. It seemed obvious the farmer was looking for more than a good meal by way of thanks for his assistance.

Waite's instructions from Sable Maude were to find DuSatoy and get rid of him, but there was no way that was going to happen here. Too many witnesses, too much risk.

What he *would* do, however, was get word to Dante Regiment that DuSatoy had returned home. Perhaps the campaigning had gone sour. Why else would he abandon it? Waite settled in to enjoy his breakfast.

~ * * * ~

In the City, Fanny rose from her chair at the side of the entertainment hall to accept the hand of the next man in line to offer a dance. This time it was

Acting Leader FitzGibbon, and she smiled in acknowledgement of his close relationship with her father in the past.

He bowed gallantly and took her hand as the orchestra struck up a sedate waltz. "Ms Master," he beamed. "I'm delighted to see you out and in such good form. It's a pleasure to meet you again after such a difficult time."

He must have seen the tears gather in her eyes, because he glanced away and manoeuvred her around General Paulo Regiment and Mildred Hart, who were moving very slowly together across the floor. Mildred's son, Puntledge, the Chief Adjudicator of the Khandarken Court of Appeal, was standing to the side of the room in deep conversation with Dr Stonsifer from the hospital.

"That's kind of you, Mr FitzGibbon. Father was pleased to work with you, you know. He had great respect for you." Fanny decided not to enhance that comment, Father was often totally frustrated by FitzGibbon's obfuscations, and had been grateful he had very little power among the members of the Board of Representatives.

"I hear you might have changed your mind about the upcoming election," she added. "Are you pulling your name from the running?"

As the man flushed a heavy red, Fanny nodded serenely. "Father would be so proud. He said you were a man of great insight, and obviously he was right. Do you support Cownden Lanser for Leader, then?"

The Acting Leader hedged his response as the music picked up speed and they executed a sharp turn near the corner of the dance hall in the Learmonth Resort Hotel. Positioned in the downtown section of the City, it was an outstanding structure, even in a part of town that was full of new and innovative architecture.

The lobby ceiling had been finished in plaster cornices and framing, most of it painted with gold leaf. The walls sagged with paintings from the old masters before the Last War, along with some new ones. The stairs leading to the second floor where the dance hall was located were carpeted in fine wool matting in every shade of rose to wine, and the huge banister that towered upward from the main floor was known throughout the country for its intricately carved design.

There were hordes of people in the crowd who had come out to support Cownden's campaign. Frank Advisor, who ran one of the major attorney offices in the City, was here with his wife and some of his junior workers. Saxby Wordsmith and his companion, Brentwood Holmes, had pulled in quite a contingent of support from the Men's Club situated in Old Towne. Cownden hadn't been impressed by that but Anatoliy mentioned that the Club was where a great many decisions were made that didn't always reach the Board of Representatives, so it was a good move to have them there and onside.

Most of the Territory Governors had stayed in their ridings, many ready to cast their support behind the campaign as Cownden's train of supporters moved about the country. Security was high, however. Cownden had insisted that Ooievaar be appointed head of the guards that accompanied them wherever they went.

Fanny glanced about and continued her conversation with FitzGibbon. "Mr DuSatoy seems to have disappeared from the campaign trail in the south. I can't imagine what he's thinking, because the date of voting draws near." She looked over her partner's shoulder. "Jack Learmonth is here in full regalia," she commented. "His whole entourage seems to be in attendance as well."

Jack Learmonth was the titular head of the Learmonth Industry now that his father had died. He had run for Leader in the last two elections, only to be defeated by Harold Master each time. Tonight he had a young woman on his arm who seemed no more than half his age, and flushed painfully each time he introduced her to a new acquaintance.

An elderly gentleman tapped FitzGibbon on the shoulder, and stepped in to dance with Fanny. She gratefully accepted the hand of Elliott, former head of the Constabulary Board. Although he was plagued by rheumatism, he moved slowly but smoothly as they navigated across the floor. "I thought I should rescue you," he muttered. "I know what an ass our Acting Leader can be from time to time."

Fanny laughed and gazed into his kind eyes. "Very good of you, sir," she replied. "He wouldn't say *yes* or *no* as to whether he's supporting Cownden."

Elliott turned his head to follow FitzGibbon with his gaze. "Yah, I'm not surprised. He's just faced the fact that with so little support, he has to step out of the race. It's hard on the ego."

"Yes, I felt sorry for him."

Elliott shrugged eloquently. "Don't waste your time. He's not the best we've had among the Representatives, but he's not the worst either. And Cownden will make a fine Leader. Maybe almost as good as your father, Harold."

She took a breath and held it. The pain in her breast was sharp, like the stab from a knife, but she welcomed that statement with her whole heart. Father *had* been good, maybe great, and it was nice to have that acknowledged by someone as informed and respected as Elliott.

"Thank you, Elliott," she said, her voice quavering. "That was very kind."

He patted her shoulder and led her to the side of the room. "With all the fuss about this election," he said, "I thought it should be stated. We wouldn't be having this vote right now if things had been different, and I mourn as you do. On the other hand," he favoured her with a sharp smile showing yellowed teeth, "Lanser has some attributes that might be needed now, with Emperor Carlton making inroads through our borders. We have to be ready for war."

Fanny shuddered.

CHAPTER FORTY TWO

Damian slogged through the mud, following the two dispossessed leading them into the temporary camp. They were well across the border now, inside Legitamia, and his official ident had been burning a hole in his pocket. Nikesh had suggested a knot in a tree and they'd both been keeping an eye out to find the right hiding spot.

When the ragged line of men stopped to relieve themselves, he'd spotted a hollow oak beside the trail. The tree was huge, taller than anything around it, but the lower branches were dying due to a rotted hollow cavity in the trunk. Damian wrapped the two idents in an onion skin and tucked them low in the space, covering them with crumbs of decaying bark. He used his wristlink to take a measure of the spot, and drifted off to converse with the other men.

The camp was just ahead and tension was rising. Yet when they arrived, it was a bit of a letdown. Just an ordinary spot, with tents down one side, flytarps tied back. A cook's space was cleared in the centre and large kettles steamed over low fires. A dog barked and was hushed by the guard near a small herd of mules.

There were dozens of men moving about. Some looked ex military and others more like youthful farm hands looking for adventure. Although Damian couldn't imagine anyone wanting this kind of escapade. He gave a silent hollow laugh. He'd been looking for exactly this kind of action at the age of some of these young fellows during the Last War. He prayed to God he didn't get caught up in a firefight sitting on the wrong side of the Khandarken border.

A young man in uniform came to greet them and got them to line up in formation. As they shuffled into rows, he blew a whistle and raised his arm. "General Elkon," he announced as an officer emerged from one of the tents and strode to the front of the line.

Elkon was a short square man, his shoulders broad and thick. He wore an old-fashioned Adar Silva-style uniform jacket with a standing collar and belted waist, with a peaked cap on his head. He saluted and seemed un-phased when only a couple of men returned the gesture. Walking down the line, he took his time inspecting the men one by one, then returned to the front.

"Welcome." His voice was low and powerful. "Welcome to the New Empire. We are embarking on an exciting and ambitious journey and we need you men to work with us for the greater glory. You'll receive a suit of warm clothes, meals every day, weapons as they become available. Most of all, you will receive the undying gratitude of Emperor Carlton. How many of you want to sign on?"

Damian looked around as he raised his hand. There were about thirty men in the group, all looking wary but eager to get their meal and whatever else Carlton would provide. His gut clenched. How big was this army? And how long would it take him and Nikesh to find out? Fanny was back in the City and he was here. It was a painful realization.

After a surprisingly good meal of llama stew, honey-coated pané and steamed vegetables, they were relaxing in the grass with the other men. Each held a bowl of ale. As the morning whiled away, the stories began to flow. One particularly weathered-looking fellow was waxing eloquent in describing his adventures during the Last War. "Fought for Aqatain," he boasted. "Heavy fighting in north Khandarken. Then we moved south to the Helmcken Trail and that was tough. Lots of boms. Never saw so many boms."

Damian's chest was tight. He and Da had been in the midst of that and it had changed them both forever.

The fellow continued. "Of course the Jiranis had left off with support of the Empire and were just fighting for themselves by then, looking to seize more territory. That's when I changed sides."

He glanced around and lowered his voice. "Didn't seem like the Emperor was going to win, anyway.

And they had too much corruption going on. Couldn't quite see helping with that."

There was muttering amongst some of the men. "What are you doing working for the New Emperor then?" someone asked. "If you changed sides, and all."

"Well." The fellow shrugged. "I haven't had a decent meal like this in months. Look at the gadget they just gave me." He pulled the ten-gear from his pocket and pressed the side button. A thin lethally sharp knife sprang forward at the same time as a hole punch fired out of the handle at the back. "Never seen anything like it. Great for hand-to-hand combat."

The other men fingered their weapons as the guy continued. "Why are the rest of you here? Same reason as me, I'll bet. Looking for somewhere to hang your hat."

Damian nodded. "Me too. I need a job and this one looks like the kind of place I can use some of my old skills." There was laughter from a few of the men.

By afternoon they'd been marched further into Legitamian territory and reached Emperor Carlton's main establishment. It seemed to consist of a large barn-like building with some smaller structures behind it. Horses and mules grazed in the fields nearby, under watch from herd dogs. It was a busy place, men working in groups, training in formation, conducting target practice albeit without discharging their weapons. Perhaps they were short of ammunition. It was the first encouraging thought

Damian had entertained since they encountered the recruiters the day before.

This place was clearly a military camp, larger than he had anticipated and there were a lot of bodies milling around. Obviously not all the recruits were here. Carlton held the village of Discovery, and there had been attempted insurgencies through the border all along the north of Khandarken. In other words, a lot more men than he could count here at the main camp.

By the time he and Nikesh bedded down in a canvas tent at the side of the barn, Damian was feeling decidedly discouraged.

~ * * * ~

Fanny arrived home to a peaceful household. Mr Weisner, the tutor, had Boulter in the den working on his studies with great diligence. The new housemaid, Tippy, was young and looked somewhat frail but was obviously strong enough to stand up to Ms Maya, because the place was dusted and orderly and she was currently poised at the counter chopping vegetables as Ms Maya went through her recipes at the kitchen table.

"Good morning," Fanny called, letting herself in through the front door. Tippy belatedly came running to take her shawl and hang it in the cloak room.

Boulter called out, "Mum?" His voice seemed deeper than even a week ago.

She peeked around the corner into the den. "Morning, Boulter." The youth grinned, his cheeks going red. He looked too big for the chair he was occupying.

Mr Weisner drew himself up to his short stature and gave a shallow bow. "Good morning, indeed, Ms. Good to see you back." He gestured at Boulter. "He learns fast, does this young man. But we still aren't there yet."

"That's good to hear." She eyed the pages laid out on the desk and Boulter's smooth flowing writing across the surface. "I don't mean to interrupt, perhaps you can join me for lunch and we can catch up then."

Seated at the dining room table some time later, the young maid served a light soup of leeks and lentils, then heartier fare of fried rabbit, a vegetable salad and roasted beetroots with a lemon sauce. Boulter talked non-stop, telling her all he had accomplished since she left. Her heart swelled with pride. He was a quick and clever boy, and so well-meaning.

"I'll excuse myself now, Mother. There are a few things I need to tend to before my afternoon lessons begin." He leaned to buss her cheek and give her shoulder a squeeze before he dashed off. She was sure he hadn't been tall enough to reach her cheek when she left here just days ago. It was alarming.

Mr Weisner sat back over his tea bowl. "He learns fast, Ms. I don't know if I've had a sharper student. Even for twelve or fourteen, he's very advanced.

Fanny squinted as a sudden headache threatened. "I'm not sure how old he is," she managed. "He's grown a lot since we got back home, but I thought it was the effect of finally having steady meals and a roof over our heads." Mr Weisner had been fully informed, when he'd joined their household, of how she and Boulter met and the conditions of their recent life.

He nodded sagely. "Well, that can certainly influence things. I don't suppose it matters how old he is. He's got an ident, so there shouldn't be any problem, and he's got a mother who cares for him. Believe me, that's a lot."

"Yes, the ident." Fanny glanced to the sideboard where she'd laid her bag. "I'd better get busy on that, because he needs his own if he's past twelve. I'll get Toll to look into it."

She smiled and let it go for the moment. "I'm very pleased to have you here working with Boulter, Mr Weisner. It's a relief to me knowing he's coming along in his studies, even if I'm absent some of the time. But once the election is over, things will settle down again."

"Yah. Well, let me get back to the schoolroom." He waved toward the den. "There are a few things I need to set up before Boulter and I begin for the afternoon."

Fanny rose and watched him depart. As the maid cleared the plates, she wandered back into the family chamber where she could see into the back garden. She had to get packed, Cownden was leaving for another trip soon, but first she'd check the flowers. Stepping through the rear door, she lifted her hand to shade her eyes from the bright light.

The garden was looking decidedly better. Boulter had obviously been keeping up with the weeding, as the pest plants had been removed and the flowers were flourishing in the early autumn heat. She glanced toward the back lane and frowned. Two tall figures hovered near the garden shed. They were clad in long grey robes and Mickens sat at the feet of the first one as if he knew him. Boulter was conversing with them, his expression especially serious. He nodded once, then the nearest figure laid a hand on his shoulder. Boulter bowed his head and seemed to listen to his words.

The figures turned and went down the lane, disappearing from view.

Mickens perked his ears and dashed forward to stop in front of Fanny as she approached, licking her hand, and she leaned down to pet his head. Boulter came more slowly up the lawn.

"Who were those men, Boulter?" Fanny frowned. "Did you know them or were they just asking directions?"

Boulter beamed at her. "They were travellers, Mother. Friendly travellers." He took her hand and led her to the table in the yard. "I've got lemon water for you. Sit here."

Fanny smiled at his enthusiasm and seated herself on the bench, leaning her elbows on the table. "This is nice. Thank you."

He poured her a bowl and handed it across, then one for himself and took the bench opposite. "Do you like the garden? I've gotten most of the weeds out, but there are a few plants that I'm not sure about, and nor was Ms Maya. We thought we'd leave them and let you decide, because they're your flowers. See that clump there? We didn't know. And there's a creeping ivy that she thought should be dug out but it has pretty violet flowers so I've left it for you to tell me."

Fanny sipped her lemon water, and ignored the tears that clouded her vision. He was a lovely child, so caring, so willing. She owed her life to him, because she was confident she couldn't have carried on alone.

"I'm glad you left the ivy. It's one of my favourite plants. We should just move it to a better spot."

"Oh good. I'll get to it tonight after my lessons with Mr Weisner."

She took his hand. "You don't have to work so hard, Boulter. I love you just the way you are."

His expression turned serious. "Thank you, Mother. I love you, too. You see, we don't have much time left."

CHAPTER FORTY THREE

M ickens lay down in the grass at Fanny's feet and leaned his head against her knee. Boulter had gone back into the house, his lessons about to begin for the afternoon and she was alone in the garden. Her hand descended and rubbed nicely around his ears and along his back. He groaned his pleasure.

We don't have much time left, he thought. *Boulter is right. The travellers came to warn us today. Fanny is going to be secure in her new home and Boulter is growing up. They won't need each other anymore. When they met, they were both in a desperate situation, and the relationship worked very well. But now it's almost time for Boulter to move on.*

Mickens clambered to his feet and paced the garden as Fanny finished her lemon water. When she rose to enter the house, he strode beside her, keeping pace. *It is going to be hard. They'll both lose someone they love.*

~ * * * ~

DuSatoy watched the programme on the infolink in a bar in a small town north of Wymark. He hadn't left Khandarken, why should he? There was no warrant out for his arrest, because they didn't have proof that he'd done anything wrong. Obviously Rutman had kept his mouth shut.

But this presentation on the link had been shown over and over and it burned him every time he had to listen to it. In the first holograph, Fanny Master stepped out of a military aircart, the small boy holding her hand, and a crowd of supporters rushed forward. They surrounded her where she stood at the foot of the steps, cheering and laughing. Several pushed forward to hug her, and from her expression these were people she knew. But the others didn't give up, they reached to touch her, many patted her shoulder and laid hands on the little boy's head.

Who did she think she was? It was as if *she* was running in the election campaign. He gritted his teeth. DuSatoy's manager had just received a letter by personal delivery from the Secretary of the Board of Representatives, telling him DuSatoy had to withdraw from the election race. But he sneered at that idea. *Either charge me for a crime or stand back. I'm running.*

He glanced again at the screen, now showing the damned Master daughter in the centre of the City, standing in the entry to the Constabulary Headquarters. She was surrounded by reporters and Cownden Lanser stood beside her. Of course. Why wouldn't he pick up on this extraordinary notoriety that dogged her steps? It couldn't last. Who would be interested in her for long? What had she ever done of any note?

"Change the link," he barked. "I've seen this a hundred times."

The barkeep looked up from wiping the counter down and glanced at the infolink. "Only line we get up here," he remarked and went back to polishing bowls. "Besides, I like that story. That little girl has guts, and so did her father. She should run for election."

There were a few laughs down the bar at the idea of a woman as Leader.

DuSatoy sat on his stool, seething with anger. So now he was supposed to withdraw? That simply wasn't in the plan. He slapped money in the bowl on the counter and stalked out.

~ * * * ~

They travelled by aircart into Buckley the next morning. Toll had arranged for everyone to stay at the Learmonth Foothills Hotel, and Fanny was tired. She'd been up most of the night with Anatoliy in a rushed effort to organize the last details for the trip.

Somehow, Boulter appearing so much bigger and more mature had thrown her badly and she wasn't sleeping well. There was no way a small boy should develop that fast. His voice had deepened, his shoulders were broad. When they walked together, she had trouble keeping up with his long-legged stride.

The first event of this leg of the tour was a reception hosted by Governor Phelong at his headquarters downtown. It was heavily attended by Constables and their families, and other officials of the area. Then they set out on a five-day tour through the province, going nearly as far as Forbidden Reach. The line of official transports was long and the roads rutted and dusty. A lead vehicle proceeded in front, followed by Cownden and Selanna with their guards. Toll and Fanny, with guards in tow came behind. It was unusual enough to see such a big number of vehicles that people in many villages came out to engage and it turned into a fun encounter.

Central hubs for the maxibus service were popular campaign spots, as were the local bars. Phelong spent some time travelling with them as he knew his territory well, and had contacts in every village.

The response to Cownden's campaign was heartening. He had started out on this task seeming very stiff and formal in his manner. But he'd slowly relaxed as he began to understand his role. People responded to the slow smile and focussed attention. He never seemed hurried and always appeared interested, and it was a winning combination on the campaign trail.

The flight back to the City after days on the move was welcome and Fanny dozed on the trip, only waking on touchdown at the airport outside town.

She was suddenly swamped with anxiety about Boulter and what she'd find when she got home. And when would she see Damian again? She ached for the comfort of his presence, longing for what she apparently could not have.

~ * * * ~

Dante Regiment's assistant Mallahide poked his nose in the doorway. "Major, secure link message coming in for you."

He nodded and clicked on his infolink. The reception was fuzzy, the holograph unintelligible, but the sound was clear.

"Dante Regiment here," he said.

There was a pause. "This is Waite calling."

Dante felt a thump in his gut. He had a number of undercover agents roaming Khandarken and beyond the borders, and he was aware just how dangerous it was for each of them. Waite was no exception. He was a military man who had volunteered some time ago to act as informant, yet any day he could be found out. The result would be disastrous for him personally and for Dante's information network. Dante would never hear from him again, and he'd never know what had happened, or who might be involved.

"I'm here, Waite," he said. "I can't see you but I can hear you fine."

"Yah, had to disable the holograph function, it eats up the power and a charge doesn't last long enough to be useful."

Dante barked a laugh. He loved these gadgets that the military provided, but half the time they were useless out in the field just when they were needed. "Go ahead, Waite."

"Okay. Sable Maude is expecting three women and a young boy in the next few days. They're coming from north this time, near Sturridge, but have to enter Khandarken along the Collaros border by Krimen. The plan is to take them past Discovery and back into Legitamia to his holding. So, the only time to stop them is when they first enter."

Dante made notes on his tomo and clarified the particulars. "How many does that make now?" he asked.

"About thirteen." There was a small silence. "It *was* thirteen but the Constable raid last month seized five women, bringing it down to eight. I think that's right. We're working with three locations, but the raid shut one down and the women were taken. The owner of the bar was arrested as well."

Dante nodded. "That's my information, too. Well done, Waite. Thanks for that evidence."

"Yah. There's something more. DuSatoy has retreated back into the north. He was at his holding yesterday, not sure what his plan is but it didn't sound like he's backing out of the election."

"Hmm." Dante tugged a sideburn thoughtfully. "He was told to cancel his campaign."

"Yah. So he said. But in his words, either charge him with a crime or back off, he isn't quitting."

"Okay. Might be time to move in and pick him up. I'll work with some of the folk here to sort it out."

"Good. That's all I have."

Dante leaned closer. "Where are you now, Waite?"

"I'm near Sprintline. Had to make a pickup here. By the way, DuSatoy knows I've been in the military base. Last time I stopped there to report, he caught me coming out of the main offices as I was leaving."

Dante thought about that. "Doesn't sound good. I don't like it. It might be time for you to step down and find another line of work. I'm uncomfortable when my men are put into danger when it isn't necessary."

Waite gave a cough. "I'm fine for now, just keeping my eyes open."

CHAPTER FORTY FOUR

Cownden paced his boardroom as Anatoliy hustled to the door. Dante Regiment had just arrived. Radha already occupied one chair, Saffi another. Puntledge Hart was planning to attend but said he'd be late so they would proceed without him for the moment. Since Saffi had taken over the duties of Assistant Chief Constable, Cownden had noticed a distinct change, not just in the atmosphere in the Constabulary Headquarters but also out in the field. Saffi had been a good choice. The fact that Duncan had been corrupted in the same role still ate at his gut, but he tried not to let it distract him from his job.

Campaigning had turned into a full-time occupation. He shrugged his shoulders irritably. Fanny Master held some tight reins in her fragile-looking hands, and Toll just followed along. She'd been a huge asset, it was just bad timing that all of these things should happen at once.

Turning, he took his place at the table. "Okay, Radha, can you give us what you've managed to wring out of Rutman about the Fanny Master assaults."

His head investigator tugged on his sparse chin whiskers for a moment, then leaned forward. "Here's what I know. Rutman was involved in the hydro-truck collision on the Violetta Bridge that killed Ms Master. He was the driver, and his task was to get rid of the family. As to why he was given that task, he's been slow to explain, telling me it wasn't his job to question the order. But it appears DuSatoy was involved because even later when Fanny Master was seen in Deep Creek, he was still getting messages from the strongman to finish the deed and get rid of her."

He glanced around the table. "We don't have any further information about Leader Master's aircart bom. That is still unsolved, although it wouldn't surprise me..." He paused and tapped the table, obviously changing courses. "That's about it. Rutman has given us enough under oath to issue the warrant for the arrest of DuSatoy. We need to do that right away."

Just then there was a short knock and the door opened again to reveal Puntledge Hart in the entry. He nodded to the others and took a seat across from Cownden. "Sorry, but got here as soon as I could," he said, taking a sheaf of onion skin from his case and laying it on the table. "It's not great news."

All heads turned in his direction, as he continued. "I tried to have DuSatoy's name removed from the electoral list, but the court turned me down."

Cownden snickered. "Just issue your own judgement, Punt. It's faster and you get the result you want."

Puntledge tightened his mouth in annoyance. "This was the Supreme Court and their decision says, and I quote," here he lifted a sheet and read from it. *"Without a criminal conviction there is no authority to authorize the removal of a name from the electoral list.* Then the judge adjudicator lectured me that I should have known that and if I want someone off the list, they have to be charged and convicted before I can make such application."

Dante reached to take the paper and read the rest of the reasoning. "Well, according to this, we're almost there. Radha just gave us enough evidence to issue the warrant, so with him in jail he can't campaign. If we can show a case even without DuSatoy's presence in the courtroom we might have enough. Therefore, we don't need to wait until he's arrested to hold a hearing."

Punt nodded. "Let's put out the arrest warrant, and hope someone turns him in."

Radha gave a shrug. "He's quite a powerful man. It's unlikely anyone will have the guts to do that."

~ * * * ~

Damian jogged down a narrow trail through the hills. It felt odd not having Nikesh with him. The two men had worked together for years, first with Makulski and now with the special forces that Cownden Lanser ran through Governor Frank Maude.

But Nikesh had insisted on staying back. "We'll lose a lot of what we've gained," he protested. "With you called back to headquarters, we won't have firsthand knowledge here, if I leave too." His black eyes had looked determined. "Leave my ident in the same spot. I'll come and get it when I think I'm done here. There's more to learn, Damian, and I plan on learning it."

Damian couldn't fault him. A brief training period at the Emperor's headquarters gave them a chance to gather numbers of men and arms, but the information was sparse and rumours nipped sharply before they flourished among the troops.

However, soon they'd been assigned to Discovery to relieve some of the men who were on duty there. They'd found the village in fair shape, a few of the residents still in their homes, but most houses stood empty or had been taken over by dispossessed in the army who were tired of living in tents. Those residents who had stayed were either too old to travel, or were in trade and had made a bid to conduct business with the Empire. The food supplies store and the small bar were most notable for their activity.

Before the first week was out, Damian had enough time to assess numbers of the army, and gather more rumours about where else the men had been dispatched. Emperor Carlton's forces were beginning to add up to a significant size. It was startling.

Damian also became aware of plans for a new offensive, but no one had information about when or where. Would they come through the border at a different spot, or try to enlarge the holding they already had around Discovery? From what he saw in the village, it looked more like a holding pattern, but that could obviously change in a hurry.

Leaving Discovery early in the morning to hunt for elk, he'd returned across the Legitamia border. Then he'd promptly abandoned the fictitious hunting expedition and headed west to where they'd originally entered weeks ago. Finding the original trail was his first priority, and once he stumbled across it, he broke into a run. His ident was hidden along this track, and he would need it once he was back in Khandarken.

He found a weak signal on his voicelink and sent a short message to Cownden Lanser, informing him where he was and the expected time of hitting the border region. Still, it was almost dark by the time he found the tree, and dug around in the rotted hollow for the rubber plastic document. He used his finger to trace the letters on the face of it, and carefully wrapped Nikesh's ident in the onion skin and tucked it back into the hiding place.

Then he found the nearest hunter's hut and bedded down. He'd long since lost the banner the Emperor's men wore across their chests, and cut the collar off his shirt to get rid of the detailed stitching. This time there was only one other man in the hut, who was already asleep. As Damian pushed his way through the warped door, the fellow sat up and glared at him for a moment, then subsided again in slumber.

Damian kicked some straw together and found his own spot. Within moments he was asleep, his voicelink shut down and tucked securely in his boot.

It took another full day of travel before he caught up to the fellow in the battered transport near Krimen. As arranged, he was waiting patiently beside his vehicle at a roadside pané and ale shop.

For the first time since they left the City, Damian felt the tension ease in his gut. He took a deep breath and climbed behind the frontboard of the vehicle. *He was heading toward Fanny now, not in the other direction.* Suddenly everything seemed possible.

CHAPTER FORTY FIVE

Damian was coming. Gazing into the plexi mirror in her office in the City, Fanny fastened a stray length of hair with an ivory pin and pinched her cheeks. This was far from her first day on the job, but suddenly she was flustered. The campaign would start up again shortly, this time in the Collaros Territory, and Toll had let her know that new guards had been appointed.

Unsteadily, she seated herself behind her desk and glanced at the infolink where the schedule for the next leg of the campaign was laid out in detail. Having already covered the south and west, they would be doing more travelling in the next weeks. She hoped Ms Maya would be able to manage at home. Thankfully, she'd been able to persuade her to keep Tippy the housemaid employed, what with the extra people in the place. Boulter ate like a horse now, and his tutor Mr Weisner had taken up residence while Fanny was away.

There was a knock on her open door and Toll poked his head in. "Damian and Linus have just arrived. Can I bring them in?"

She flushed, the heat climbing her throat. "Yes, of course." *By all the angels, was she going to blush every time she laid eyes on the man?* This could get very awkward. Yet she'd been hoping, praying to see him again. The night they'd had together in the Transit Hotel had been like a dream—a fairy tale. The way his arms surrounded her, his body moved against her and in her...

She grabbed a jug of cold water and quickly poured some into a bowl to take a drink as Toll backed through the door and Damian stepped forward, a second man hovering behind him. He looked magnificent, tall and lean, shoulders and arms heavy from his fighting arts training. She hadn't forgotten how he looked, but seeing him again just reminded her anew of his physical presence. His face was different, thinner, the expression more distant and shuttered with lips pressed firmly together.

Cownden had mentioned Damian had been sent north on a mission and would be gone some weeks. Obviously, it had not been an easy task.

She smiled but Damian didn't respond. It was as if he'd forgotten their time together, the bonding that took place during that long night. Her heart stuttered beneath her breastbone.

"Ms Master," he said in a formal tone. "I understand we have a job to do here, as your bodyguards during the travelling campaign. Linus is going to work with me, if you don't mind."

"No, I don't mind. Greetings, Linus." She nodded at the man and he saluted with a smile.

Turning to Damian, she said, "We leave tomorrow for four days travelling through the Collaros Territory then back to the City before we go into the Northern Territory. Do you have the schedule?"

He gave an abrupt nod. "We do. Is there anything else?"

"Yes. Just have a seat and perhaps Linus can find himself a tea and wait in the entry."

Damian went red and Linus nodded as he gave a shallow bow and left the room, closing the door behind him.

Fanny moved around her desk to stand before him, placing her palm on his chest over his heavily beating heart.

His face went from flushed to pale and beads of sweat formed on his forehead. "Don't do this, Fanny. I beg you." His voice came out ragged.

Tears appeared in her eyes. "Do you not care for me at all, Damian?" she said.

His arms slowly went round her waist and he tugged her uncertainly against him. "I care. It's killing me, but I care. I don't know how I can do this job, guarding you, when I can't forget that night we had." He closed his eyes. "It doesn't work, us being together this way."

Fanny wiped a tear away with the back of her hand. "I think it works very well. I've been waiting for you, Damian."

His gaze was fierce as he turned back. "What do you mean?"

"I've missed you. "

"By the God of heaven," he murmured. "I've missed you too. It felt like I was dying." He lifted his head. "But I'm to be your guard, not your man. I can't court you."

"I know." Her eyes shone up at him. "We can't be together for now. While we're travelling on the campaign trail, everything has to be done right or it will reflect on Cownden. But I'll be safe. I feel safe with you."

He tugged her up against him and leaned his cheek against her hair. "I'll keep you safe, Fanny, I swear."

She sighed as the knot in her chest unwound. *She'd be all right now, Damian was finally here.*

~ * * * ~

There was a thunderous banging on the door and the doorman leapt from his stool in the kitchen to answer. DuSatoy leaned from the dining hall to watch his progress. "Be careful who you let in," he called.

He'd begun to have nightmares. In his dreams, his staff had deserted and he was alone in the house, the horses untended in the stables, when a group of Constables rode up to the door. Perhaps it was time to make a decision, because things were definitely not going his way at the moment.

The door crashed open and the doorman was knocked back against the wall from the impact. "They're coming!" It was the guard he had posted down by the corral, running with the news. The man stood on the doorstep, head hanging in exhaustion. "They're here," he gasped again, "Right behind me."

DuSatoy grabbed his napkin from around his throat and jumped to his feet. "Saddle horses out back," he barked. "Get my case, I'll meet you in the stables. Run!"

"You." He pointed to the doorman. "Keep them here, tell them I'm upstairs and you'll send someone to fetch me."

DuSatoy was on his horse in minutes, his case jammed in the saddlebag. He left at a gallop, two of his men keeping pace, with the sound of yelling and crashing receding in the distance behind them as the Constables forced their way into his manorhouse.

He knew the track like the back of his hand. He should have taken this step before. But definitely now it was time to get to the Monarch's establishment. It wasn't so bad there, even though it was outside Khandarken borders. The main floor rooms were all finished, he'd heard, and Sable had a competent cook.

The main problem was having to look at Sable's torn face, it was a disgusting sight. But there were ways around that, too. Perhaps he'd just take his meals in his room.

CHAPTER FORTY SIX

Collaros Territory was a sparsely populated area and in the fall, like now, the barren plains were dry and brown. Fanny had planned seven campaign stops once the events in Martonosha were over. Governor Norcross had given them a fabulous reception, with every conceivable member from government and military officials to business in attendance.

Fanny had been hard pressed to tell if all these people actually supported Cownden Lanser, but the enthusiasm was so effervescent, she was caught up in it anyway. The mood was uplifting, and Cownden and Selanna were laughing as they moved around the centre of the town greeting the residents. They were buoyed up by it and set out on a round trip tour of the territory in a good mood.

The first stop was Krimen and everywhere Fanny turned, Damian was one step behind her, his body tense, his eyes roving the crowds. She was warmed by his very presence. At dinner that night in the Northern Lights Hotel, Cownden and Selanna ate in their room. Toll joined Fanny at a table in the dining hall, but didn't stay long.

"I'm fine, Toll," she said, when he offered to escort her to her room. "I need to talk to Damian, and then he'll take me up."

Damian seemed reluctant to sit. "Fanny, I should be standing against the wall like Linus, not joining you at your table." His teeth clamped shut as he reluctantly lowered himself to the chair.

"I want you here," she said with a gentle smile. "I need to talk to you."

He nodded and waited, his eyes on her face. "About what?"

"About Boulter. You saw him in Deep Creek, you know what he looked like. How old would you say he was?"

He stilled and then carefully glanced around the room at the few remaining guests. "I'm not sure, Fanny. He was an undetermined age. What did his ident say?"

"It didn't."

He glanced back at her. "The ident usually gives an age, or date of birth."

"But it didn't, Damian. No age. And I've had Anatoliy do a search for his information, given we have his mother's name, and we can't find anything.

We're here in Martonosha where the ident was issued, so I thought…"

She gave him a desperate look. "The thing is, Governor Norcross had his people conduct a search but they found nothing. If you saw Boulter now, you'd think he was twelve or fourteen. It's so strange. He was just little, maybe four years old when I found him in that ditch. And now he's almost grown. There's something not right, and I'm not sure…" She looked down and tears fell on the tablecloth before her.

Damian took her hand in his and held it. "Calm down, Fanny. It's alright, I think I can help. Listen, when we get back I'll have Da come and take a look at him. He's already given him a medical exam, the day you left him with me in Deep Creek. Remember? Well, Dr Stuke had some ideas as to what's going on."

She gazed at him hopefully, the tears still running down her cheek. "You didn't tell me. What did he find?"

He moved uncomfortably and used his thumb to wipe her tears away. "I didn't completely understand it, myself, so it'd be better if he told you. That way you'd know what he was saying and could question him if need be. So hold onto that thought. The minute we're back, Da will come and see you at the house. I'll arrange it."

"You'll be there, won't you Damian?"

His jaw firmed. "By the graves, I will. If you want me there, Fanny, no one can keep me away."

She watched his cheeks go dark under the force of her smile. "Thank you."

"Now," he said, glancing away uncomfortably as he rose from the chair. "Linus and I will take you up to your room. You need your rest, and I can't take much more of this—sitting beside you but not being able to touch you." His smile was rueful, his gaze determined. "Let's go."

~ * * * ~

Fanny paced twice around her tiny room in the Northern Lights Hotel. Linus occupied the room on one side of her, and Damian the one on the other. Selanna and Cownden had a similar setup down the hall. Toll was meticulous about attending to details and the security arrangements worked well. But having Damian right next door was too stressful for words.

She paced once more between bed and door, from the window to the desk on the far wall, then reached for her voicelink. Entering the particulars, she waited no more than a second.

"Fanny?" Damian sounded startled. "Are you all right?"

Fanny's throat suddenly had a catch in it, and she struggled to reply. "Can you come over here, please? I need to see you."

"Why? What's wrong?" She heard him shift on the sheets. He must already be in bed, they were doing long days on this tour.

"Nothing's wrong. I just need to talk to you."

There was a pause. "Fanny, if I come over there…"

"I know," she breathed into the speaker. "I need you."

"By all the gods…" He was silent for a moment. "Are you sure, because I'm just balancing on the edge right now, Fanny. I'm holding it together, but I can't take much more."

"I'm sure."

"I'll be right there." The link clicked down and a moment later she heard a soft rap on the door.

She leaned against the panel. "Who's there?" she called low. She wasn't a total idiot, even though she'd just invited Damian over didn't mean there couldn't be someone else entirely at her door.

"Open the door, Fanny." His voice held a wealth of intent in the firm tones.

Fanny pulled the lock off and twisted the handle as the door swung inward. Damian stood there, his head turned to check the hallway behind him. "Let me in," he said, and herded her back with his body, closing the panel behind him.

He wore his pants and unclipped boots, a shirt thrown over his shoulders and he looked dangerous and wonderfully familiar. She leaned in and pressed her face to his chest as his arms wrapped tightly around her. The feel of his body, the scent of him was almost more than she could bear. Something quaked in her belly, and she hung on tightly to steady herself as her head spun.

Since the death of her father, life had been out of control. Even now, things were in flux. The campaign was going well but they were coming from behind both DuSatoy and Jack Learmonth, who had begun work on the election much earlier. Boulter was a confusing puzzle that tugged at her heart with both hope and fear, and Damian had been almost out of reach. She panted, her ear pressed to hear the steady strong beat of his heart.

He bent and swung her into his arms, laying her gently on the pallet.

"Lie beside me, Damian." She reached toward him.

His shirt hit the floor, followed shortly by his pants and boots shed in one quick motion. She was still wrestling with the tie on her blouse when his fingers pushed hers aside and swiftly conquered the task. He tugged her skirt and smalls over her hips to toss them at the foot of the bed.

Then he pressed a knee to the pallet and leaned over her. "Fanny, marry with me," he said. "I don't have much to offer but what I have is yours. I can't live like this, not knowing if you're mine, or if I can see you. It's tearing me in two. Marry with me."

Her heart stuttered in her chest at the aching look in his eyes. She reached out to him, pulling on his shoulders. "Lie here, Damian. I need you now."

With a muttered imprecation, he gently lowered himself to the pallet and wrapped his body around her. Her heart eased, her breath slowed. Something shifted within, and the tension seemed to flow away. Damian was here, everything was going to be okay.

As he lowered his mouth to hers, she lifted her face and welcomed him. Lovely soft kisses, a soothing connection that slowly grew in strength until his breath came shallow in his throat and she panted heavily against his shoulder. His hands were powerful and knowing. They roved her body, finding all the places that ached for him and assuaging that ache, yet causing it to increase and focus until she felt she couldn't take any more.

Then he rose above her, positioning himself and steadily forcing his way in. It was slow torture, heavenly reward. He nudged deep and she rose to welcome him. Sweat dripped down the sides of his face and she wiped it away with her fingers. Still he moved, the motion steady and hypnotic.

Suddenly she couldn't wait, rising and straining against him. Yet he held her back, a hand on her hip to pin her to the pallet.

"Slow," he gasped. "Just slow, baby. Soon now." She bucked under the tension and he drove himself home. It was too much. When she opened her mouth, he crushed his lips over hers to contain her cries. Then he moved faster and with such purpose that he followed her down.

CHAPTER FORTY SEVEN

Damian gathered her close, running his fingers through the beautiful golden strands of hair. She seemed to doze for a few moments, but he was wide awake.

Would she marry with him? She hadn't answered, yet it seemed the best thing to do. It was going to be a devastation when she learned about Boulter. When the child left, as was bound to happen, she would be alone again. Damian had no illusions about who he was —a damaged man. But Selanna had straightened him out yet again, so the nightmares had vanished as if they'd never been. Didn't mean they wouldn't be back, but he had a way to deal with them.

What about Fanny's nightmares? Being abandoned must be her worst fear. She seemed to need him, and by all the gods of heaven he needed her. Even a damaged man had his uses.

He couldn't stay here in the room with her. He was on duty and this was the last thing he was supposed to be doing. Nor could he allow anyone to find him here and compromise his woman that way. He rose quietly and tugged on his clothes, shoving his feet into the boots.

When Fanny raised a pale face, he leaned to give her a kiss good night. "Lock the door behind me, Fanny. Lock it tight."

~ * * * ~

Sable was waiting in his great entry when DuSatoy finally strode through the door. He waved at his houseman to fetch ale and watched as his visitor settled on the lounge opposite. Purposely Sable turned his head to give DuSatoy a good view of the ruined side of his face, and had to suppress a laugh when he looked back to see the man had lowered his gaze to his hands where they clasped tightly in his lap. Squeamish, the man was squeamish.

"Well, what brings you here today?" Sable looked innocently at his guest. Not that he didn't know. Waite had gotten word to him last night about a raid at DuSatoy's enclave and the race into the night. It had only been a matter of time before he showed up across the border at the Monarch's door.

For a man who couldn't stand the sight of Sable's face, he had nerve to trot in here looking for sanctuary. As it was, the strongman was of no use to Sable now. With the Constables searching for DuSatoy inside Khandarken, and his network of mercenaries who controlled the border in shambles, Sable was ready to write him off. If a relationship didn't work, there was no reason to hold onto it. He'd done this before.

DuSatoy shifted in his seat and lifted his gaze as far as the midway point on Sable's lean chest. "I need a break from the campaign," he said. "Things are getting heated in the south, so I'm taking the time to visit all my contacts and reinforce our business arrangements."

Sable nodded and sipped his ale. He swished the liquid on the other side of his mouth and carefully swallowed, holding a cloth to his cheek to catch what managed to leak out. His guest quickly glanced away, looking out the back window to the construction in the rear of the compound.

"Have you seen my new barns?" Sable remarked. "I see you've just noticed them. We finished a couple of weeks ago. Come and have a look."

He rose to his feet, heading for the back door, and DuSatoy reluctantly fell into step beside him. The huge yard was now surrounded by a new rock wall with gates at the back. Sable was thrilled with the progress he'd made. It was starting to feel like a home, if he could call it that. There weren't many people here – his doorman and houseman, a chef and odd jobber for the manorhouse. Then there were a few men who cared for the animals and rode as guards when he left his holdings, and a trio of workers who continued with the construction. But it was slowly coming together.

Standing in the walkway of the stables, he turned to his unwanted visitor. "How long do you plan to stay?"

DuSatoy's face went a dull red. "Not long. Just trying to catch my breath. A week or two perhaps. I have to complete my campaign for Leader and need to take some time to get further plans in place."

Sable felt a smile coming on. *A couple of weeks? That was plenty of time to complete what he had in mind.*

DuSatoy's tone turned sullen. "After all I've done for you, it shouldn't be a problem."

Sable shrugged. "I've paid for everything you've done, DuSatoy. Everything." He strolled down the aisle, checking the horse stalls. His stallion nickered as he approached and he stopped to smooth his hand over the satin skin of its nose.

"My houseman will show you to a room," he said over his shoulder. "Dinner is at seven."

CHAPTER FORTY EIGHT

Damian sat in the entry of Fanny's home, her hand in his, as they waited for Da. Dr Stuke had taken Boulter into the back room and the silence emanating from there was deafening. Finally the door opened, and Boulter came out, his stride confident, face serene.

"Mum, he'd like to talk to you now." He leaned to give Fanny a hug. "Just go right in, he's waiting."

Fanny's gaze was searching as she stared at her son, then she rose and made her way down the hall. Damian watched her disappear behind the closing door, then switched his gaze to the boy. "What did Da say?"

Boulter shrugged self-consciously. "He already knew that I was a traveller. You know, from the other world. He guessed it last time he saw me, remember?"

Damian grunted in reply. "When did you discover it for yourself, Boulter?"

The boy's face paled. "I saw the travellers just before we left Deep Creek. It was kind of scary, you know?" His face scrunched up like the child he had been in those days. "But they explained that my other mother had died and Mum came along and offered to look after me when I needed it most."

He gazed down the hallway uncertainly. "I'm not sure when I have to leave. Last time they came, they told me there wasn't too much time left."

Damian clamped a hand on his shoulder. "Don't worry, son. I'll look after her. But it's going to be tough. She loves you."

Boulter's eyes shone. "I know. I love her too." He rubbed his hands down his young face. "She's been a great mother for me. I'm so lucky she came along when she did. I might have died." His shoulders shook, and Damian wrapped an arm around him as he cried.

When the door opened again, Dr Stuke emerged, his medicine bag in hand. Boulter had already left to finish his work in the garden and Damian waited alone. He rose. "How is she, Da? Can I see her?"

Da looked older, his shoulders stooped, his hand thin where it gripped the handles of his bag. "She's laying down, son. Give her some time, it's been quite a shock. And she's had a lot to deal with in the last while."

"Yah, I know." Damian glanced at the closed door. "Is she sleeping?"

Da nodded. "Be patient. She needs to process all this. Best to let her rest."

"So, what now? How old is Boulter, do you think? That was the question that got us here in the first place." He moved his shoulders impatiently and frowned at his father.

Dr Stuke lowered himself to the lounge. "Right now, I'd say he's fifteen, give or take. Amazing, really. I mean I saw him those few months ago, and he was no more than five. He's a strapping boy, strong, intelligent, and caring. She's very proud of him, and rightly so."

Damian paced the room. "I don't know what to do. Should I take you back to the City? I really need to be here. I have to stay close. This is a tense time."

Da smiled, his implanted teeth glittering a bright white. "No worries, son. She's asked me to stay for dinner. Just relax, see that Boulter is doing what he should, and she'll be ready to talk in a bit."

~ * * * ~

Fanny rolled over on the lounge in the back room and propped her head against the arm rest. Someone had draped the throw over her and she was comfortably warm. She stared out the back plexi where Boulter was talking animatedly with Damian and gesturing toward the back of the garden.

She smiled fondly at his constant enthusiasm, then her heart stuttered in its beat. Her son would be leaving soon. That was the main message she'd taken from what Dr Stuke had to say. She already knew in her soul that he was different – his growth had been astounding, his leaps in intelligence, his knowledge improving daily. She'd understood that he was not a normal little boy growing up under her care.

But that he would leave her – it broke her heart. One more loss to add to all the others. She closed her eyes in distress. She wasn't crying, but still the tears crept down her cheeks. Impatiently she brushed them away and threw the quilt off.

She glanced to the back of the yard, but Damian was gone and Boulter stood talking to two men in long plain robes. Mickens patrolled beside his feet.

No! Was now the time? She dashed through the back entry onto the grass. As she approached, Boulter glanced up and gave her a brilliant smile. He held out his hand to her. "Mum, these are the travellers. They wanted to meet you."

Fanny looked into those still, softly glowing faces and felt a pang in her chest. "He can't leave yet. He's not ready."

"No, Mum. It's not time yet." Boulter squeezed her fingers and Mickens leaned on her leg, rubbing his head back and forth.

One of the men reached to place a hand on her shoulder. It felt like a light caress. "I see Boulter, and it is good. You've done a fine job." His voice seemed to fade away in the breeze.

Fanny smiled. "He's been a good boy." Trembling, she placed an arm around his sturdy shoulders and glanced back, but the men were gone.

CHAPTER FORTY NINE

Fanny lay sleepless in her bed. Dr Stuke's news had left her rudderless and she'd spent days wrestling with it. Wasn't it enough that she had to deal with Boulter's situation, that he was leaving her soon? But no, as she had trembled in her chair listening to the medic's news about her son, trying to take it all in – that Boulter was a traveller, an angel, and would soon be leaving to join his own people, Dr Stuke had mentioned something else.

"You look tired and drawn," he said. "I know how busy you have been, working with my daughter Selanna and her husband Cownden, and I admire you for that." His kind eyes smiled into hers. "But this is something else, let me take a quick look."

He took her hand, using a probe to hover over her wrist, then her chest, finally her belly. He nodded as if simply confirming what he had already suspected.

"You are with child," he pronounced and grinned. "This is good news, my dear."

Good news? Her world had turned upside down once more. She was to have a baby. *How had it come to this, that she was so unaware?* Too many events piled one upon the other in the last months. Too many decisions and steps to be taken that had left her no time to care for herself.

As she rolled once more to her side, and adjusted the bolster beneath her head, she thought of what this meant. First, it meant if Boulter left, she wouldn't be alone. The comfort of that thought was immeasurable. Not that she could exchange one child for another. There was a firm and fixed place in her heart for Boulter, and that would never change. But the feeling of abandonment was not so strong, the thought that she would be totally alone didn't have the same hold on her.

She shifted the other way and adjusted the cover. She had to tell Damian, it was only right. But still she hesitated. There never seemed to be any privacy. Linus was on duty tonight and Damian would have retreated to his own room. With Ms Maya, the new house maid, and Mr Weisner living with her and Boulter, adding two guards to the ménage created a very crowded home.

She sighed and glanced restlessly through the plexi. The half-moon shone low in the sky and lit the corner of her room like a handlight. It was too bright to sleep.

Catching her night dress from the post at the foot of her pallet, she shrugged it on. Maybe a bowl of hot tea would be enough to soothe her nerves and allow her to rest. She crept silently down the stairs.

Moonlight shone through the plexi in the garden door and illuminated the heavy rocking chair in the back room as low music rose from the speakers. A pair of sock feet twitched in the beam of light, then Damian rose from the chair. "Fanny?" He strode into the hall and peered up at her. "What's wrong? Are you ill?"

"Damian, I thought you'd be asleep." Her heart hammered in her chest. She had to give him the news, she just wasn't as prepared as she thought she would be. What if he was angry, felt betrayed or trapped?

"No, not asleep." He came forward and climbed the first step toward her. "What do you need?" he said.

She smiled. That part was easy. "You," she said. "I need you."

Later, as she lay boneless on his shoulder, he tightened his arm around her and pulled her full against him. "Fanny, we can't continue to do this. Boulter might discover me here, he'd be shocked. Or Mr Weisner might hear me, let alone Linus. It won't be good for your reputation."

She nodded and smoothed her fingers across his chest. "I know we can't."

He grabbed her hand to get her attention. "Marry with me," he urged. "I can help you. When Boulter leaves, you won't be alone. I can do that for you, Fanny."

She rose up on one elbow. "You need to know everything about me before you decide that."

"There's not much I don't know," he murmured, his fingers pushing back through her hair.

She giggled and his kiss drowned out any more words for a long time.

Later she came slowly awake as Damian slid from the pallet. "Wait!" There was so much to say and she hadn't even started. "Damian, we need to talk."

"Talk?" He leaned down and tugged the blanket up over her shoulder. "I have to get out of here before Linus comes looking for me to start my shift. Go to sleep. You need your rest."

"Damian, I'm to have a baby."

He stalled, then sagged back onto the pallet. "A baby? A child? By the graves..." He gazed in wonder at her. "Really? When did you... Ah." He blinked as light dawned. "Did Da tell you?"

She nodded. "He guessed, I didn't even know myself."

"I'm not surprised." He smoothed his fingers down her cheek. "You've been busy for a while now."

She laughed. "Yes, since our night in the Transit Hotel in Deep Creek."

He cradled her in his arms. "Yah, that night. You changed my life, Fanny." He threaded his fingers through hers. "I never imagined being a father. It didn't seem... Well, it didn't seem likely, in my line of work."

Her smile was gentle. "You'll make a wonderful father, Damian. I can see you now. Just the way you've been with Boulter, instructive and patient, so attentive."

His expression grew determined. "Fanny, we can't delay. We have to marry now. I'll look into the license."

She smoothed her hand down his naked back. "I haven't agreed yet," she teased.

"Very funny." He leaned down and she saw a new determination in his eyes as he pinned her to the pallet with a fierce kiss. "When shall we marry?"

She blushed. "Right away," she replied. "As soon as we can."

CHAPTER FIFTY

Fanny tried to organize the wedding, but between Selanna and Julianne the reins were taken out of her hands almost from the beginning.

"You have way too much to do right now, Fanny," Julianne decreed. "And I've done this before so I have an advantage in the organizing department."

Selanna had snorted elegantly at that statement. "Don't listen to her. Have you heard the story of her marriage? The ceremony was performed on the deck of a fish boat on the Catastrophic Ocean. She was wearing a dress with the hem dragging on the ground and her husband had a borrowed shirt and boots from the tribesmen. Luckily he removed the bells before the event took place."

The women laughed and Fanny turned to her friend. "Is that true, Julianne? I have to hear that story. But right now, we need to focus. This is just a small ceremony, right? Boulter will stand up with me as my family, and Damian will have you, Selanna, and your father. There won't be many guests. But you will come won't you, Julianne?"

Julianne took her hand. "Nothing can keep me away. Let me take care of the guest list. Selanna says she can organize the food and refreshments."

Selanna grinned. "That just means I pass it on to Anatoliy to arrange. You know that, right?"

Fanny began to relax and enjoy herself. A small gathering, in her back yard if the weather held, and she would be married. However, things didn't turn out quite that easy to manage.

Soon a cook named Hannan showed up at her door. "She's the best," boasted Julianne. "She handles everything in the kitchens at Farmer Holdings and she volunteered to organize things for you." Three days of baking and cooking later, Ms Maya was in a frenzy. The fourth day, a string of helpers filed in loaded down with baskets of food.

Fanny began to worry at the volume of preparation, but Selanna distracted her with the task of re-writing Cownden's speeches for the final campaign tour through the north of Khandarken. "I know you won't be coming with us, Fanny," Selanna said. She rearranged the flowers on Fanny's desk, sent that morning by Damian.

"But that's fine. You've got us organized and trained now, and we aren't as helpless as we were when you first started work with Cownden. Just make sure he says all the right things and we'll handle the rest of the tour. By the way, what are you wearing for the wedding?" Selanna asked. "Do you have your mother's dress?"

Fanny shook her head. "I can't find anything like that in the trunks upstairs. Anyway, my mother wasn't built like me, I took after Father in that regard. Not the girth, but the short stature. Although..." She glanced down at her midriff. "I imagine the girth will arrive."

Selanna hugged her. "I'm so happy for you, Fanny. I'm so happy for my brother. Damian has changed, just since he met you. It's wonderful to see." Her eyes filled with tears. "I never thought he'd create a life for himself like this – with a family, children. I hope you are both very happy."

Fanny felt a thrill run beneath her breastbone. It was exciting that Damian's family had been so welcoming. Dr Stuke was the kindest man and now Selanna was becoming a true friend.

The next day Selanna arrived at her front door accompanied by Julianne. Beth Farmer, with her little baby, was also there and the transport driver who escorted them to the door carried a large package under his arm. It held a wedding dress.

~ * * * ~

The guest list grew. Many people from her parents' lives contacted her, insisting they would like to come. The ceremony itself would be held at the tiny neighbourhood church that Mr and Ms Master had attended.

The middle-aged priest had known the family well and was very pleased to conduct the service. The nave was tiny, and Damian and Fanny, with Boulter and Selanna standing with them, barely fit into the space as the binding words were said. Guests were packed into the pews and stood against the walls along the back of the building.

Fanny looked up into Damian's dark eyes and felt a thrill of wonder. Finally, a positive step. Finally, things were going right for her. She loved this man with her whole heart. He looked handsome and solemn in his new suit.

Boulter was maturely solemn and childishly giddy by turns but he managed to bear witness with aplomb and signed his mark, alongside Selanna's, like any adult. Fanny was so proud of him. He'd learned a lot from Mr Weisner, who reported they were charging through the lessons as fast as he could manage.

Arriving back at the house, she realized the yard was packed. Her good friend Julianne was there with her husband Abe Farmer. She'd been introduced to the family and liked what she saw. Julianne was obviously happy. Abe's sister Bethlehem arrived with Major Dante Regiment and their very young son. He was a beautiful baby, dark skinned like his father with the luminescent pale blue eyes of the Farmers.

General Paulo Regiment came, announcing that Fanny was almost like family so he couldn't stay away. With him was Governor Frank Maude. It wasn't common knowledge, but with Damian working for Maude, the connection was close.

FitzGibbon arrived, and was exceedingly civil to Cownden Lanser, an obvious change of heart about who he supported for Leader. John Longo, the minister of defense accompanied him, his connection to Cownden close since her father's death.

Fanny's heart felt blessed when Elliott walked in, accompanied by two booksellers from Old Towne, Saxby Wordsmith and his wife, along with Brentwood Holmes, businessmen her mother had worked with in her search for rare tomes for her book collection. Mr Weisner was obviously acquainted with them as well, their membership in the Men's Club in Old Towne the common thread. Many increasingly jovial toasts to the bride and groom were made, to their huge enjoyment.

The lawn milled with people. It reminded Fanny of the affairs she used to attend in the heart of the City, usually at the Learmonth Hotel. Jack Learmonth, minus the young woman he'd had with him earlier during the campaigning, arrived with his son. Fanny grinned and introduced them to Damian, who looked so much more mature to her eyes than the young heir to the distillery estate.

Boulter was very social, moving around with a group of young people his age who'd attended with their parents. Jack Learmonth's young daughter seemed very taken with him, and he grinned good-naturedly at all the attention.

CHAPTER FIFTY ONE

W ould you like to hold the baby?" Fanny took a seat beside Beth Farmer and looked down into the sleeping infant's face. His large eyes were closed, the eyelids translucent.

"I'd love it." As she took the small bundle in her arms, she felt a thrill beneath her breast. She would have one of her own soon, a little child just like this one. She stroked a finger along the downy cheek. "His skin is so soft. It's like silk."

Beth smiled and nodded. "Yes, it's amazing. I didn't know until the moment I held him in my arms how exciting it would be."

Fanny glanced at her. "Thank you for the loan of this dress. Ms Maya adjusted the hem and it fits like a glove, as you can see. Damian liked it immensely."

"I'm not surprised." Beth chuckled. "You look like an angel in it. Did you know Selanna wore it for her wedding? My mother chose well, that three of us wore her wedding dress with pride."

Tears came to Fanny's eyes. "That's a wonderful gift, that you shared it with me. I'm proud to join that group of women."

"You're welcome, Fanny." Beth squeezed her fingers. "Julianne would have worn it as well, I'm sure, if Abe hadn't been in such a hurry that he couldn't wait to get on dry land to say his vows."

Fanny laughed and rocked the child in her arms.

"Your husband is trying to get your attention. Perhaps you'd better see what he needs."

Fanny glanced up to see Damian impatiently listening to a long lecture of some kind, with Cownden on one side of him, Dante on the other taking turns adding their comments.

~ * * * ~

Damian helped Fanny into the transport and tucked the skirt of her beautiful wedding dress in beside her before carefully closing the door. Then he got behind the frontboard and pulled out into the street. A string of well-wishers were lined up along the verge, waving and calling what sounded like less-than-helpful advice for the coming night. He was glad he couldn't hear most of what was being said. Hopefully nor could his wife. His wife. The very thought made his breath catch in his throat and his stomach clench. He tugged at the tight collar of his new suit.

Glancing at Fanny, he saw she had turned to wave to the crowd, blowing a kiss to Boulter. He stood in the midst of a group of young people, cheeks bright red, cheering the vehicle as it pulled away.

Then she straightened and leaned against the bolster, sighing a long breath.

"You okay?" He took her fingers and held them in his hand.

She smiled at him. "I'm fine, more than fine." She looked so beautiful, his eyes watered and he blinked at the sight of the strand blurring in front of him until his vision cleared.

They didn't have far to go. He'd booked a room in the Learmonth Hotel for the night. Cownden had warned him. With the event being held at the house, he wouldn't be able to get her alone for hours as the guests took their time socializing and expressing their best wishes to the couple before slowly departing the scene. It had sounded like torture. This way, he and Fanny could wave goodbye and be on their way, leaving Julianne and Abe, Selanna and Cownden to handle the crowd. Best advice he'd had in a long time.

Linus was already at the hotel, canvassing the place and ensuring their rooms were secure. But the news had reached them that day. Dante had called, reporting that one of his special forces had confirmed DuSatoy was still on the run, the would-be politician was somewhere along the northern border of Khandarken working on his election campaign.

Cownden had later confirmed that Sable Maude was in conflict with DuSatoy, perhaps too many strongmen in one region, or a clash of wills in an area where only one man got to dictate how things turned out. There was a regional battle going on, that his constables did their best to circumvent.

Damian had been relieved to hear hear the news. He could assure Fanny that she was safe for the moment. Rutman was in jail, DuSatoy had travelled north. The election campaign was drawing to a close, and the wedding was finally over.

He glanced at his wife. She was his now, finally his. And they had a child on the way. His breath caught again and he concentrated on the sharp turn into the hotel entrance. Climbing out, he helped Fanny from the vehicle, grabbed their luggage and handed the transport over to Linus. Then they were inside the Learmonth.

The lobby was luxurious and welcoming, decorated in warm colours of rose to wine from the dyed silk wall coverings to the hand-woven carpets. The detailing of gold and silver leaf added just the right touch of opulence.

A greeter escorted them to their room overlooking the inner courtyard and gardens. Candle lights in plexi shades were planted amongst the flowers to give an amber glow in the square below.

Closing the door on the greeter, Damian placed their bags on the bench and turned to his wife. "How do you feel? We can just relax here and have a glass of wine, or we can go down to dinner. What would you like to do?"

She looked into his eyes and his heart stopped for a moment, then started again to a slower, steady beat. She was his now, he would take care of her.

"I'm tired Damian. I'd like to go to bed."

The teasing look was enough to start a smile at the corner of his mouth. "Don't play with me, wife. I'm hanging on by a thread. I'm trying to do the right thing here."

Her laugh prompted a full grin.

"Okay, if you want to play like that, take your clothes off," he instructed. "If you can." He examined the back of her dress. "I'm not sure how this works."

"I think I can manage," she said, reaching to unfasten a tiny row of buttons across one shoulder and under her arm. "Just here," she said and he stepped forward to help. The fasteners were very small and his fingers felt all thumbs as he fumbled to ease them through the holes, but finally the last one released and the bodice of the dress sagged forward.

"Oh, Fanny." He tugged it lower. "You are so lovely. What a fortunate man I am, how did I get so lucky?"

By the time Fanny crawled up onto the pallet, Damian was right behind, settling beside her to pull her body on top of his. "Kiss me, wife," he said and sealed his lips over hers.

When he came up for air, he took a moment to smooth her hair back, the curls curving around his fingers and hanging on. "Marry with me, Fanny," he said. She smiled and there was no need to say more.

Later they ordered dinner in their room and a sumptuous feast arrived with two footmen to attend. Damian allowed them just enough time to set the dishes out on the small table by the plexi before banishing them from the room.

He propped Fanny up in bed and fed her bits of roasted llama, pieces of smoked cheese and curdled astrofruit. "You see," he said, passing her a bowl of pale wine, "everything is new again. Our whole lives begin from now, but in a different way. You've given me a new life, Fanny."

She leaned on his shoulder, lingering over a plate of ripe dumplings. The warm weight of her seemed to press on his heart. To think he was no longer a gamer's man, enforcer of debts, but instead a member of the special forces and married to someone like Fanny. He closed his eyes a moment.

"Damian," she murmured, "when the baby comes, things will be different again."

He nodded and put his arm carefully around her bare shoulder. "Yah, I know. I can't wait. Boulter was so cute when he was little, he pulled at my heart strings, you know? Even now that he's almost grown, I can still see the child he was as well as the man he'll soon become."

Her gaze was anxious. "He'll be going soon."

"I know that, too." He tightened his hold. "It'll be alright. You've been a wonderful mother. It's a gift that you were given time with him. Be glad." He wiped a tear from her cheek. "Be glad."

CHAPTER FIFTY TWO

"Mum, can you come? They want to talk to you." Boulter looked anxious as he poked his head around the kitchen door.

Fanny looked up in surprise from her perusal of soup recipes that Ms Maya had handed her. "Boulter, what is it? Who wants to see me?"

"It's the travellers," he said.

She glanced around for Damian. She was still nervous, hadn't totally settled down and acknowledged the fact that Rutman, the man who tried to kill her, was in prison and his boss was dead. Just then her husband walked in, laying a hand on Boulter's shoulder. "What's going on?" he said.

Fanny felt her shoulders relax at the sight of him. He gave her a cheeky grin and her face flushed as she thought of what he'd done to her just this morning when she woke in the marriage bed. He was a very attentive husband.

She firmed her mouth. "I'm coming, Boulter. Where are they?"

Boulter led her out the garden door into the back yard, Damian following close behind. Mickens ran in circles excitedly, then dashed toward the back lane. The men were waiting at the bottom of the lawn, their long gray robes shifting in the slight breeze.

Why were they back so soon? Fanny glanced nervously at her son, but he was focussed on the men.

The tallest of the strangers held out his hand as she drew near and Fanny extended her hand in greeting. He held her fingers for a moment as he looked deep into her eyes. He had such a light touch as to almost seem imaginary. He released her and bowed his head. *We wish to thank you for your care of Boulter. He needed you and you were there for him, even in your own distressful condition.*

Fanny's heart staggered in her chest. This sounded too much like a farewell speech. "You needn't thank me. Caring for Boulter has been more than rewarding. I would not have survived without him."

Boulter's eyes shone as he looked at her. He laid his head on her shoulder for a moment.

"It's true," she said, "you gave me courage and purpose. You came along at just the right moment."

The man nodded. *And you also,* he said. *Just the right moment. And now a new moment has arrived. Come, Boulter.*

Boulter's mouth looked determined as he turned to her. "Goodbye, Mum. I love you so much." His hug was tight and then he let go and shook Damian's hand. Turning, he stepped in behind the two men. As they walked ahead, he looked back for a moment, then ran to her for another hug. When he walked away, it was only a second before he disappeared down the lane, Mickens trotting at his side.

~ * * * ~

Mickens kept pace as Boulter walked with a steady pace behind the two travellers who had come for him at last. *He's nervous, that's not surprising.* The hound moved closer to brush against the young man's leg. He felt a hand on his head for a moment. When he glanced up, he realized Boulter's robe was gray like the others, shifting lightly in the breeze.

That's better. He'll be all right. This is where he belongs, where his future lies. And Ms Fanny has done a wonderful job of preparing him.

Mickens settled down to a steady pace at Boulter's side. They had a long way to go, but the excitement was building. New horizons, new tasks rose before them.

CHAPTER FIFTY THREE

Nikesh stepped off the aircart along with a flock of other passengers arriving at the airfield near the Sprintline. He knew he'd lost weight while he was away, and his hair hadn't seen a barber since long before he and Damian departed the City months ago, so now it stuck up like an out of control firebush. The worn outfit Cownden's men had supplied for the undercover operation was in near rags, the shirt hanging limply from his broad frame.

Damian came forward to meet him and clasped arms, giving his shoulder a squeeze. "Good to see you," he said gruffly. "I was afraid I'd lost you there for a bit, out of communication for so long."

Nikesh grinned and slapped his back. "Never happen," he said. "I'm too tough for that." He felt a breath of relief leave his lungs. It had been tough out there, at times dangerous. He was powerfully glad to be heading back to more welcoming sites. And it was good to see Damian again. They'd worked together for a long time, in sync with each other.

Damian pointed him in the direction of Cownden in the waiting transport. Their meeting had been set up for the military base where Dante Regiment had an office. He would be debriefed there.

After a couple of hours with the crew of men, Damian, Dante Regiment and Cownden Lanser settled with him around the dining table at the base. Nikesh drank the last of his Chilean tea and brushed a hand through his thick hair. He glanced at the expectant faces around him. Damian looked happy, maybe for the first time since they'd met along the Helmcken Trail years ago. Marriage must agree with the man. They'd have a chance to catch up soon, he knew.

"My main information is this," he said, lowering his voice against the nearby tables where military men were having their midday meal. "Emperor Carlton has sent the call out for recruits, as Damian will already have told you. Dispossessed are arriving at the Emperor's camp in a steady stream from the northern territories of Khandarken, as well as from Jiran and Legitamia. The training has been sharply accelerated, and they've sent out a request for mules and horses. Not sure how they pay for their supplies, but they keep pouring in."

He took a last bite of his meal and laid the fork across the empty plate. The faces opposite him were grim.

"There's no doubt, General Elkon is laying the groundwork for a new offensive," he continued. "The organization could be better, but it's functional. The men are put through their paces on a daily basis, and it won't be long before there is a real army ready and waiting. No one talks about what the target will be, not even a whisper of speculation out there. But Emperor Carlton is preparing for an all-out military assault."

Nikesh felt his gut clench. This was the worst news he could have delivered.

From the Author -

I love to write and my readers are the life blood of why I write. If you enjoyed this book, please consider giving a review.

You can contact me at my website
www.sylviegrayson.com,
Leave a review at Amazon
Or email me at sylviegraysonauthor@gmail.com.
All comments are appreciated.

Sylvie Grayson

The Last War series is a stunning portrayal of a new world created from fire and consumed at the edges ...- sci fi and fantasy at its best...

The Emperor has been defeated. New countries have arisen from the ashes of the old Empire. The citizens swear they will never need to fight again after that long and painful war.

Bethlehem Farmer is helping her brother Abram run Farmer Holdings in south Khandarken after their father died in the final battles. She is looking after the dispossessed, keeping the farm productive and the talc mine working in the hills behind their land. But when Abram takes a trip with Uncle Jade into the northern territory and disappears without a trace, she's left on her own. Suddenly things are not what they seem and no one can be trusted.

Major Dante Regiment is sent by his father, the General of Khandarken, to find out what the situation is at Farmer Holdings. What he sees shakes him to the core and fuels his grim determination to protect Bethlehem at all cost, even with his life.

Ms Grayson has created a fascinating new world with a lot of the same old problems. Sci fi and fantasy rolled into one with a sure hand and enormous imagination

From the mud and danger of the open road to the welcoming arms of the Sanctuary, from attacks by the dispossessed army to the storms of the open sea, Son of the Emperor takes us on a wild ride into danger and on to the dream of freedom.

With the Emperor defeated after a seemingly endless war, the citizens pray they'll never need to fight again. But already unrest is growing in the north of Khandarken.

After Julianne Adjudicator's father disappears, she seeks to escape the clutches of her vicious stepmother Zanata, who has posted a reward on her head. The Sanctuary, near the Legitamia border, is rumoured to be the safest place for a woman in need of shelter in a sometimes hostile world full of unrest and roving dispossessed. But when Julianne seeks asylum, it soon becomes clear all is not as it first appeared.

Then Abe Farmer arrives at the Sanctuary seeking medical help and she seizes the opportunity to leave. Abe isn't interested in taking a young woman with them, as he and his injured bodyguard struggle to return to the Southern Territory. Yet when he discovers her fate if she stays, he finds he has no choice. But the journey becomes more dangerous as they encounter the army of the New Emperor. Caught in the middle of a firefight, they flee toward the Catastrophic Ocean. Can Abe keep her safe till they reach home?

From the mud and danger of the open road to the welcoming arms of the Sanctuary, from attacks by the dispossessed army to the storms of the open sea, Son of the Emperor takes us on a wild ride into danger and on to the dream of freedom.

...a whole new world with the same old problems - fantasy at its best...

TRUTH AND TREACHERY

THE LAST WAR
BOOK THREE

SYLVIE GRAYSON

The Last War is over and the next one is about to begin.

From attacks by Emperor Carlton to conspiracy in the ranks of the police, Khandarken is in more danger than at any time since the end of The Last War. But when the Young Emperor makes an offer, can Chief Cownden Lanser resist? Khandarken's future hangs in the balance.

The Young Emperor has been backed into a corner. He holds a bit of land in Legitamia where he marshals his troops, but the skirmishes they've launched to expand his empire have had limited success. Now, his ambitions are aimed at overthrowing everything Khandarken has cobbled together since the Last War.

Cownden Lanser, Chief Constable of Khandarken, is a private man with a close connection to the Old Empire that he doesn't divulge to anyone. Although he's dedicated to his position, things are not what they seem in the rank and file of the police.

Selanna Nettles is a sookie, trained in Legitamia but working near her family in the Western Territory of Khandarken, healing the injured mine workers and the dispossessed. But her life takes a startling turn when Chief Cownden Lanser hires her to attend a set of high-level meetings in Gilsigg.

When these three meet up in Legitamia, the result is explosive. Not just for them but for the future of Khandarken. The Emperor makes Cownden an offer that might be everything he's secretly dreamed of. How can he refuse?

The Last War series is a stunning portrayal of a new world created from fire and consumed at the edges... sci fi/fantasy at its best...

Contemporary romantic suspense from author Sylvie Grayson...

Some secrets are too dangerous to keep...

A thrilling novel of romantic suspense from author Sylvie Grayson.

After losing her husband to a deadly illness, Julia Butler is determined to look after her family, but this is the 1930's and times are tough for everyone. As the endless string of jobless men trudges past her farm, she does her best to hang on. Then two strangers suddenly appear at her home. They are hiding something that places her family in danger, and nothing will ever be the same.

Dr. Will Stofford has become disillusioned with women. In an effort to heal his broken heart, he leaves his brothers behind and sets up his medical practice in the Kootenays where no one knows him.

Meeting Julia throws his plans into chaos. Will can't turn his back on a challenge and he won't rest until he solves this puzzle and puts things right.

In the 1930's, can a country doctor and a determined widow save the lives of these abandoned strangers?

When a police detective falls for his main suspect, life gets complicated…

When Chloe Bowman woke to find her husband gone, never did she imagine it would take so long to find him, or that in the midst of the search she'd discover she didn't really know this man at all. She soon realizes she has been left alone with her young son and a time bomb on her hands. Then the earthquake throws everything into question. Lurking in the shadows is the mysterious Rainman who travels under an unknown name.

Police Detective Ross Cullen was already investigating Chloe's husband when he disappeared. Although he's powerfully drawn to Chloe, Ross also knows that when one member of a family disappears, the first place to look for the suspect is among those closest to him. No one was closer than Chloe.

But the deeper Ross digs the less he knows, and the more he's attracted to the young wife as she struggles to put her life back together.

Can Ross break through the Rainman's disguises to solve the case so he can be with Chloe?

Can Rain solve his last case without getting his girlfriend arrested?

Rainier is a survivor. He's made some mistakes, and now he's paying for them. As a condition of his probation, he must work with the police on investigations where his skills might be useful. There is one more case to solve to complete his commitments.

Then he'll be free. As he heads undercover to work this last case, Sophia arrives in town. She is a childhood crush who means a great deal to Rain, and she is obviously terrified of someone.

Sophia has made a bad choice in the past, and now she's in hiding to avoid dealing with it. Still, it follows her, and Rainier is the only one she can trust to help her deal with it.

Rain's problem? The clues he uncovers on his final case all seem to lead directly to Sophia. Can he solve the case without breaking his heart or pointing the police in his girlfriend's direction?

Jake never expected his investigations would prove deadly.

Sylvie Grayson delivers another thrilling romantic mystery that will keep you on the edge of your seat— a gripping story of suspense with characters that you'll root for and a plot that pulls you in.

After years of taking courses and jumping

through hoops to get licensed, Jake Murdoch is more than ready to open his private investigator's office. Leah Bonnar, a family friend and childhood irritant who blames him for a past disaster in her life, steps in to volunteer as his assistant. Given he's not making money yet, he needs her help to get things up and running. Yet as the cases start pouring in, she organizes the hell out of him. Jake is attracted to Leah, and grudgingly grateful for her help in equal measure. Despite their history, their relationship heats up.

But in the midst of one of his investigations, Jake steps on the toes of a couple of very determined con men and Leah is sitting right in the crosshairs of their revenge. Can Jake find the evidence he needs to stop the criminals, while protecting Leah from their efforts to bring his investigation to a halt?

SYLVIE GRAYSON

Sometimes you get a second chance...

MY BEST MISTAKE

Jordie let her get away the first time. He's determined it won't happen again.

Jordie was heartbroken when he returned to town to find Jenny had married another man. Now she lives beside him, and he'll either go crazy or do what he should have done before - claim her for his own.

Jenny is back and she's angry, her husband cheated and she can't let it go. But when her boss dies and someone comes after her, who will she turn to?

With her cousin living right beside her it's becoming harder to ignore the chemistry they have always shared. Can Jordie help put her life back together?

SYLVIE GRAYSON

LEGAL OBSTRUCTION

Emily moves to a new town to hide her secret, but it follows her. Can Joe protect her from her past?

When Emily Drury takes a job as legal counsel for an import-export company, she does it because she needs to get away to safety. Joe Tanner counts himself lucky. He's charmed a successful big city lawyer into heading up the legal department of his rapidly expanding business. But why would a beautiful woman who could easily make partner in a high profile legal firm give it all up to come to Bonnie? As Joe realizes she has become essential to his happiness, his first reaction is to protect her. But he doesn't know the whole story.

Can Emily trust him enough to divulge her secret? Will he learn what he needs to know in time to stop the avalanche that's gaining speed as it races down the hill toward her?

Katy Dalton's friend has disappeared with her money and bad things start to happen. Can Brett Rome save his father's company, and the woman who causes chaos in his heart?

Katy Dalton needs her money back, but Bruno has stopped answering his phone and bad things start to happen.

Brett Rome is frustrated. The last thing he wants is to leave a promising career in hockey to come home and run his ailing father's trucking company. What he discovers is a company teetering on the very edge of bankruptcy and a young woman demanding the return of her money.

But danger lurks in the form of Bruno's dubious associates. What secret are they hiding and why are they willing to kill Katy? Can Brett put this broken picture back together, and is Katy part of the solution or the problem?

Please visit my website at
www.sylviegrayson.com and sign up to receive my
newsletter. You will be the first to hear the latest on new
book releases, book giveaways and author presentations.

I'd love to hear from you. You can leave a comment on
my website or contact me at
sylviegraysonauthor@gmail.com

ABOUT THE AUTHOR

Sylvie Grayson loves to write about suspense, romance and attempted murder, in both contemporary and science fiction/fantasy. She has lived most of her life in British Columbia, Canada in spots ranging from Vancouver Island on the west coast to the North Peace River country and the Kootenays in the beautiful interior. She spent a one year sojourn in Tokyo, Japan.

She has been an English language instructor, a nightclub manager, an auto shop bookkeeper and a lawyer. Now she works part time as the owner of a small company, and writes when she finds the time.

She is a wife and mother and still loves to travel. She lives on the coast of the Pacific Ocean with her husband on a small patch of land near the sea that they call home.

If you enjoyed this book, please consider giving a review.

Sylvie loves to hear from her readers, you can Visit her at her website – **www.sylviegrayson.com or** find her on Facebook.

Please consider signing up for her newsletter at http://sylviegrayson.com/newsletter/